THE
FIRE
SHE
FIGHTS

A Novel

Sept. 2021

TRACY MOORE

Tracy Moore

ISBN 978-1-63489-476-0
Library of Congress Catalog Number has been applied for.

Printed in the United States of America
First Printing: 2022

26   25   24   23   22   5   4   3   2   1

Cover design by Emily Mahon
Interior design by Kim Morehead

Wise Ink Creative Publishing
807 Broadway St NE
Suite 46
Minneapolis, MN, 55413

For the women of the Minneapolis Fire Department
and
for the woman who inspired me first—

my mom

PART
ONE

LATE 1990s

CHAPTER 1

Ruby

Every rookie is granted *one first fire*, and Ruby would be ready. She climbed into the back seat of Engine 7 and rechecked the level of air in her tank for the third time. After three months on Engine 7 she had become the master of preparedness. Fire would come, Ruby was certain, and she'd finally be free of the title of *fire virgin*.

The sun shining through the window grid of the firehouse garage door cast a shadowy glow in the back of the cab. She snapped the air bottle of her self-contained breathing apparatus (SCBA) into its bracket. The station lights flickered. The shadows dissolved into the intruding fluorescent light. Fire tones vibrated through the station in six loud blasts. Her heart rate quickened, outpacing the alarm. Tyler, the driver of the rig, stepped up and into the cab. Ruby searched his face for a hint of whether he thought this was another false alarm or an actual fire.

He smiled and said, "Don't get too excited, rookie. It's probably just someone burning leaves."

Hector got on the rig next with one hand through the sleeve of his fire coat and the other holding a cup of coffee. He sat next to Ruby and pulled the straps of his tank over his shoulders. "Or the whole city could be on fire," he said.

Ruby barreled off the rig and into her boots. She pulled her turnout pants over her hips and climbed once again into the back seat.

John, the captain, took his place at shotgun, patted his chest and then his lap, and said, "Spectacles. Testicles. Let's go." He pulled a cord hanging from the ceiling to activate the apparatus doors. The rubber protecting the bottom of the massive garage doors scraped on the concrete as they separated like a stage curtain at the start of a play. ·

The engine rolled out of the station and rumbled over a pothole. Ruby wriggled into her fire coat and glanced at Hector. Seeing him balance his half-filled cup of coffee made the emergency seem almost trivial. The engine raced down Franklin Avenue. Ruby caught her reflection in a store window. The red lights swirling above her and the intense wail of the siren matched the pride she felt as a Minneapolis firefighter.

Ruby leaned to the left when the engine made a right turn onto the parkway. A curtain of smoke closed across the landscape. The undeniable odor of a house on fire was the final precursor—Ruby's first firefight had arrived.

Hector flung what was left in his cup out the window and said, "Them's some mighty big leaves."

Tyler drove through the smoke and stopped on the far side of a two-and-half-story stucco home. Black smoke poured from the eaves. Ruby's eyes widened, reflecting the flames licking from the first-floor window. The fear of not being enough and the anticipation of proving herself flashed like flint striking steel.

Ruby tightened the straps of her air tank and leaned forward, forcing her SCBA from its metal bracket. She adjusted her yellow helmet and hurried to the back of the rig to retrieve the tank line. With the hose draped over her shoulder and the nozzle in her hand, she walked alongside Hector across the lawn. A woman dressed in a puffy pastel-blue robe ran toward them and grabbed Hector, screaming, "My babies are in there!"

Ruby fought the urge to rush in. She knew her primary task was to ready the water, making a rescue more feasible. She spread the hose on the lawn leading to the doorway and grasped the nozzle in her gloved hand. The nozzle jerked as water entered, stiffening the hose.

Hector readied his mask. "Ma'am, where did you last see them?"

She hugged herself tight. "I couldn't find them."

Hector put his hand on her shoulder and shouted through his mask, "Don't worry, I'll get your kids." He turned to Ruby. "Wait for John while I do a quick search." Then he disappeared through the smoke-blackened doorway.

Ruby pulled back on the handle of the nozzle, clearing air from the line. A stream of water spat across the sky. She closed the nozzle and dropped it to the ground. Radiant heat grazed her face. She loosely fastened her helmet strap below her chin and pushed her helmet back, letting it dangle behind her. She pulled her mask from the bag clipped at her side, but the air hose tangled with the harness straps. She fumbled to make it right.

John joined her at the entry. He took her mask, slipped it through the strap, and handed it back to her before bending for the nozzle. She covered it with her boot, remembering the warning in rookie school to "never give up the line."

"I'm just gonna hand it to you," he said.

Hector stumbled out through the front door. The bell of his air tank screeched, indicating low air. He peeled his mask from his face and dropped to his knees. Ruby looked for the kids he had gone to rescue. Instead, three soot-covered kittens clutched the arm of his fire coat. Another clung to his left shoulder while the one peeking from his side pocket bawled like a fire engine siren.

John lifted his chin. "The pied piper of kittens."

Ruby had regarded Hector as gruff and unapproachable. With fire on his heels, as the savior of kittens, he appeared heroic and almost tender. She pressed her mask to her face. The click of her regulator let her know air would soon fill the space inside her mask. She tightened her helmet strap and lifted the nozzle, letting John know she was ready.

Beneath his mask she saw only his eyes. She envied the fear she imagined they had conquered and longed for the confidence they conveyed. As they stepped through the smoke-framed door, the homeowner's voice faded behind them: "My babies! You got my babies."

John pushed on Ruby's back. Smoke banked down from the ceiling, creating darkness like a midnight void of moon and stars. She bumped into what felt like a kitchen counter. Holding her gloved hand in front of her mask and seeing nothing, she widened her eyes. She peered into the blackness, listening for the muffled crackle of a hiding flame. Squeezing the hose between her bicep and ribs, she took another step, tightening her grasp on the nozzle handle.

Fire rolled over their heads. Light blasted into the room like the crack of thunder on a clear day.

"Don't let it get behind us," John yelled. He reached around Ruby and tugged on the nozzle handle. She turned, holding the handle tighter, and forced the handle back, directing a powerful stream of water on the flames gathered at the ceiling.

"Hit the fire, not the flames," John shouted.

She slammed the handle forward. Releasing the pressure threw her off balance. John nudged her through the doorway to the living room. Devoured by fire, the furniture and window frame were reduced to ash. The floor glowed. Heat raged. Ruby sank to her knees, straining for cooler air, even as the force of the hose pushed her up and forward. John followed behind, lifting the hose and driving her into the heat.

The fizz and pop of fire amplified. Ruby stepped over the threshold and waited, resisting the temptation to open the nozzle on flames overhead. Instead she tracked the rolling flames down from the ceiling to where crimson cinders pulsed at the floorboard. She pulled back on the trigger, discharging a hundred and fifty pounds of water pressure on the seat of the fire. The fire flashed, fell, and transformed into gray smoke. Ruby chased rogue flames from the blackened floor to the wall and then to the ceiling. Light poured through a burned-out window, filtered by steam.

Ruby turned toward John and raised her gloved hand for a high-five. Her mask chirped, signaling low air. Instead of slapping her hand, John cupped her shoulder and pointed to the door. She dropped the nozzle and headed toward the exit, passing the ladder crew armed with axes and hooks.

Lights from fire rigs on the curb flashed through the windows, reflecting two eyes shining behind the kitchen trash can. Ruby swept up the stray kitten and tucked it inside her coat.

Walking with John to the rehab truck, she spotted the woman

in her blue robe coaxing the mother cat from under a neighbor's hedge. Hector sat on the curb next to an empty granola box full of kittens, dumping Gatorade into his wide-open mouth.

"Hey, Catman," Ruby joked, "you missed one." She reached inside her coat and pulled out the gray ball of fur, humming Batman's theme song.

Hector threw his empty can into the box with the kittens. "Careful, rookie. You might wanna get some time on the job before you start givin' out nicknames."

The affection she had felt for him flattened. She shot back, "It's a compliment. It's like Batman, except you're a cat."

John slapped the back of Hector's coat, loosening lingering smoke. Through a cough he said, "Like Catwoman, but for a dude." He turned to Ruby. "How 'bout you and your pal Catman"—he smiled at Hector—"get this hose picked up. We might still be able to get dinner before the sun goes down."

On the way back to the station John said, "Hey, Ruby, you were part of real live heroism today." It was the first friendly conversation he'd initiated with her. He winked and sang, "Da da da da da ... Catman."

Hector scowled at Ruby. She returned his expression with a satisfied smile. *Finally,* she thought, *I'm fitting in.*

———

Tyler backed the engine into the stall at Station 7. Ruby was first to get off the rig. She heaved the dirty, wet hose from the tailboard, and Tyler splayed it next to the floor grates to wash it down. Ruby poured truck-wash soap over the canvas, and together they pushed long-handled brushes over the hose. Hunger grumbled in Ruby's stomach.

Tyler leaned his brush against the wall and handed a clean section of hose to Ruby. "Dinner will be out in less than an hour. You're gonna love my famous hot dog hot dish. It's double hot," he said. "Get it? *Hot* dog *hot* dish?"

She stuck out her tongue and scrunched her face. She liked Tyler. She hated hot dogs but realized if she wanted to be part of the crew, hot dog consumption was mandatory.

She dragged the hose to the back of the fire station and into the three-story drying tower that doubled as a mop closet. Commercial mop buckets tipped over the drain in the darkness seemed to be waiting for her to begin floor duty.

"Not this time," she said, and kicked one to the side, feeling superior to the routine firehouse task. Ruby secured the hose to the hoisting hook and began to pull. That was when she felt him.

Hector pressed his body against her back and breathed into her ear as he reached for the rope above her. She looked toward the gloomy yellow light bulb at the top of the tower. His breath moved her hair from behind her ear and onto her face. It was hot and smelled like orange Gatorade masking dehydrated saliva. She swallowed, not sure if her fear was justified. The wet canvas hose brushed her cheek, and the heat of Hector's sweat-drenched uniform shirt pressed against her back.

"I got it," she said.

He squeezed the rope above her and pulled. The hose ascended. She buried her face in the dangling canvas, intensifying the mixed odor of mold, truck soap, and lingering ash. He slid his free hand around her waist and pushed it into her uniform pants. She wondered for a moment if it was a coupling from the hose jammed against her. No, it was Hector's fist. He forced his hand deeper into her pants, manipulated the crotch of her underwear to the side, and penetrated her with two fingers.

"Double hot," he said.

Terrified, Ruby froze.

Hector pressed harder into her back, slowly pulling his hand from her pants. "You might want to get used to eating *hot dogs* around here."

Her eyes darted from one side and then to the other. She wanted to run, but that would mean going forward. More than anything, Ruby wanted to go back. Hector moved to tie off the rope, letting in a path of light. She pushed her hair back behind her ear and wedged past him, following the light out of the tower.

Tyler climbed down from the top of the engine and said, "Good job today, Ru. To celebrate your first fire, I'm adding tofu into the hot dish especially for you." When she didn't respond he added, "That is, if you help me load this hose."

The red gear lockers lining the wall flickered, appearing as flames sprouting from the concrete. The flames rose and spun in circles. She stumbled.

Tyler approached her and held out his hand. "You all right?"

She steadied her hands on her knees and recalled the voice of her mother—more like criticism than encouragement—saying, "Ruby, you have to be strong."

Ruby raised her palm. "I'm fine." She picked up the dry hose from the floor, coupled it to another, and handed it to him. She focused on the task, one detail at a time. Couple the hose, load it onto the rig, couple the hose, load it. But with the hose bed full of fresh, dry hose, the sanctuary of mindless work faded.

Hector stood in the doorway of the engine with his head bowed, replacing his air bottle. Ruby imagined slamming the door and cracking his skull. She had been faced with this conflict before, with the choice to confront or avoid. *Be still, stay silent. If you tell we'll both be in big trouble. Isn't this how the predator convinces its victim to keep secrets?* Fight or flight—Ruby chose flight and headed into the station.

John met her at the door. "Not so fast, rookie," he said. "I noticed you got your mask tangled up on the fireground today. I want you to practice donning your mask a few times before you shower up. Imagine the fire we fought. Feel the heat. Take a deep breath and try not to fuck up your air hose. When you can get your mask on in ten seconds, hit the shower."

Ruby put on her fire coat and strapped the tank on her back. She loosened the chin strap of her helmet and pushed it behind her head. She closed her eyes to imagine the fire, but instead she saw the blurred yellow light of the hose tower. Instead of the heat of fire on her face, she felt Hector's breath choking the air around her. She squatted. *One detail at a time.* Smelling the soot mixed with sweat on her face, she swiped her tongue across her upper lip. She pressed her eyes tighter, squeezing him from her mind.

Ruby stood, set her watch to ten seconds, and unsheathed her mask from the bag clipped at her side. With her mask pressed against her face, she secured the side straps. She slid the protective hood from her neck over her head and dragged her helmet over the hood. She turned the knob on her tank. Hearing the bell, she inhaled a long, deep breath. Her ten-second timer beeped. Finally, Ruby could hit the shower.

Of the two side-by-side shower stalls, the left was missing the lock, leaving a hole that someone had stuffed with toilet paper. Ruby chose the one on the right. She placed her dry clothes on the bench inside the changing stall and locked the latch.

Warm water hit her skin, and tears filled her head. She held them there. She squeezed the soap and scrubbed soot from her arms, creating a trail of clean skin through the black ash. She rolled the bar in her hands, filling them with soapy water. Gray suds dripped down her body, surrounded her feet, and swirled down the drain. Ruby surrendered her face to the shower stream. Afraid to close her eyes, she covered them with her hands.

The faucet handle in the next stall creaked. Her paralysis returned.

"Hey, Ruby," came Tyler's voice. "Pass me the soap, would ya? Some asshole only left a sliver."

She looked at the white slab marbled with the black she had washed from her body. She dropped the soap to the floor and squished it through the grate with her toes. "All out over here too. Sorry, Tyler."

A click, like the sound a cowgirl makes to summon her pony to the fence, warned them of an incoming call. The subtle sound is the first in a series of alerts designed to slowly signal the firefighter. Next, the thickened glass light bulb flashed in a metal cage fixed above their heads.

"I guess I won't be needing that soap," Tyler said.

Finally came the whooping tones of a medical call. Ruby pulled on her pants. Her T-shirt clung to her wet body. She quickly wrapped her hair in a towel and, in unison with Tyler, slammed open the shower door.

"Nice turban, Swami." Tyler laughed. He pulled his shirt over his wet torso as they raced to the rig. She threw her turban in the back seat of the engine. Sitting next to Hector felt like a betrayal of common sense. She opened the medical bag at her feet and checked the inventory she knew she had stocked.

Focus on the task, one detail at a time.

Arriving on scene, Tyler parked the engine next to the river embankment behind two Minneapolis Police squads. John approached the officers, who were bending and pointing under the bridge spanning the river. Ruby checked the captain's computer screen—*Possible suicide under the bridge on West River Parkway*—and hurried to join the crew.

The silhouette of a hanging figure swayed from the bridge support beams. A steep hill, sandy and mottled with rock, sloped down toward the river. Tattered shoes dangled inches above the sand.

"Swinger's been there a while," the officer said. "We got what we need. Coroner is en route. Jus' need you to cut him down."

John said to Ruby, "Grab the rescue basket."

She pulled the basket from the compartment and donned her turnout coat—the firefighter's first layer of protection and the gear that guards the guardian. It's fireproof, reflective, and a barrier against contaminants. It's the armor that emboldens a firefighter to betray the urge to run away. But when things go bad, and no layer of protection is enough, the false promise of invincibility becomes the turncoat.

Ruby, Hector, and John started down the hill, leaving Tyler with the rig to wait for the coroner and block traffic, while the officers managed curious onlookers. Ruby squeezed the rope of the basket and dragged it behind her like a sled. Reaching the slope, she cinched the rope to keep the basket from getting ahead of her. The hanging figure's black overcoat matched the dark shadow of his face, his eyes obscured by matted hair.

"You're up, rookie," John said.

She whipped her head around. Wet hair slapped her in the eye. "I'm up?"

"Hold him steady while Hector cuts him down. Create some slack."

Ruby lifted, but the slumped mass was too heavy for arm strength alone. She let go and stepped back. Her intrusion started him swinging. She stepped closer and steadied him. She crouched, dug her boots into the sand, wrapped her arms around his thighs, and used her leg strength to lift.

Hector sidestepped closer and reached for the rope. With scrunched eyes Ruby focused on the moon reflecting on the river. The click from Hector's jackknife blade pulled from the handle told Ruby to run. With nowhere to go, she pushed her forehead into the hanging abdomen. The stench of decomposing flesh intensified. The black coat jerked back and forth as Hector sawed. Suddenly, the tension released and the weight of the cadaver forced Ruby to her knees. John steadied the basket. Half of the body hung over the sled; half slumped on the sand.

"Roll him into the basket," John said. Ruby wedged her arms

under his coat and pushed. When he didn't budge, John said to Hector, "I'm not sure who is more dead weight here, you or the dead guy."

Hector grumbled and knelt next to Ruby. Together they rolled him into the basket.

"Okay, Ruby. Pull him up the hill." John handed her the rope.

She draped it over her shoulder and bowed toward the hill. Using the rocks anchored in the sand as steps, she started the climb. Sweat dripped down her chest. Her thighs burned, and she bent closer to the hill, pulling her passenger to the top of the embankment.

"Those assholes," Tyler said when she crested the hill. He grabbed his gloves and ran to the edge to help. She turned from him and squeezed the rope tighter.

"I don't need your help."

"I know you can do it by yourself. I'm saying you don't have to. You don't have anything to prove."

The fuck I don't.

CHAPTER 2

Auditorium Raise: *Climbing an extension ladder without the support of a building or other fixed object.*

Dana

Dana hadn't seen Ruby since they graduated rookie school together. The friendship they had formed sharing sweaty fire gear and coming up with techniques to work smart instead of hard, the daily support she had needed for survival during the climb, had become an afterthought once they reached the summit, and Dana felt a little guilty. She swung into the lot at Station 7 for a surprise reunion.

"I let the cat drag me in," Dana announced, tousling the short, wavy layers of her dark hair into their natural messy style.

Ruby kept her eyes on the rescue basket she was disinfecting and mumbled, "I've had my fill of cats today."

This wasn't the reunion Dana had expected. "Miss me? Seems like a century since rookie school. Station life is aces compared to the training tower of torture, right?"

Ruby lifted the basket to stow it on the rig. Dana rushed to help.

"I can do it myself, Dana."

"I know you can. But you're the poster girl for *everything is better with two.*"

"Everything but hot-fudge sundaes. Grab the heavy end, would you?"

Feeling the change in Ruby's optimistic, all-for-one attitude, Dana pressed, "I know I should have stopped in earlier but—"

"It's not about you. It's nothing."

Dana understood keeping secrets. At a young age she'd learned the fragility of happiness and the lies we believe to hold onto it.

It was before dawn on the day after Christmas. Three days before Dana's fifth birthday, she woke to the squeals of her two older brothers. A gust of wind cut through the open door of the cabin where her family had spent Christmas break. Dana ran to the door, pushing past her brothers. The newly fallen snow meant one more slide down the big hill. Her dad had packed up their station wagon with unwrapped gifts, suitcases, and skis. The sleds leaned against the lodge.

"Okay, kids," Dana's mom said. "Get dressed. Grab your sleds and put them in the back of the car."

Dana's dad winked and nodded toward the sleds. "One last ride before we hit the road?"

Dana pulled her snow pants over her pajamas and grabbed her coat from the hook. Her boots were still untied when she hopped onto her silver saucer. Dad pulled her to the top of the hill while her brothers dragged wooden toboggans behind them. He gave the metal sled a push and a spin, and Dana surfed down the hill with snow splashing in her face. At the bottom of the hill she rolled off her sled. Snow glistened in the shadows of the morning moon lingering low in the sky. She looked for her dad, who was still at the top, taking the toboggan rope from her brother.

"You two double up on the flyer," he said. "I'm taking this one. The race is on!"

Her brothers sat on their sled and pushed off, claiming a head-start advantage. Dad thrust his sled in front of him and did a belly flop that propelled him down the hill. He pumped with his arms against the snow until he could no longer keep up with the speed of his sled. Dana cheered for her dad while her mom cheered for the boys.

Dad hit a patch of ice and veered off the path, but he maneuvered the steering bar and got back on course. Dana felt sure he would catch up. "Faster, Dad! Faster!"

The boys glided past Mom and Dana—the official finish line. They screamed in unison, "We win!" Dad slid in behind, grinning despite the loss.

Then they packed the sleds in the station wagon and headed home. New snowflakes started to fall.

Seat belts left unclicked, Dana sat in the front on her mom's lap. Her brothers sat in back, arguing about who'd contributed most to the sled race victory.

"It's because Dad's sled turned," Dana chimed in.

Her dad turned to her and winked. When he looked back, a deer was standing in the road. Dad swerved, crossing the centerline to avoid the deer. The tires skated on the icy surface. Dana felt fear in the squeeze of her mother's arms as the car slid toward the shoulder and the edge of a ravine.

Dad jerked back toward the centerline. The car slid again, now toward the steep embankment, and Mom squeezed tighter. Dad's fingers clenched the wheel and steered the station wagon away from the cliff, back to clear pavement and a slow stop.

No one dared to speak. The silence was finally broken by the sound of the gearshift thrown into park. Dad got out of the car. He leaned on the hood, and if not for his trembling, Dana would have thought his face was wet with snow. No, she could see he was crying. He turned his back to them and faced the ravine. Then he ran his hand through his hair, got back into the car like nothing happened, and said, "Who wants to go for pancakes?"

Dana felt her mother's arms loosen. She said just three words: "Good drivin', Jack."

The fear Dana had felt in the squeeze of her mother's arms became her obsession. She needed a place where she could bring calm to the chaos.

Twenty years later she answered her calling and joined the Minneapolis Fire Department.

———

Dana and Ruby had been two of five women in their training class of thirty rookies. Growing up with only brothers, Dana was competitive among men—gender wasn't a factor. While most of the women in class were challenged by lifting the 175-pound dummy, the auditorium raise became the holy grail of obstacles for the men. Dana quickly mastered the dummy lift and was unique in her excitement to confront the auditorium raise.

The task was performed outdoors, over a wide-open space of concrete, where four cadets used tether ropes to support a forty-foot ladder extended into the open sky. Two more cadets butted the ladder as one cadet climbs dressed in full gear, including the tank. The challenge is most difficult at the top, and it demands trust. With no rungs above to hold onto, the climber must swing a leg over and come down the other side. Failure to complete the exercise results in termination.

The training captains demonstrated the setup of the ladder but not the climb, and the chatter intensified. Dana stood next to Ruby on the pavement, looking up at the raised ladder.

"A literal stairway to heaven," Dana said.

"We're idiots for doing this," one cadet complained.

"It's like Jack and the Beanstalk, 'cept no branches," another said.

"What if we all refuse? Do we all get terminated? Maybe we should stick together," Jared, the biggest guy in class, suggested.

Ruby nudged Dana and said, "I'd like to see Jared stick by me. Would we ever lift a fire victim's face into the smoke? Why not just drag the damn dummy!"

During lunch Dana and Ruby sat together on the curb. Dana said, "I can't believe we get to do the auditorium raise tomorrow."

"Get to? You're not worried? You do know you're the fifth favorite in the betting pool, right?"

"Favorite for what? What pool? How did I not know about this?"

"You're number five to fail—but I'm number one. Ryan's holding the cash."

"We're totally not failing. How am I five? Who'd you bet on?"

"I didn't. I'm the smallest of the women, so I guess that makes me number one. You're the biggest, I mean tallest, so—"

"Dumbshits. Climbing over that ladder takes courage, not strength. Rung by rung. You're small, Ru, but it's your humongous heart that'll get you over the top. Plus, less weight means less ladder sway. Where the hell is Ryan?"

She scanned the training ground and saw him sitting on the steps. She threw what was left of her sandwich in the trash and approached him.

"How much to get in the pool?"

"Pool's full if you're betting on Ruby. Basically, you get your ten bucks back."

Dana reached in her pocket and dropped a ten into Ryan's lunch box. "My money's going on Jared."

The buzz of Dana's alarm clock pulsed, matching the honking of an oncoming car in her dream. Its tires were exaggerated, outlined like in a cartoon. She sat up. The smell of brewing coffee calmed and oriented her: today was the auditorium raise. She imagined Jared swaying at the top of the ladder. She couldn't blame him for trying to start an uprising.

Her girlfriend, Lily, called from downstairs, "You up?"

Dana sauntered into the kitchen, still wearing her boxers and a tank top. Lily handed her a coffee cup and said, "Big day."

"Every day is big at the training tower. Just when I think I got it down, the training captains change it up. Last week, after we all breezed through the obstacle course, they made us go on air."

"On air?"

"Tank air. Strap on an SCBA and breathe through the mask. They warned us, 'Run out of air before finishing and stay after to chop holes.' Six guys ran out before finishing, and all the women still had half a tank. The captains decided it wasn't relevant for firefighting. Don't ask me how breathing tank air isn't about firefighting."

"That's what I love about you, Dana. Don't you see? They want the women to fail. It's a *boys' club*, and you're not a boy. I mean, you're hot in those boxers, but underneath you are all girl."

"Everyone is betting on us to fail. Ruby is the favorite to mess up. I bet on the big guy."

"What do mean 'bet'? You bet? Dana, that's gambling. And worse, you bet on someone to fail?"

"I had to. Everyone was betting on Ruby."

"That's bullshit and you know it." Lily glanced at the clock on the microwave. "I'm gonna be late for work. Maybe you're a little more boy than I thought."

"Lily. You're mad? I need you to not to be mad at me today."

Lily grabbed her keys from the counter and kissed Dana. "I am mad, and I love you. Good luck."

Dana filled her cup halfway with cream and topped it off with coffee. *Did she just wish me good luck?* She watched through the window as Lily backed out of the driveway and then glanced at the thermometer—forty-two degrees, a perfect April day for a ladder climb.

The recruits stood in a semicircle around the extension ladder resting on the pavement. The training captain divided them into teams of seven. *Lucky number*, Dana thought. Two cadets to butt the ladder, acting as anchors, four cadets on the guide ropes, and one climber. Ruby's group was up first.

Dressed in full turnout gear, including tanks and helmets, Ruby chanted in unison with her team, "Raise ladder, raise."

One firefighter pulled the rope extending the ladder to its forty-foot maximum while the others steadied it. Two cadets held the rails while the other four seized the tether ropes. Ruby placed her foot on the bottom rung.

"Hold the ropes taught," the training captain instructed. "Steady."

Dana whispered, "Number one in the pool, and number one to climb."

Ruby climbed quickly to the top, locked one leg in, and threw the other leg over. Then she unlocked her leg and climbed down the other side, making it look easy. Dana let out a communal breath with the rest of the class.

Cadet after cadet climbed, swung a leg, and came down the other side. The confidence of the class grew, and the camaraderie felt more like a party than a test.

Jared was last to climb. He pulled his extra-large gloves over his massive hands and stepped onto the bottom rung. Dana thought, *Betting on Jared to fail is messed up.*

Jared had just reached the top when a light breeze passed over the toggle ropes. The cadets held tight, and although the ropes remained taut, the ladder swayed. Jared froze. His 240-pound, muscled silhouette dwarfed the sun above.

Seeing Jared squeezing the top rung with both hands, she thought of her dad's hands grasping the steering wheel, like somehow holding tighter could make everything right. "Let go," she whispered.

The semicircle of cadets shuffled closer, looking up at Jared's back. Clouds moved above him, turning the sky gray. When snow-flakes started to fall, the training captain yelled, "Come on down."

Ryan stepped closer. "Cap'n, he's at the top. Give him a minute."

"Can't do this exercise on wet pavement. Jared, come on down."

Dana rounded the ladder to see Jared's face. "Swing the leg and climb down," she called.

Ryan joined Dana. "Step over. Coming down is easy," he said.

Dana cupped both hands around her lips to add, "Swing that leg!"

Ruby rounded the ladder, and the three shouted, "Swing that leg!" The entire class followed, taking up the chant: "Swing that leg! Swing that leg!"

Jared threw his leg over the ladder, and the class cheered. He climbed down the other side and landed safely on the snow-dusted concrete.

"Lower ladder, lower," the rookies holding the ladder announced.

The training captain ordered the entire class to line up in front of wooden railroad ties and chop. The consequences for the mutiny of teamwork would be worth it. *Jared was right*, Dana thought. *We do need to stick together. Maybe Lily is wrong. Maybe it's not as much of a boys' club as it is a rookie club.*

Snow fell on the cadets while side by side they chopped, the blows of Dana's axe fueled by a feeling of solidarity.

After class, on the way to the parking lot, Ryan caught up to Dana and Ruby. He handed Dana the wad of tens. "You were the closest. Way to bet against the one most likely to succeed."

She rolled the cash into a wad, draped one arm over Ryan's shoulder and the other over Ruby's, and said, "We can all use a drink after that ass chewing. Drinks are on me."

"Rail Station?" Ryan proposed. The bar was just around the corner from the classroom.

"Rail Station," all three agreed.

———

Dana and Ruby slid the rescue basket into the stowage compartment. Ruby clicked the compartment closed and said, "As torturous as the training tower was—we shared the persecution. I miss us all being in the same boat."

"I'm still in your boat. What about the guys at your firehouse?"

"I haven't exactly become part of the brotherhood."

Tyler shouted from inside the station, "Tofu is served."

Dana widened her eyes and whispered, "There is no tofu in brotherhood, Ru."

Not wanting to rock Dana's blissful boat of brotherhood, Ruby shifted. "Stay for dinner? Tyler made hot dog hot dish."

"Tempting, but I just ate. I am impressed you got him to make you tofu."

Ruby walked Dana to the door, and Dana couldn't help but notice the drag of her feet as she headed to the kitchen for dinner.

CHAPTER 3

Coop: *The office area of a fire station.*

Lanyard: *A handheld remote horn, attached by a coiled cord at the back of fire engines and trucks. Used primarily to signal the driver to back up or stop.*

Ruby

The crews from the engine and the ladder filed through the galley kitchen, heaping Tyler's hot dish onto their plates from a casserole pan on a commercial stove.

"Any later and we could've called this breakfast," John said.

"I call it dinfast. Too late for dinner and too early for breakfast." Hector laughed at his own joke.

Tyler defended his timing. "Dinner before nineteen thirty after a fire—I deserve a medal."

Last in line, Ruby was relieved to find most of the hot dog chunks trolled out, leaving noodles and peas at the bottom of the pan. Tyler peeked around the wall separating the kitchen from the dining table. "Look inside the oven," he whispered.

Ruby pulled open the oven door and retrieved a small fry pan filled with what looked like a sponge cut into small squares.

"I told you I'd make you tofu. I'm a man of my word."

John came from the other side of the dividing wall and looked into the pan. "Some promises are meant to be broken."

Ruby spooned tofu on top of the peas and noodles and piled what was left in the salad bowl onto her plate. She took her seat at the table. Mouths being stuffed with hot dish silenced firehouse banter. She glanced at Tyler, who sat at the end of the long rectangular dinner table, to make sure he wasn't looking. Then she slid her tofu nuggets from the heap of peas, hiding them under the iceberg lettuce.

"Mmm-mmm," John said. "Tyler, this is one of your best. Don't you think, Ruby?" He lifted his fork like he was toasting and then shoveled hot dogs into his mouth.

Busted—she quickly dragged a piece of tofu from under her salad and swept it onto her fork. With a mouth full of noodles and tofu she said, "Mmm-hmm. Super good, but I'm stuffed."

She went to the sink and rinsed her plate. The crew cleared dishes, and Ruby washed the pans. Everyone helped clean except Tyler. The cook never cleans. He sat on the couch to play video games.

Ruby dumped food scraps into the garbage bag, tied it closed, and started toward the door to take the trash to the alley. John joined Tyler on the couch.

"Shit," John said. "Every time I get to the clearing I run out of ammo and I'm a sitting duck."

Walking through the TV room, Ruby stopped to look at the screen, which read, *In war there is no prize for runner-up.*

"You're wasting ammo on targets that don't matter. If you're out, you gotta hide behind the barrier next to the helicopter and wait for the pilot," Tyler said.

Ruby stepped outside and flung the trash bag into the can. Satisfied that the evidence of uneaten tofu had been properly disposed, she headed in. She stopped short of the TV room, noticing that the floor Hector had mopped was wet. The temptation to stomp all over his work boiled inside her. She considered the consequences of pissing him off and recalled her mother's warning, *You can't just be strong, Ruby, you have to be smart.*

John and Tyler were no longer discussing the video game.

"You know, if you're too nice to her she'll never last. Plus, those WMDs don't exactly help her," John said.

"Weapons of mass destruction?"

"You know, her PFDs. Her tits?"

Ruby heard a thud. She assumed it was Tyler punching John in the arm and felt defended.

Tyler continued, "I think the city's water bill has doubled since she was assigned here. She got bucketed twice yesterday, and those boys weren't aiming for her head. I admit, I can appreciate a good wet T-shirt contest."

The thin layer of protective chivalry Ruby had sensed in Tyler roused her anger at Hector. Tyler was a safer target. Ruby stepped onto Hector's newly mopped floor and charged toward them. Tyler's eyes widened in surprise, and John's narrowed in defense.

Hector emerged from the kitchen as a dark silhouette outlined with the bright kitchen light behind him. Ruby tried to slow her stride. She slipped on the wet surface before regaining her balance and stood blocking the TV. The men stared. The urge to run and the compulsion to pick up the television and smash it on the ground froze her in place.

Tyler dropped the game controller on the coffee table in front of him. "Damn, Hector. Did you need to use that much water on the floor? You created a hazard zone."

Ruby leaned close to Tyler. "I don't need you to defend me, and I don't want to hear your bullshit." She picked up a magazine from the table. "I'll be in the coop on watch." She turned to leave. "Oh, and your tofu tastes like wet socks. Don't do me any more favors."

In the coop, Ruby kicked off her shoes, rested her feet on the desk, and buried her face in the magazine. Behind her she heard the bathroom door slam. She leaned back in her chair and noticed Hector wiping his wet hands on his untucked shirt. She wasn't sure what motivated his smile, but she wouldn't return his expression.

"You might wanna stop, drop, and roll," he said, rolling his arms like a disco dancer.

She was confused by his suggestion, and then more confused by the heat at her heels—smoke wisps curled from her socks. John crouched below the desk, holding a lighter custom-wrapped with holographic spheres to the soles of her feet. The lighter's flame was adjusted to its maximum. She furiously slapped at the smoke and then stood to stomp her feet. John held his gut laughing. Ruby turned toward him, her ponytail whipping around like a flag caught in a tornado. "You asshole!"

A click chucked from the station speaker. The red button next to the door to the apparatus floor flashed, and the station lights brightened.

"Incoming," Tyler yelled from the TV room. The medical tones followed, resembling the siren of a European ambulance.

Ruby was out the door first, stepping in her socks to the beat of the dispatcher's voice: "Baby not breathing, Cedar high-rise, language barrier. Caller waiting in the lobby."

"Probably a Somali with a cold," Hector said.

John slapped the red button, signaling dispatch that they were responding. He followed Ruby out the door. She quickened her pace. A bucket of water thrown by a truckie hiding behind the ladder truck missed Ruby and doused John.

"Instant karma." Ruby smiled.

John stopped at his gear locker, threw on a dry shirt, and hopped on the rig.

The multistory apartment complex, nicknamed the Somali High-Rise, was a few blocks from the station. Engine 7 turned into the parking lot on Cedar. John silenced the siren, and the engine crept through the lot under the swirl of emergency lights.

Women dressed in burkas crowded the entrance to the building. The engine crew pushed their way through the mob to get to the lobby, looking for a sick baby.

A Hispanic man approached them, speaking in Spanish. John turned to Hector, "What did he say?"

"You think I know Spanish?"

"Well, your name is Hector."

"I'm named after a French artist. I don't know any fuckin' Mexican."

Ruby slid the medical bag off of her shoulder and nodded toward a woman sitting on a bench next to the elevator. "His wife is having a baby."

"You speak Spanish?" Tyler said.

"I don't need to. The woman over there on the bench with the puddle at her feet looks like she's about to pop."

John keyed the mic on his radio and said, "Dispatch—Engine 7. Inform the medics we have a woman in labor. Her water broke. Can we get an ETA for the ambulance?"

"I'll get the OB kit," Hector said and headed for the rig.

Ruby sat next to the woman. "Do you speak English?"

The man Ruby assumed to be her husband said, "No English."

Ruby put her hand to her chest, "Ruby." She pointed to the woman.

The woman doubled over and moaned, "Alba."

Ruby helped Alba lie back. Hector made his way back through the crowd and dropped the OB kit next to Ruby. "You got this? I'm gonna help clear the lobby."

In a few minutes the lobby was empty, leaving only the smell of uunsi, the aromatic perfume of many Somali women. Ruby lifted Alba's skirt and removed her undergarment to check for crowning.

"Medics are still ten minutes out," John said. "How's it lookin'?"

With no sign of a baby's emerging head, Ruby gestured a thumbs-up.

Alba shouted, "El bebe está llegando!"

"She say baby come. Pero la cabeza." Alba's husband paused, searching for the English words. "The head. The head is wrong."

Alba screamed. One tiny foot suddenly dangled between her legs.

"Breech," Ruby said.

John keyed his radio and updated the paramedics. Tyler knelt beside Ruby, and together they spread out the OB equipment. Ruby smiled at Alba, feigning reassurance and hiding that she was scared shitless. Tyler unfolded the OB pad, and Ruby tucked it under Alba's legs. She mentally reviewed her training: to let nature take its course. *Don't pull, and don't tell the mother to push. Wait. Let the mother and child do the work. Provide arms to catch it when it comes out naturally.*

Ruby repositioned the pad and grazed the protruding foot. The baby's toes stretched as if reaching—and the other leg flopped through, joining the foot. Next came the baby's bottom and torso. The head remained inside. Ruby held the infant's body, motionless and opaque, shiny like an antique porcelain doll.

"Pull it out," Tyler said.

"We're supposed to wait."

"The baby's turning blue. I don't think it can breathe."

Ruby pressed her fingers inside and held the infant's face, creating an opening for air. Ruby couldn't see blue. She felt the infant resting lifeless in her hand, and then she felt panic.

"Push," Ruby said. "Empuje!"—the Spanish word she recalled posted above the handle on a convenience store door during a trip to Cancun. "Empuje!" she said again, louder. She looked into Alba's exhausted eyes. "Empuje," she whispered.

Alba pushed. The baby moved, and Ruby pulled. The infant gushed into her palms but remained still. She avoided Alba's eyes and focused on the baby, yet to take her first breath. She rubbed the tiny foot that had first emerged. She held the infant close to her lips and whispered, "Breathe." She rubbed again, listened for breath, and rubbed once more.

Like the pop of a cork on a champagne bottle, the little girl's eyes blinked open. Ruby released a quiet laugh. "Hola, little niña. Welcome to the world."

Tyler's crinkled brow softened. He suctioned the baby's mouth and nose with the bulb syringe. "I thought you didn't know Spanish." He handed the scalpel to Ruby. "Here you go, gringa. You get to cut the cord. Ten inches out and four back."

The new life Ruby held in her hands reminded her why she'd joined the fire department. She didn't simply catch a baby. She saved a life. Some might say it was heroic, and she would argue. But, secretly, she knew she was part of something extraordinary. Secretly, for one moment, Ruby felt like a hero. She handed the baby to Tyler, carefully placed the scalpel between the clamps, and cut. "Ten-four, Tyler," she said and smiled, letting the anger she had felt for him melt away.

The paramedics entered the lobby. Ruby handed the baby, now wrapped in a blanket, to Alba and said, "She's muy mimosa. She's beautiful."

Tyler picked up the medical bag and handed it to Ruby. He mouthed, "I'm sorry."

Ruby looked past Tyler and said, "Mimosa? I may have just called her baby champagne mixed with orange juice. Shit."

On the way back to the station, Ruby glanced at Hector, expecting to feel fear. Instead she felt a flash of anger, like a trapped fire getting a breath of air.

Tyler steered the engine onto the station apron, and Ruby hopped out to guide him back into the stall. He motioned to the roof and winked, alerting her to the ladder guys ducked behind the parapet, armed with water buckets.

John slammed his door and stood next to Ruby. "No more buckets today, guys. That's an order."

Confident that she could work without getting drenched, Ruby removed the lanyard from its holster and pressed it three times, signaling that Tyler was safe to back in.

Tyler and John returned to their game, and Ruby went to the kitchen to sweep. John's video soldier was just about to die again in the exact same scenario. He threw the controller on the table in frustration. Ruby rested her broom against the wall, lifted the controller, and selected *Try Again*.

John informed her, "Toggle to the left—you can choose a lady soldier."

She toggled. Her choices included an oversized muscled character sporting a crew cut and dressed in full combat gear, a wiry character with a handsome face and full combat gear, and a character dressed in a cropped camouflage tank shirt, with enormous breasts, hot pants, and army boots. She chose the handsome face.

John protested, "That's not the lady."

"I don't like her uniform."

Ruby maneuvered over a barbed-wire fence, crawled to a bunker, and waited. Potential targets scurried past. She remained behind the bunker.

"You gotta shoot the red team," Tyler and John said together.

"Move the joystick in a circle to get out of there. They'll ambush you before you get to the helicopter," John added.

Ruby let a few more enemies pass, maneuvered from the bunker, and threw a grenade at the red-team mob. She pushed every button as she made her way, jumping, hopping, and sometimes walking to the helicopter.

"Now just wait for the pilot and you're home free," Tyler said.

Ruby ignored his advice. She moved the joystick in a circle and jumped into the helicopter. She pulled down on the handle and flew the bird over the building, yielding a view of the carnage below.

"Beginner's luck," John said.

"Or maybe I'm just better at not relying on someone to bail me out. Next time you want me to choose the lady, make sure there's an option for high heels."

The next morning Ruby woke to masks chirping on the apparatus floor. Rookies were assigned to night watch on the rollout bed in the coop, closest to the noisy apparatus floor and station entryway. But last night, Ruby had fallen into it, exhausted, and slept hard. On a slow night, night watch was preferable to the thundering snore of men in the dorm. Now the dings of the morning mask check by the incoming shift meant it was time to go home.

Ruby removed her sheets from the coop bed, dropped them in the laundry bag, and went out to the rig. Her relief had arrived and placed his gear in a neat bundle next to the engine. Her bunker pants had been thrown behind the engine. One boot was under a locker, and the other was MIA. Her coat sleeves had been pulled inside out and her mask stuffed inside.

She yanked her mask from her coat sleeve. She found her gloves sitting next to Tyler's tidy bundle with his bunker pants rolled down around his boots, spanner belt clipped through the loops, coat tucked through the belt, and his helmet and mask attached to the carabiner. Properly relieved, Tyler threw his bundle in his locker.

"Must be nice," Ruby said. She pulled the sleeves of her coat right side out.

"They can be assholes."

"*They* sure can."

"Fair enough. Present company included. But in my defense, I didn't know you were spying from around the corner." He smiled.

"If I don't hear it, that makes it okay? It's not like a tree falling in the woods. If no one is there to hear it fall—the tree is still dead."

Ruby searched for the missing boot. Tyler got down on his stomach, retrieved it from under the engine, and handed it to Ruby.

She accepted her boot. Tyler's hand grazed hers. She wondered if the squeeze in her stomach was telling her to run or to hope for an ally in Tyler.

"Let me make it up to you. We're going to Bunny's for a Bloody Mary. Come. First round on me."

Hector slammed his locker door hard, causing it to pop back open. "Yeah, it'll be fun." He put his bundle in his locker. "What the hell you invitin' the rookie for?"

Ruby resisted the temptation to flinch at his tantrum. "Maybe another time." She stowed the last of her gear, headed for her car, and started home.

When Ruby turned into her alley and hit the garage door opener, the slow movement of the rising door was like a hypnotic seduction to sleep. She dropped her keys on the counter in her pristine kitchen, kicked off her shoes in her tidy living room, and dropped her uniform shirt in the hall. Her bedroom was the place where she let her guard down, free of judgment and others' expectations. She pushed the clothes piled high on her bed to the floor, dropped on the comforter, and fell into a deep sleep.

She woke in the early afternoon and showered. Sitting on the edge of the tub to pull on her socks, she gently rubbed her heel, still tender from John's asinine prank. *These feet have secrets,* she thought, tracing the pink circular scar on the pad of her foot.

She had been seven years old, living in a row apartment on Grant Street. Her mom was one of the only divorced parents in their small town. In spite of relying on welfare for support, her mother made sure that Ruby and her three brothers were clean and well-dressed. She worked at the local factory, leaving the kids to fend for themselves during the day. At night she was too tired to give them the attention they needed.

Stan Franken lived on the next block. He was the cool adult in the neighborhood, always surrounded by kids. Preteen girls competed to rub Stan's shoulders. They sat side by side on stools on his screened-in porch, combing one another's hair and waiting for their chance to be his favorite masseuse. Little boys slicked their hair back and sported short-sleeved white T-shirts to look just like him. They sat on the stoop, pretending to smoke cigarettes and telling the girls they're pretty, like Stan did. After Stan finished his cigarette, he flicked the butt into the street. The boys raced to be the first to stomp it out.

One summer evening after supper, Ruby sat with the girls on the porch. She was bored with hair combing and slipped down from her stool to sit on the bottom step with the boys. Stan inhaled his smoke. The boys mimicked him, dragging on the invisible cigarettes they held between their thumbs and forefingers. The last drag was the longest. Stan pulled in the smoke, and the end of the cigarette glowed red, burning the paper to the filter. Ruby looked at her bare feet. Stan loaded the butt between his middle finger and his thumb. He catapulted it into the air, and Ruby was already moving to the street.

The cigarette hit the curb and bounced before hitting the pavement. Ruby covered the red tip with her bare foot and stomped. The boys didn't have a chance. Stan stood, pointed at Ruby, and said, "You're my idol." With the same finger he motioned for Ruby to come to him.

That was the first time Ruby believed she was *someone special.*

CHAPTER 4

Dana

Unlike Ruby, who'd landed at a more modern station, Dana had snagged the oldest station in the city. The red-brick walls at Station 10 boasted historical significance. The second floor that once stored hay to feed the fire horses still creaked when firefighters rushed to slide down the shiny brass pole.

As the newest rookie assigned to a ladder company, the toolbox of the fire department, Dana had an opportunity to shine. She removed the chainsaw from the truck bed and yanked the cord. It whirred into service. "One pull," she said. The hum of the engine felt like applause rising in a crowded stadium. She looked from side to side; assured she was alone, she took a bow.

By the end of the day she had cleaned toilets, mopped the station floors twice, and responded to a fender bender. For dinner she consumed overcooked spaghetti noodles with meat sauce from a jar. *So much for gourmet firefighters*, she thought. After dinner she sat in front of the TV with the crew.

"Hey, rookie," Gabe said. He leaned back in his recliner. "Isn't there some housework needin' to be done? How 'bout you get some whiskers before you think about puttin' your feet up."

Dana glanced at the table she had cleared and the trash can she had lined with a new bag.

Gabe stroked his clean-shaven chin. "The floor could use a once-over, and the tools on the truck need a fresh coat."

After mopping the floor one more time, Dana checked the tools. She found one hook with a small chip. "One for all and all for one," she said and painted the lot.

Confident in glistening tools and completed station duties, Dana had a question she couldn't put off any longer.

Barbells clanged in the basement. Reggie was working out, and of all the guys, he seemed most approachable. She slapped down hard on the concrete steps to announce her approach.

She caught his eye and cleared her throat. "I was wondering." She buried her hands in her pockets and shuffled her feet. "What clothes do we sleep in?"

"Ha!" he replied. "Rookie, you won't be sleepin' tonight. This is firefightin' station number 10. Busiest house in the city. You made the mistake giving up your night watch. Rookies never let durgans—"

Dana squinted in confusion. He explained, "Veteran firefighters. Never give up your watch to a durgan."

"You mean Gabe? He said he can't sleep in the dorm."

"Durgans don't clean toilets and we don't take night watch. Whatever you wear to bed tonight, make sure when the tones go off, you're not last on the rig. You will be left behind."

Dana turned to leave and noticed a broken wooden axe handle leaning against the wall. She reached for it, figuring that a fire station is no place for broken tools.

"That's mine. Leave it," Reggie said.

She climbed the steps to the mixed-gender dorm, arranged with twin beds six feet apart. Her bed was closest to the fire pole. Taped to the footboard was a strip of masking tape with *ROOKIE* written on it in black marker. She made her bed with bleached white sheets and the standard-issue red wool blanket provided by the city. She got under the covers, fully dressed in her uniform. Her belt poked her side, and she flopped onto her back. Footsteps shuffled in the darkness. She opened one eye and saw Reggie's silhouette peel back the blanket on his bed. He kicked off his shoes, unbuckled his belt, and dropped his pants to the floor. He tucked the broken axe handle under his mattress.

Dana shut her eyes and listened—more shuffles across the floor, more belts unbuckled, and all pants dropped. Under the covers, she wriggled out of her pants and dropped them on the floor. Finally she fell asleep.

At 02:20 fluorescent light slapped against her eyelids. The dispatcher's voice squawked like a flock of geese in flight. Opening her eyes, a blur of blue shirts being pulled over torsos raced past her bed and disappeared down the fire pole.

"Shit, shit, shit." *I can't be last on the rig.* She grabbed her pants from the floor and shoved her feet inside.

"What the—" Her feet didn't come through the bottom.

She tore them off and inspected the legs. Knots were tied at the ankles. Frantic, she worked to untie them, but the knots were too tight. The last of the awakened firefighters disappeared down the pole.

She pulled the waist of her knotted pants to her knees and hopped. Her thighs squeaked on the brass as she slid. She pressed her pants-covered feet against the pole, hit ground, and stumbled to the truck, tripping on her dragging pantlegs. She threw them to the side and pulled her bunker pants over her bare legs. Safe inside the cab, she listened to the dispatcher describe the call: "One possibly trapped."

Ladder 10 screamed through the night to a residential home. Dana followed Captain Smitty up the walkway. He knocked on the door with the butt of his radio and called, "Minneapolis Fire Department."

A woman answered, shouting above a child's screams. Dana looked over the woman's shoulder. A toddler clung to the railing, one leg wedged between the rungs. An empty cup sat at the bottom of the steps in a puddle of water. Two older children sat on the top step in their pj's.

"Cap'n, should I grab the saw?" Dana asked.

"We're gonna try before we pry," he said and then asked the woman, "You got any dish soap?"

She brought soap from the kitchen, and he slathered it on the toddler's leg. The leg easily came free.

Although disappointed she wouldn't use power tools, Dana appreciated the new strategy "try before we pry." She was sure the child agreed.

On the ride back to the firehouse, the liner of Dana's bunker pants rubbed on the inside of her thighs, tender from the friction of the fire pole. She recalled advice from rookie school—if you don't get pranked it means they don't like you—and resolved to take the hazing in stride.

"I sure could've used that dish soap coming down the fire pole in my skivvies."

"You might want to keep a bottle under your bed." Smitty winked.

Laughter filled the cab. A joke at Dana's expense in exchange for bonding with her crew felt worth it.

"Kinda like that stick under your bunk, huh, Reggie?" Dana slapped her knee laughing. The others' laughter retracted like a hand on a hot stove. *Sensitive subject?* Dana wondered.

Arriving at the station, Dana found her uniform pants waiting on the apparatus floor, rolled in a ball. She threw them over her shoulder and started toward the dorm, still wearing her bunker pants.

"Hold on," Smitty said. "No turnouts in the dorm. They're contaminated."

Dana cupped the back of her neck and wiped the nervous sweat at her hairline. "I'm in my underwear under here."

"It's against MFD protocol to wear your fire gear in the living area."

The crew stood with crossed arms. Dana peeled down her fire pants and stepped out of her boots. She left her uniform pants draped over her shoulder and walked the steps to the dorm in her boxers.

Lying in bed, she wasn't sure if this is what it took to be one of the guys. But she was sure this wouldn't happen again. Dana tucked her pants under her pillow.

The next morning, she got in her truck and grabbed her sunglasses from the dash. On her way home she stopped at the grocery store for coffee. In the reflection of her pickup window, she tousled her hair and straightened her badge before crossing the lot and entering the store. She pushed her sunglasses on top of her head and noticed people glancing and returning for a second look. She basked in the pride she felt in her uniform. Two teenage girls covered their mouths, whispering and laughing.

"Mommy, look. A football player!" The child's mother made hushing sounds.

Dana was confused. *Football? Do football players wear badges? Haven't these people seen a woman in uniform before?*

She went to the checkout line with a pound of coffee. The cashier did a double take and quickly looked away. She giggled handing Dana the receipt. Dana wiped her nose with her sleeve. *Geez. Do I have a booger on my face?*

In her truck, Dana checked her face in the rearview mirror. Startled, she yanked her glasses off her head. The black grease smeared on the rims had transferred a perfect dark circle around each eye. Dana couldn't contain her laughter at the prank. Retaliation would be expected and anticipated, and most of all, it was mandatory. The traditional bucket of water thrown from the hose tower on an unaware firefighter wasn't creative enough.

———————

The next day she returned to the station armed with bananas and five pounds of flour.

The entitlement of veteran firefighters to sit around and drink coffee while the rookie works was the perfect opportunity for revenge. *Shit, they even have a made-up name to label their superiority— durgan. What the hell does that mean? Maybe "lazy ass."*

As Gabe relayed a story about his wife and his girlfriend, she put her scheme into action. She quickly scrubbed the toilets and mopped the dorm. Then she broke open the flour and sprinkled white powder between the sheets of every bed, careful to replace the blankets as she had found them.

After a quiet morning, the truck crew went into the community to do inspections while the engine crew went to the grocery store to shop for the clutch. *It's like learning a whole new language,* Dana thought.

Dana was assigned to noon watch, again. Durgans drove their cars into the station and washed them before taking a one-to-three, or what civilians call a nap, in the dorm. Time to put the bananas into action.

She cut the peels into skinny slices. She tucked them under the windshield wipers of each durgan's personal vehicle, quietly singing to the Chiquita banana jingle,

"You're most digestible, my friend,
under the wiper end to end.
You can put them in a pie or use them to . . .
get back at all the guys."

She switched the wipers to the on position so the moment the ignition turned, voilà! Smeared banana! It was good fun, and Dana was determined to let the guys know she was a worthy opponent.

At 13:45 the fire tones boomed through the station. The dispatcher described the emergency in detail, but Dana heard only two words—*house fire.*

The dispatcher's voice, steady and calm, clashed with the accelerated beat of Dana's heart. She imagined flames shooting from the roof as residents waited to be rescued from second-floor windows.

She lifted the collar of her coat, anticipating the crackle of stiff Kevlar soon to become worn in. She pushed her arm through the sleeve, trusting the promise of protection in the thermal lining. Dana's heartbeat settled. Then she remembered the flour.

Footsteps pounding like thunder. The whoosh of each firefighter sliding down the pole in a blue uniform shirt covered with the floury dust, like snowflakes falling in a blizzard. Smitty lifted his suspenders over his shoulders and smirked. Suppressing her smile, Dana shrugged. She waited for the final white-speckled shirt to disappear under the black soot of a firefighter coat before closing her door. Satisfied with her prank, Dana was ready for what she had signed up for—she would fight fire.

Arriving at the address, Smitty silenced the siren and keyed his mic. "Dispatch, Ladder 10 and the engine arrived. Single-family home, nothing showing."

Dana leaned forward, releasing her tank from the bracket. Reggie turned and said, "False alarm, rookie, you don't need that tank."

Dana shoved the tank back in its bracket and followed Smitty to the door. Two college-age guys waited on the step. One mumbled, "The smoke detector keeps going off. The beeping is driving us crazy."

Smitty returned to the rig. Dana unscrewed the detector from its bracket and removed the battery. The date on the back registered fifteen years expired. She handed it to the young man and said, "Time for a new one."

Dana expected to get a few shots from the guys after her flour prank. She welcomed it. Instead, when she took her place at the dinner table, everyone got up and left. After eating alone, she cleaned alone.

She went to the apparatus floor and found Reggie at the workbench.

"Did I do something wrong?"

He scanned the garage, making sure they were alone. "I'm gonna tell you this just once. Besting your crew when you're still a rookie won't go well for you. I suggest you lay low for a while. They'll forget about it in a few years."

Dana retired to the dorm early and got under the covers still wearing her pants. *A few years?* she thought. *Fuck 'em. If they're gonna dish it out, just fuck 'em.*

The next morning, the start of a car engine and the swish of windshield wipers hurried Dana's exit from the station.

"Son of a bitch," came the voice of a durgan.

The scent of banana wafted through the station. Dana flung open the door to the parking lot and said, "How do you like them bananas?"

CHAPTER 5

Ruby

After six months of rookie hazing, the physical test required to graduate from probation loomed. Parked in the lot at Station 7, Ruby scanned the roofline for potential water bombers. Seeing movement above, she dashed into the station. Water hit the ground behind her. She dragged a garden hose across the apparatus floor to the ladder leading to the roof scuttle hatch, ducked behind a vending machine, and waited. *They have to come down sometime.* Determined to get her revenge, she aimed the hose at the middle rung.

The ladder vibrated, and she squeezed the trigger. A warning shout came from the coop, "Chief's on deck."

Ruby dropped the nozzle. "You're lucky," she said. "Chief's here." Water wars were technically against the rules.

The durgan stepped off the ladder and said, "It's your big day. It's bad luck to dodge a bucket on test day."

Ruby flexed her bicep and said, "I won't be counting on luck."

She was in the best shape of her life and knew she could complete the course in eight minutes, allowing a four-minute cushion for hiccups. She loaded her gear into the chief's Suburban and took shotgun, anxious to shed her rookie status.

———————

In spite of her confidence, Ruby's stomach jittered as the chief steered through the gate to the training tower. As she got out, she eyed the course and spotted Jared as he high-fived the training chief and bundled his gear, obviously successful. She dressed in her turnouts and clapped her gloved hands together. Approaching the starting line, she cinched up the straps of her air tank and pressed her mask to her face.

"On your go," the stopwatch keeper said.

Ruby took the step that started the timer. She slid a twenty-five-foot straight-beam ladder from the truck bed and butted it against the building. Recalling her first attempt nine months earlier at the start of rookie school, when she dropped it on her helmet, she relied on experience. A rung-by-rung method was choppy and clumsy, so she placed her hands on the rails, leaned forward, and used her legs for momentum.

She climbed the ladder to a parapet. She retracted the cord on a mock saw for the required nine pulls, chopped on the simulator, and pounded down the stairs to drag the hose and climb the stairs again to the dummy.

That 175 pounds of dead weight outfitted in a plastic fire coat was once her nemesis. After arranging it into a seated position, she squatted behind and reached around its waist, then pushed with her legs to stand. The burn in her quads signaled her to take the first step back. Step by step, she backed through the maze with its head towering above hers. She was close to the finish. Two steps remained—throw the dummy into the waist-high window and hang the fan. Ruby was well ahead of her best time.

Descending the stairs to the final obstacle, she visualized lifting the fan. *Lift it to my waist, rest it on the carabiner of my spanner belt, heave it onto my shoulder, crouch and jump.* Probation would end with the slight jump she needed to secure its floppy rubber hook over the top of an eight-foot-tall door. Everything at the tower was bigger than in life, but Ruby had adjusted and found techniques to use her 5'6", 130-pound frame to her advantage.

A yellow square painted on the pavement marked the final hurdle. Inside it she expected to find the familiar red, forty-pound square fan—the same fan that her entire class had conquered during training, identical to the square fan used at the house fire she had recently fought. Instead, in its place was a round fan, still red, but with rigid metal hooks welded to its side.

Certain she could jump a little higher to compensate for the rigid hooks, Ruby lifted the fan to her waist, surprised at its increased weight. She approached the door, hoisted the fan to her shoulder, and crouched. She jumped, and as her boots left the ground, she pushed the fan from her shoulder to hook the door.

The hook scraped against the door before falling back on her shoulder. Ruby crouched lower, jumped, pushed, and missed. Her shoulder ached. She crouched, jumped, pushed, and missed again.

"Thirty seconds remaining," the timer said. "Maybe you should quit."

Ruby crouched again but, exhausted, she dropped the fan and fell to her knees. She lifted her mask and vomited in her helmet.

The chief drove Ruby back to the station in silence. John was waiting in the coop. He handed her a letter on official Minneapolis Fire letterhead.

Firefighter Ruby Bell:

Your failure to successfully complete the six-month probationary test extends your probationary period for 30 days. Report downtown to headquarters at the start of your next shift for a fact-finding hearing. Failure to meet physical standards, required of a Minneapolis firefighter, will result in termination.

At the bottom was a rubber-stamped Chief of the Department signature.

CHAPTER 6

Tiller: The firefighter driving the back of an equipped hook-and-ladder truck; the box containing the steering wheel, perched high above the end of the rig, is the **till**.

Truckie: Firefighter working on a ladder truck rather than an engine. Trucks are ladders-and-rescue vehicles. Engines are water-and-medical-response vehicles.

Dana

After completing her six-month probationary test, Dana was moving on to till training. Her stomach flipped like she was waiting in line for the roller coaster. She set her gear at the back of Ladder 10. Proficiency in the till would earn her the title of Ladder 10 tiller and increased popularity. Most of the guys were talking to her again, and Gabe's complaints droned on about being stuck in the box while the rookie sat in comfort of the cab.

The arrival of the first snowfall of the season on her first day of till training felt symbolic. Like the white snow covering the muddy streets, she was ready for a fresh start. The more slack she pulled by doing undesirable tasks, the more she would be appreciated.

She climbed the steps to the second floor, grabbed a sweatshirt from her locker, and went to the bathroom to change. Reggie was standing at the bathroom sink.

"Till day," she said, and closed the stall door.

He pulled the razor down through the shaving cream, tracing his jawline. "Don't throw me off back there. Follow my lead." He swiped the stubble into the sink. "Hang onto the wheel. I'll do the rest."

The stall door thumped. Cold water drenched her fresh uniform shirt. She covered her mouth. No way would she let them hear her scream. She threw the door open, slamming it into the wall. Reggie glanced at the exit and continued his shave.

She tossed her soaked shirt into her locker and pulled a dry shirt over her soaked hair. Anxious to get in the till, she set to the housework.

As Dana pushed a mop bucket down the hallway, Ryan met her holding a toilet brush. Another rookie at the station took off some of the heat, but she'd been especially happy to see Ryan Leon. The bond formed as they helped Jared over the auditorium raise had grown into a partnership.

"Should we hit this, Rin?" she said.

Ryan held up the brush. "Livin' the dream, Tin-Tin—the heroic work of a firefighter."

Dogging it during the daily five-mile run in rookie school had earned them their nicknames, consistently last to finish and shepherding in the rookie herd. After the toilets were scrubbed and shaving stubble was cleaned from the sinks, they mopped the floors. She helped Ryan wash the engine, and he helped her wash the truck—partnership in action.

Reggie joined them for the final rinse-down and then said, "Hop in the till and we'll pull her out on the apron. When we start rollin', don't force it. Just hold onto the wheel."

Dana pulled on her bunker pants and climbed up to the till. She slid open the door to the small, one-person cockpit perched above the tail end of the elongated truck, squeezed in, and ran her hands around the steering wheel, repeating Reggie's advice. "Just hang on and keep the back in line with the front."

Reggie watched her from the concrete apparatus floor. "It's kinda like backing up a boat, but you're going forward." He turned to walk to the cab and then turned back. "When I turn a corner to the right, you steer to the left. Don't oversteer. Make small adjustments. If you're unsure, let go and the back of the truck will right itself."

He pointed to a little speaker above her head. "You can hear us from the cab on the speaker, but we can't hear you, so don't bother yelling. The pedal for the horn is by your right foot. I'll hear it. If you're in trouble, step on the pedal. I will stop. I won't be happy, but I will stop."

Reggie walked the fifty feet to the driver's seat and climbed in. When he signaled Dana with a thumbs-up through his open window, she pulled a string hanging from the ceiling, triggering the garage door opener. This was the first time she truly felt the grandiosity of the huge doors. The sun reflecting off the snow-covered streets flashed like a mob of paparazzi cameras. She was a rock star and the glimmering snow celebrated her as she steered the back of the rig onto the apron.

"Okay, good job going forward. Now we're going to back it in. Hey, Leon, grab the lanyard. If she's gonna hit anything, lay on that horn."

Dana waited while Ryan grabbed the yellow bungee-like cord.

He pressed the button three times, signaling the all-clear to back up. The truck began to roll back, and a waterfall dropped from the roof, drenching Ryan.

"Ahhhhhhh," he screamed, his voice pitching high. "It's freezing. Ahhhhhh." He squeezed the button on the lanyard in one long drawn-out honk. Reggie slammed on the brakes. Ryan dropped the lanyard and bolted into the station.

"Whiny little baby," said Gabe from above. "Leon the Lion my ass. More like Lioness, I'd say."

Ryan was instantly dubbed Leon-ess. Although Dana was happy to have a second target in the house, she knew they got it wrong—the lioness is the strong one in the pack.

Smitty joined the group. Steam from his coffee cup rose into the snowy spring air. He grabbed the lanyard with his free hand, looked to the clear blue sky, and said, "Must be warming up to drop that kind of rain."

Dana steered into the garage, pushing the wheel to the left, and parked at an angle. She knew she wasn't done. A crooked rig could slam into the wall when pulling out for an emergency. Reggie pulled forward. Backing again, Dana landed cockeyed. The incessant beeping of backing into the station attracted most of the guys to assemble and shout out tips.

"Ten and two doesn't work. Hold onto the underside of the wheel at six and four. Push your thumbs out. Follow your thumbs!"

Even Ryan, now in a cozy dry turtleneck, joined in. "Hold on. Don't turn."

"Use the string you pulled to open the door as your target. Drive the cab to the string! Don't take your eyes off it."

Dana swerved again, too close to the wall. She stomped the

pedal on the floor, engaging the horn with one long blast. Reggie hit the brakes. Dana climbed out of the till and stood on the ledge. Instead of hanging next to Dana's cockpit, the brown piece of twisted twine rested on the roof of the till. She looked down at the gathered firefighters and wiped the sweat from her upper lip with the collar of her shirt.

"I can't see that damn string. It's the same color as the wall."

"Here, catch." Smitty threw her a white dishtowel. "Tie this on the string."

The towel did the trick. Dana backed into the station twice, perfectly straight.

The next part of training was navigating the city streets. Dana was flawless at going forward. Towering above traffic, she looked over neighborhood fences. She spotted a snow-covered gas grill next to a garage and the banana seat of a girl's Huffy bike jutting from snow.

The speaker above her head vibrated with the dispatcher's voice. "Ladder 10 report to King's Highway Nursing Home for a head injury from a fall."

Reggie tapped the air horn. Smitty engaged the siren. Dana maneuvered through the streets, reacting to Reggie's every move. She turned wide at the corner, avoiding a car parked too close to the intersection. To stay in line with the cab she focused on the flashing red lights. That was when the till slid sideways toward the curb.

Dana tightened her grip on the wheel and turned to the left. Still sliding. She spun the wheel to the right. "Four and six," she said. She grasped the underside of the wheel and stuck her thumbs out, then pushed the wheel in the direction of the thumb pointing toward the street and away from the curb.

Ahead, a bicyclist with wide mountain-bike tires cut a slushy path through the snow-covered bike lane. Dana blinked, certain the biker was a snow mirage. But as the ladder angled up the street, the pedaling legs of the mirage came into focus.

Reggie's voice crackled over the wail of the siren. "There's a medical waiting to happen. What kind of idiot rides a bike in the snow?"

Dana hovered her foot above the pedal. *I will stop, but I won't be happy.*

The front cab raced down the middle of the street. The back slid at a ninety-degree angle. Axes vibrated in the tool bed. Dana screamed, "Hit the brakes!"

You can hear us, but we can't hear you.

Frantic, Dana jerked the wheel. The street, the snow, and the steering wheel became a blur, the biker more vivid. The impact imminent. Dana closed her eyes. She heard her mom's voice, "Good drivin', Jack."

If you're unsure, let go. Dana took her hands off the wheel.

She opened her eyes, and the till was in a straight line behind the cab. They passed the biker. He waved. Dana sat tall, thumbs at the ready and her boot suspended above the horn she had refused to honk.

At the nursing home, Dana climbed down and retrieved the medical bag. An elderly man held the door open, his chest puffed out and his hand tilted in salute. The crew crowded into the elevator as the siren of an arriving ambulance whooped. Smitty pushed the button for the fifth floor, the Alzheimer unit.

"It's Marjorie again," said the attendant at the desk outside the elevator.

The attendant led the crew down a dimly lit hallway. Fluorescent light spilled into the corridor through the open doors of the residents' rooms. Children's drawings taped on the walls above twin hospital beds acted as reminders for the strangers who cared for them—*I once had a vibrant life. I am loved.* As they turned the corner into the dining area, the stench of urine faded and the aroma of shepherd's pie promised a partitioned tray filled with mashed potato, ground beef, and corn.

Marjorie sat on the floor, smiling. The legs of her stretch pants were bunched above her knees, and her gray hair was tangled and matted.

"My head hurts."

Dana slid her hands into medical gloves, tugged her turnout pants to create slack, and crouched next to Marjorie. "Do you remember falling?" She separated the strands of Marjorie's matted hair and discovered an egg-sized bump.

"I didn't fall. My head hurts."

Dana slapped an instant ice pack on the floor to activate the cold. She wrapped it in gauze and held it to Marjorie's head. "This will help."

Gabe handed Dana an oxygen mask. Smitty filled in the arriving medics, and together they loaded Marjorie onto the stretcher. Smitty, Reggie, and Gabe crowded into the elevator with the paramedics.

"I'll take the stairs," Dana said. The elevator closed, and Dana made her way to the far side of the dining hall in search of the activity room. Lily worked on this floor, and she wanted her girlfriend to see her in her fire gear. In the dining room a resident with perfectly groomed white hair, matching the pearls around her neck, played solitaire. As Dana passed by, the woman smacked the table with a card and said, "Go fuck your mother."

"Hi, Rita," Dana said, recalling Lily's venting sessions about her charges in this unit.

She found Lily standing in front of the TV with her back to the residents, fiddling with the DVD player. She was obviously unsuccessful in getting it to work. Looking frustrated, she turned to the group and said, "I hope you all enjoyed the movie. Time for your afternoon snack in the dining room."

Dana leaned in the doorway with her arms crossed. She caught Lily's eye and shook her head. "Shameless."

Lily giggled. "Why explain something they won't remember in a few minutes? Happiness is not overrated." Dana stepped into the room, making way for the last of exiting residents.

"Look at you in your hot truckie turnout pants. What I'm thinking right now—that's shameless." She tugged on the waist of Dana's pants. Dana gave in to Lily's pull, leaned in, and kissed her.

"My crew's waiting. I better go."

Lily exaggerated a sad face.

"Someone has to protect the city."

She kissed Dana on the cheek. "Honestly, how many fewer runs do you get on that truck compared to the engine?"

"We don't get paid for what we do. We—"

Lily rolled her eyes and joined in, "Get paid for what we're prepared to do."

Dana jogged back through the dining hall. Turning the corner, she heard, "Fuck your mother."

"Bye, Rita."

Dana caught up with her crew and climbed into the till. Following

Reggie, she made small adjustments, navigating the streets with little effort. At the firehouse, Reggie made a wide turn onto the apron, and Dana mirrored his turn and prepared to back into the station.

Steam from the wet garage floor rolled through the opening door and into the snowy afternoon. Dana looked over her shoulder for her dishtowel target.

Hanging from the rafters, one hundred white towels flapped in the wind of the widening door. The scene resembled a battlefield of soldiers waving white flags in surrender.

She soaked in the salutation and homed in on one towel. Ryan stood inside the garage and grabbed the lanyard to guide her. She tapped the horn at her foot three times and beelined to the original dishtowel. Her firefighting brothers stood in a line, holding half-eaten sandwiches in the air and cheering.

Dana exited the till and stood on the ledge, high above the cheering crowd, and took a bow. She felt sorry for Ryan, soaked again in his second uniform shirt of the day.

"Hey, Rinny, help me get these towels down. You need 'em more than I do."

CHAPTER 7

Reach Down: Passing over faster and stronger candidates to hire firefighters from an underrepresented group. The Minneapolis Fire Department labeled women as reach downs for thirteen years.

Ruby

Dressed in her class-A white uniform shirt, Ruby sat in the back seat of Engine 7, gripping her warning letter. For most firefighters, the formal uniform finds its way to the back of the closet, hanging next to prom formals from years gone by. The rest of the crew, dressed in blue, accompanied her as Tyler drove downtown to headquarters. Ruby skimmed the details outlining her unsatisfactory performance. Her eyes caught again on one phrase: *failure to meet physical standards will result in termination.*

"I tried to tell 'em," Hector grunted. "Women aren't strong enough for this job, but they reached down and got 'em anyway. Now I gotta miss my morning shit while we tote her princess ass downtown."

"Kapow! Really, Catman?" Tyler said. "Who are you to bitch? Weren't you in the class of the lollipop kids?"

John joined in. "That's right. You were part of the bullshit lawsuit for the short guys." He turned to the back seat. "If it wasn't for *reach down*, you'd still be making Spam in Hicksville, Minnesota."

Tyler let out a bellowing laugh. "Literal reach down," he said.

Ruby looked up from her letter and stared into Hector's eyes. *Such a hypocrite,* she thought. He turned away. Tyler stopped at the curb in front of city hall.

Hector hopped off the rig and lit a smoke. Ruby opened her door and glanced once more at the letter.

"Don't forget to mention you crushed the rest of the course," Tyler said.

The sound of Ruby's shiny patent-leather shoes echoed through the wide marble stairwell as she marched up the center. John held the railing and walked behind. She intended to appear competent. *Act it until you feel it,* she thought.

The blood pumping through her carotid flushed her cheeks red. Inside the waiting room of MFD headquarters, she peered into a glass cabinet displaying framed photos of white men standing next to horse-drawn fire rigs. Others, sporting bushy mustaches, wore vintage white hats adorned with brass bugles, commemorating the fire department's long history. Her white shirt and bell cap, reflected in the glass, made her almost appear as one of them.

A woman in civilian clothes sitting at a desk said, "They're ready for you."

Three chiefs sat at a long white table, wearing pressed white shirts decorated with shiny gold badges. The bugle insignias pinned on each side of their collars shined under fluorescent light. Their chairs were pushed in so far, they could do nothing but sit up straight, folded hands rested on the tabletop. John took an empty chair at the end of the table.

The chief sitting across from the remaining chair and a microphone set on a pedestal gestured. "Have a seat."

"Ms. Bell," he began as she took the open chair, "you were unable to complete your probationary test in the required time." He shuffled papers and cleared his throat. "Excuse me, you were unable to complete the test at all. You gave up and were unable to hang the fan."

"I am able to complete the test in the required time. The fact is, Chief, when I reached the fan I was ahead of my best time." She paused, smiled, and said, "I was crushing it."

In the silent room Ruby's breath echoed in her head. *Had minutes passed or just seconds?*

Ruby broke the unbearable silence. "I have no excuses." She leaned close to the microphone. "I can and I will finish the test within the time limit, given an opportunity to familiarize myself with the required equipment."

"You have thirty days to get to know that fan," the chief replied.

———————

After the inquisition, the identity of cadets who had failed the test had spread like a leaky ink pen. One of the shorter men and all the women, except for Dana, had been unable to hang the fan.

For the next two weeks Ruby carried the round fan with her at the fire station. She named her new pal Fanny. At lunchtime Fanny sat between Ruby and John.

"I'd think you'd hate that thing," John said.

"Hate it? This is my biggest fan."

"FANtastic! Well, love it or not, can you hang it on the door?"

She couldn't. She could shoulder press it five consecutive reps, but the extra few inches of height she needed to reach the top of the door seemed impossible. Gossip among the rookies swelled: "It's a conspiracy. The round fan is obsolete. Human Resources should be notified." Ruby ignored the chatter and focused on overcoming her height disadvantage.

———

Too quickly, thirty days passed. Ruby's retest day had arrived and still, she hadn't hung the fan. The ladder truck captain approached her and said, "The new class of rookies is out today. We got Bettina. Show her around a bit."

Today of all days he wants me to be tour guide. Ruby was glad to have another woman in the station, but if she didn't pass this test, the new girl would be on her own.

Ruby started the tour in the bathroom. "After you clean the toilets, move to the sink. Mop the bathroom floor last. Be careful not to splatter mop water on your pants. It'll leave bleach spots that don't come out."

"Do we clean the men's bathroom or do they?" Bettina asked.

"This is it. We share."

Looking confused, Bettina took in the layout. Two shower stalls on the left, three toilet stalls on the right, and one urinal. Three sinks hung from the wall opposite the toilets. John entered the bathroom with a newspaper, proceeded to the end stall, and closed the door. Bettina looked wide-eyed at Ruby.

Ruby laughed. "Let's go outside. The patio could use a quick shovel."

After directing Bettina to the shovel closet, Ruby grabbed her turnout coat, strapped on her SCBA, and disappeared into the basement. With one last opportunity to practice, she lifted Fanny to her shoulder. "Fanny, any ideas? We need three damn inches."

Fire-department shoes slapped onto the bottom concrete step. Tyler said, "Any good tips from Fanny?"

"Now who's spying from around the corner?" Ruby teased. She lowered the fan to the ground. "I meant to thank you. I had no idea Hector was a lollipop kid."

"He's harmless. I'm pretty sure he's just glad for a new scapegoat."

Ruby's stomach churned and her legs weakened. She sat on the fan and covered her face with her hands.

"Listen, you'll do great today. It's bullshit since we don't use that fan anymore, but I'll be on the sideline cheering you on."

She stood and looked into Tyler's eyes. "Enjoy the view from the sidelines."

"Whoa. Excuse me for coming down here to let you know I'm on your side."

Ruby lifted the fan. He took it from her shoulder and lowered it to the floor. "You're ready," he said.

"I'm not."

Tyler held her hand. "Ready to go?"

She pulled it away and checked her watch. "Shit. It's time." She sprinted up the steps and jogged through the coop to the dining area. Hector and a truckie stood in front of the patio window, sipping coffee, as Bettina bent over to chip ice from around the grill.

"Wow, Big Butt-Tina. About seven axe handles wide," said the truckie.

"I wouldn't mind slippin' my axe handle in there," Hector said.

Ruby wondered, *Am I invisible, or do they not care that I'm here?* The engine horn blasted from the apparatus floor. Startled, Hector dropped his cup on the table and started toward the door.

"We don't wanna be late on your last day," he said, rushing past her. His back grazed her chest. Ruby flinched and brushed the front of her shirt like somehow she could wipe Hector away.

A ladder truck waited at the four-story cement tower, loaded with the equipment she would use to perform the test. A twenty-five-foot straight-beam ladder rested on the ground. Fanny waited at the far end of the tower on the faded yellow line. The original square fan from rookie school sat next to Fanny, wedged into a newly shoveled pile of snow.

The training chief approached, glanced at Ruby, and addressed John. "Came straight from HR. Each candidate will be given a choice to use the square fan with floppy hooks or the round fan with rigid hooks."

Ruby smiled at her best friend of the last few weeks and said, "Thank you, Fanny."

John broke out in song, "I am woman, hear me roar."

Ruby stretched her suspenders over her shoulders and flung her coat on like a cape. The miracle she'd hoped for had manifested. She pulled on her gloves and clapped her hands together, signaling she was ready.

Ruby clicked the respirator into her facepiece. She slapped the ladder against the building like it was made of bamboo. The rhythm of the sledgehammer hitting the chopping simulator inspired her like dance music during a workout. She reached the dummy a full forty-five seconds ahead of her best time. She approached the two fans set side by side like competitors on a starting line.

Ruby glanced at her crew watching from the sidelines. *Hang the fan and I'm done. Hang the fan and I'm one of them.*

Tyler gave a thumbs-up. She met Hector's eyes. He shook his head. "Fuckin' figures," she read on his lips.

Ruby lifted the floppy-hooked square fan. It was lighter than she had remembered. She cocked the hook and bellied up to the door.

The training chief instructed, "Hang the fan on the door to complete the test. Five minutes remaining."

Ruby raised the fan to her shoulder. She eyed her target at the top of the door. "Fuck it," she said. She carried the lighter fan back to the line and dropped it. She wrapped her hands around Fanny and lifted the round fan to her belt. "You didn't think I was going to do this without you."

She crouched in front of the door and jumped, throwing the round fan with all her strength. It was as if Fanny's rigid hook was reaching to take its rightful place atop the steel-framed door.

The sound of metal scratching metal came first. Next came the crash of the fan hitting the pavement. Hector let out an involuntary "Whoop!" John resumed humming "I am woman, hear me roar," because he didn't know any more of the words, and Tyler's eyes remained fixed on Ruby in disbelief.

The top of the door might as well have been a star in the sky. She took one step back and then another. The loosening straps of her harness made her tank feel like a lead weight. She bent forward to gain some slack and tightened the dangling straps. Resting her hands on her knees, she rested for a moment and then, in one swooping movement, removed her helmet and threw it like a Frisbee to the bottom of the door. She picked up Fanny, stepped up on her helmet, and hooked the fan on the door.

The air in Hector's whoop deflated to an oomph. John and Tyler high-fived. The chief pressed the button on the stopwatch and confirmed her passing time, "Ten minutes flat."

Ruby eased the fan to the ground and retrieved her helmet. "We did it, Fanny."

───────

The engine traveled across the familiar bridge spanning the river. Sheets of ice floating on the river's surface gathered at the shore and joined its border. Smaller pieces swirled and diminished in the flow, nearing the bliss of invisibility. She knew how close she had been to disappearing. She'd surprised herself in choosing Fanny over the lighter fan. *This will show them,* she thought. *I don't need— No, I don't want special treatment. I just want to be part of the shore.*

───────

At the station Ruby snapped a fresh, full air bottle into her bracket. As she headed toward the coop, she felt Hector approaching. She quickened her pace. She paused to open the door, and Hector reached over to hold it closed.

Whispering, his voice rose above the shush, vibrating like irritating chatter in the back of a classroom. "You think because you know how to use your helmet like a stepstool, we're gonna trust you? This changes nothing. If I, or if any of us, go down in a fire, we know. You can't fuckin' pull us out."

She pushed Hector back and returned to the rig. Tyler was setting up his boots and pants next to the driver's door. "I need to check my air bottle," she explained.

"Again? Hey, nice move with the helmet toss." He lifted his chin toward Hector. "Don't let him get to you. He treats everybody like that."

Ruby raised her eyebrows.

"If he didn't like you, he'd ignore you. If it makes you feel better, he had a rough childhood."

"We all had a rough childhood, and then we grew up."

Ruby clicked her tank into the bracket again and went to the coop, where she found Bettina on watch with her feet up on the desk.

"Hector told me about your helmet trick. Slayin' it," Bettina said.

"Thanks. Watch out for that guy."

"I figured. He said you cheated. He's an asshole. Still, I don't get it. Why choose the heavy fan? You had the choice, right? You could've been fired. Why risk it?"

"We don't have a choice. I realize it doesn't matter to them, heavy fan, light fan—throw up in my helmet giving it all I got. They will always see me, see us, as less. I'm just trying to avoid being *that girl*."

"That girl? The one who does the job with the equipment we have?"

"The girl who enters a room and everyone else walks out. I'm doing what I can to fly under the radar."

"I'm more of a buzz-the-tower kind of chick," Bettina said.

Good luck with that, Ruby thought. "I'm glad you're here. And not just because it's nice to have another female in the firehouse."

"I know why," Bettina interrupted. "You're not the rookie anymore. I mop the floors, and you get the cush job of taking out the trash."

———————

After dinner, Ruby carried the trash across the perfectly shoveled patio. The cold air caught her breath. Flickering stars competed with the city lights. *A twinkle is better than total darkness, but shining bright is not overrated.*

Returning, she let the station door slam behind her. The air on the apparatus floor was a dusty contrast to the clear night sky. The smell of cigarette smoke and the sound of water sloshing from the mop bucket onto the floor drew her toward the tower. She heard Hector's muffled voice and Bettina giggling. *Nervously?* Ruby wasn't sure.

She approached the cracked sliding door of the tower. The voices inside went quiet. Light from the fixture thirty feet overhead reached the ground dim, like the yellow smoke on Stan Franken's porch.

"You're my idol" had felt so good to her as a seven-year-old.

———————

It was dusk. Boys in white T-shirts played in the street, taking turns pitching rocks and swinging bats made from sticks. Stan had told the older preteen girls to go home. From his cot, positioned tight against the wall of his screened-in porch, he motioned for Ruby to come closer. He patted the empty space on his cot, and Ruby sat beside him. The red ember on the end of his cigarette glowed as he inhaled. He took her hand and placed it over the zipper of his pants. He pressed her hand against him. It was dark. Ruby was unsure. She was afraid.

"Do you like how that feels?" he had said.

Why didn't I say no? Why didn't I run outside and throw a rock at the tallest boy's head?

Finally, her opportunity for a do-over had arrived.

Ruby stormed the hose tower. Hector was leaning against Bettina's back as she rinsed dirty water from the mop. A section of dangling dry hose draped over Hector's shoulder. Ruby grabbed the back of his shirt and spun him around. She snatched the cigarette from his lips and threw it into the mop water pooling around the floor drain. With a fistful of his collar scrunched in her hand, she wrapped the hose around his neck and squeezed.

"Listen, you midget prick!" She squeezed harder. "You better keep your fuckin' axe handle—You better not go down in a fire. It's your helmet I'll be using as a stool."

Bettina grabbed Ruby's hand and pried her fingers from the hose. Hector fell to his knees and massaged his neck, coughing.

"Wow!" Bettina said. She leaned close to Ruby. "What the hell! He was helping me hang the mop. Hector, are you okay? I'm getting the captain." Bettina started toward the station door.

Hector looked up from the floor and raised his hand. "Wait."

He stood up, rubbing his shoulder. "No need for the captain. Just a misunderstanding."

He reached into his pocket and pulled out his pack of smokes. He shook the pack, and one cigarette emerged. He cupped it with his lips and pulled it from the pack. Ruby looked into Hector's eyes, and for the first time she noticed she was a little taller.

"Good call," she said, and followed Bettina out of the tower.

Bettina whipped around to face Ruby. "Next time you're planning to fly under the radar, give me a heads-up. I don't wanna be part of your flight plan."

The click of the intercom cut into the argument. Ruby started toward the engine, and Bettina ripped for the ladder.

"Bettina, wait," Ruby said. Bettina kept moving. Whining tones indicating a medical call drowned out Ruby's words. "He deserved that, and more."

Bettina had stepped into her boots and was lifting her suspenders when the ladder captain pushed open the door from the coop and said, "It's a medical. Stand down, Tina."

Ruby took her spot on the engine. She watched Bettina remove her fire pants and skip toward the coop with blissful ignorance.

You can't pull us out, Hector had said. *What if I go down in a fire?* Ruby wondered, *Would Hector pull me out? If I go down, will people mourn less because I'm a woman? What will they say? "It's her own fault. Women don't belong on the fire department. They reached down and got 'em anyway."*

CHAPTER 8

Spanner Belt: *Belt with a large carabiner, used to carry an axe and for securing rope for rappelling.*

Ruby

The rising sun peeked through the crumpled shade into the otherwise dark dorm. Ruby woke to fluorescent lights flashing. "Engine 7 to a jumper on the Hennepin Bridge. Respond to the lower lock and dam."

The whitecaps of the Mississippi crested and surrendered and crested again. John announced Engine 7's arrival at the lower lock and dam, and while the rig was still rolling, Hector jumped off. The brakes hissed. Ruby's tension eased.

Hector clicked open the life-jacket compartment. He handed one vest to John, one to Tyler, and dropped the third on the ground. Ruby fastened her spanner belt around her waist and lifted the vest from the pavement. She slipped her arms through, clipped it in front, and tamed her windblown hair into a ponytail.

They headed for the boat launch; the mens' jackets were left un-clipped over their heavy turnout coats. All that distinguished them as individuals disappeared into the blur of orange vests with *MFD* scrawled in reflective letters on the back.

Tyler and Ruby jumped from the dock onto the fire rescue boat. John's radio crackled. "Caller reporting seeing the jumper in the water, ten feet from shore and floating toward the lock and dam."

Tyler ducked into the cabin and started the engines. Hector re-leased the tether rope from the cleat and jumped on board. Ruby tested the hinged platform on the bow, ensuring it could be lowered for the rescue. Tyler steered the boat over the waves, and John searched the surface through binoculars.

Hector pointed out over the water. "There's our Einstein," he said.

John tracked Hector's arm to the object in the water. "It's a log," John shouted over the engine's roar.

"He's holding on to it. Don't ask me why they jump to their death and then fight for their lives."

John motioned to Tyler to steer toward the log. Ruby readied the rescue basket at the bow. John cupped his mouth and yelled to Tyler, "Approach him from the side. Careful not to run him over."

Hector kneeled beside Ruby. Together they released the plat-form and lowered it into the water.

"Hold the basket steady, and I'll pull him in," Hector said, reach-ing over her and toward the victim.

"I'll help pull him in," she said.

Hector made a *tsssst* sound. "I got it, rookie. Just hold the basket steady."

"He's panicky," John said. "Grab the back of his jacket."

Hector reached out over the water from the edge of the platform. He grasped the jumper's jacket and spun him around, pinning his back against the side of the platform. The jumper's flailing arms reached for Hector.

"Relax!" Hector shouted. "I'm gonna pull you up."

"I'm not crazy. Don't let me sink," the man pleaded.

Hector tightened his grasp. Ruby steadied the basket. Hector grunted and heaved the victim toward the basket. The wind gusted, and boat and basket bobbed in the river's current. The victim's head dipped under the waves, and when he emerged from the river his eyes bulged in terror. He grabbed at the air and seized Hector's vest.

Ruby let go of the basket to free Hector from the panicked man's grasp. She pried the jumper's fingers from Hector's vest, but he grabbed on again, clenching tighter.

"I can't swim. Don't let me fall under," he begged.

Cold water splashed Hector's face. "Son of a bitch."

Hector's shoulder sunk under the waves. Ruby grabbed his arm, struggling to keep him on the platform. The victim thrashed until he'd hooked Hector's open vest in the crook of his arm, and then he climbed Hector's body like a ladder out of the water. Pressing his drenched sneaker into the side of Hector's head, he hopped safely on deck with Hector's life vest dangling from his arm.

Hector splashed into the river.

One slap on the surface of the water and then he disappeared into the swirling Mississippi. Ruby threw the rescue rope out near the spot where Hector had submerged. The yellow tangle floated on the surface.

Unable to see Hector, Ruby threw her end of the rope to Tyler and jumped into the river. She dipped her face under the water. The reflective trim of his fire coat flashed in the sunbeams beneath the surface. She reached for him, but her life jacket prevented her from diving. Ruby unclicked her vest, grabbed the floating rope, laced it through her spanner belt, and dove.

Hector's limp body sank farther. Her fingertips grazed the collar of his coat—she gathered the fabric and pulled him to her. She wrapped the rope around Hector and kicked for the surface. Icy water rushed inside her turnout coat. Her coat and the water, two allies she counted on for protection in a fire, conspired to pull her down.

Ruby let go of Hector but was tangled with him in the rope. Her gear and Hector's weight dragged her down like an anchor. As the brown murky river swallowed them, Ruby lifted her chin for a last glimpse of the light. And then everything went dark.

The peace she felt drew her deep toward the darkness of euphoric slumber. The river was warm like her mother's womb. The rocking current sang a muted lullaby of nothingness. Hector's weight pulled her toward the riverbed. Unable to fight any longer, Ruby rested.

Their descent jerked to a halt. She resisted the slow drag from the stillness even with Hector dangling below.

Light shocked Ruby awake when she broke surface. She sucked in the sun-scorched air. Her eyes bulged, not in terror but with purpose. She reeled in the rope, pulling Hector from under the water and to the side of the boat. Tyler dragged him onto the platform and then extended a hand to Ruby. He threw a blanket around her before he returned to the cab, racing toward shore where two ambulances waited.

John kneeled next to Hector on deck and felt for a pulse. "Ruby, you good?" He lowered his ear close to Hector's face. "No pulse, and he's fucking not breathing." John retrieved the defibrillator and med bag from where they rested next to the jumper, also huddled in a blanket. Ruby started compressions. She wasn't good. Her arms ached, and she shivered under the blanket in her soaked clothes. But her adrenaline-fueled superpower of denying reality urged her on.

Tyler cut the engine. They'd reached the dock. Medics from one ambulance attended to the jumper while John, Tyler, and Ruby assisted the second pair of medics in loading Hector onto a stretcher.

"We hooked him up to the AED, but no shock was advised. His pulse came back after two rounds of CPR. He's still unconscious," John reported.

Hector woke as the medics pushed him across the slushy, rocky ground. Looking confused, he tried to stand.

"Whoa," John said. "Where you goin'?"

"I need to get to shore."

"We got you buddy. You're on shore," Tyler said.

Hector squinted at Tyler and then stared at Ruby. He raised his hand to his chest and flinched in pain. Still, he made it to his feet, and the medic led him by the elbow to the side door of the ambulance.

Hector winced again. "My ribs."

The medic said, "You're gonna be sore for a while. She didn't hold back on those compressions."

He pulled his arm from the medic. "She? What?" He stormed toward Ruby, who was assuring a paramedic that she was okay. He tapped on her shoulder. She turned.

"Sorry," Hector said. "I mean. Why?"

Ruby steeled her stare. "Why what?" She leaned close to him. Absent fear, Ruby felt superior. She whispered in his ear, "Why bother saving a fuck-up, you mean? Do you really think you being an asshole is going to change who I am?"

She turned and caught up to Tyler on the way to the engine. Then she turned back and shouted, "You might want to get used to tofu. I'm not going anywhere."

Tyler chuckled and waited for Ruby. He put his arm around her and said, "I thought you didn't like tofu."

"He doesn't need to know that." She glanced at her watch. "We're officially off shift. How 'bout that Bloody Mary you promised me?"

CHAPTER 9

Eductor: *A device that connects to a water supply and infuses foam concentrate into the water stream. The aqueous film-forming foam (AFFF) cools and blankets the fuel, decreasing the possibility of ignition.*

Dana

Dana steered the till with just one hand, clutching an ice cream cone in the other. She was lucky to be in the district with the city's only year-round Dairy Queen. A ride after dinner to indulge in discounted ice cream for firefighters was one of the many perks of being a community hero. The voices of her crew in the forward cab were white noise in her overhead speaker. Happy she couldn't be heard, she sang loudly.

"Rockin' in the till top all day long,

Watchin' the city to make sure nothin' goes wrong.

Rockin' Dana, twee deeda leeda deet!"

In the till, more than anywhere else, Dana felt invincible. The truck rolled onto the freeway overpass. In the distance a high-rise apartment building pierced the pink sky. Headlights blinked in the traffic below as dusk fell. Something moved in the grassy area next to the freeway. While Dana didn't see it launch, a white-tailed deer landed on the freeway and froze in the slow lane—its disorientation fracturing the peaceful twilight of the evening.

A semi-trailer truck veered toward the concrete center median.

"Holy shit!" she said as its trailer jackknifed. Dana set her foot on the horn pedal. The long, drawn-out honk signaled Reggie, and the ladder truck bucked to a stop.

"Holy fuck," Gabe said.

"He's gonna roll," came Reggie's voice.

The crew hurled half-eaten ice cream cones out the windows. Dana took one last lick and did the same.

The semi teetered, took out the deer, and rolled onto its side booming like an M-80 on the Fourth of July. The trailer collided with a van before crashing into the median. The cab ricocheted and skidded along the freeway until smashing through a metal guardrail. The guardrail wrapped the cab like a slap bracelet and then settled on its side, with the roof wedged against the concrete and the cab crushed to a third of its size.

Smitty radioed, "Dispatch, Ladder 10, we have a rollover on the freeway, 35W and Hiawatha, southbound. We're on the overpass. Send a ladder and an engine."

Dana climbed down from the till as her speaker clicked and Smitty added, "Dispatch, we need the rescue rig and two ambulances. Send traffic control. We'll be approaching the scene on foot."

Dana dressed in her turnouts and retrieved the rescue basket and a backboard. Gabe and Reggie filled the basket with essentials—medical equipment, hand tools, and ropes. Together they carried the basket down the grassy hill to the freeway.

Smitty instructed Gabe and Reggie to assess the van and then said, "Dana, you're with me. We need to check on the semi driver."

The cab rested on its side with the driver's door suspended a foot above the ground. The guardrail encircling the passenger side made opening that door impossible. Dana slid close to the ground, under the cab to see if she could reach the driver.

"Check on him quick, Dana. I don't want you under there without cribbing to stabilize the semi."

Sirens wailed in the distance. Truckies working without the truck and all its tools were like Wonder Woman without her superpower bracelets. All they could do was assess, treat injuries, and wait for equipment.

Dana crawled through diesel fuel pooling on the ground and shouldered her head and torso through the shattered driver's window. The driver was conscious but his body was folded in half with his left leg straight up in the air above his head.

"Hey, I'm Dana. We're gonna get you outta here. What's your name?"

"Kevin. My name's Kevin. Shit. Where the hell did that deer come from?"

Dana's stomach turned. She remembered her dad's hands white-knuckled on the steering wheel and her mom's arms squeezing her five-year-old body tight. Dana wiped her face with her gloved hand; the scent of diesel fuel sharpened her focus like smelling salts.

Sirens screeched as Engine 7 and Ladder 3 approached the scene.

"Tools are here. I'll be back."

"Wait. Don't go."

"I promise. Be right back."

Dana crawled out and rushed to the ladder. She pulled wooden blocks of cribbing from the tool bed, determined to keep her promise to Kevin. Smitty began triage. He assigned Ladder 3 to help Dana build a support structure. He instructed John with Engine 7 to lay a precautionary hose line to protect the semi in case of diesel fuel ignition. He sent the medics to assist Gabe and Reggie treating the injured in the van and enlisted police to control traffic.

John said, "We got the line laid, Smitty. What else do you need?"

"The cab is resting in a pool of diesel. Have Tyler add foam to the hose line."

Dana poured sand on the diesel and said, "Cab's stabilized. I'm going in."

"Wait until we have foam in the line," Smitty ordered.

Tyler set up the foam eductor while Dana helped Ruby pull five-gallon buckets of foam from the engine compartment. Mixing foam with water would create a protective blanket, blocking oxygen—necessary for ignition—from the diesel fuel. Ruby readied the line and Dana prepared to crawl back into the cab.

"Damn. The eductor's clogged," Tyler said.

Ruby dropped the nozzle and rushed to the engine. "Dump all three buckets into the tank," she called to Tyler, but he kept trying to flush the eductor.

Dana caught Ruby's eye with the look women share while waiting for the men who ignore them to catch up. Kevin couldn't wait, and neither would she. Being a rookie had its advantages, and detailed knowledge of rarely used equipment, like foam, was one of them.

"Ruby is right," Dana said. "Fifteen gallons of foam are carried on the rig for a reason: three percent of the five-hundred-gallon tank is the perfect mixture."

Ruby winked at Tyler and climbed to the top of the engine. Tyler handed Ruby the buckets, and she dumped them in the tank.

Dana rushed back to the semi, crawled into the cab, and handed Kevin a blanket.

"Told you I'd be back. Cover yourself with this. I can't reach around you."

The roar of extrication tools revving into service sounded like the cavalry charge to Dana. With his leg jammed, it would be impossible to pull him out. They needed to widen the space, and the Jaws of Life was the tool for the job.

Kevin glanced at his leg, wedged next to his face. "I don't think my leg belongs there, and I'm sure my hip's broken."

She pulled off her glove and took his hand. "We have a doc on the way. We're gonna open it up in here. The doc is bringing medicine to take the edge off that hip pain."

The sun had set. Dana felt a chill on her neck. Smitty called from outside the cab, "Dana, come on out and warm up a bit. We'll send someone else in."

"I'm okay," she said.

"Come on out. Time for a break."

She ducked out through the window. "I'm not leaving. I don't need a break." She popped back in and said to Kevin, "Breaks are overrated."

He winced in pain. Dana tried to distract him. "Where you from?"

"Prior Lake. My wife and I have a six-year-old girl."

"What's her name?"

"My wife is Rachael. My daughter's Samantha. We call her Sammy. She's the star of the T-ball team. She's fast. She gets that from me."

"I'm sure you're not biased at all," Dana teased.

"No, honest, she is by far the fas— Ahhhhhhh! Something's stabbing my ribs."

Dana looked, but nothing had changed. The muffled sound of hydraulic tools faded into the background. The cramped quarters of the cab seemed to be closing in rather than opening. The golden hour to transport a critical patient to a trauma center, increasing their chance of survival, had passed.

A private trucking company arrived on scene with a crane and a strategy: raise the semi just enough to slide Kevin out.

"Dana, the doc is here from HCMC," Smitty said.

"The doctor is gonna hook you up to an IV and take a look at your options. I'll be right outside."

As Dana exited, a jolt rocked the cab and Dana felt a shift. The crawl space under the cab increased by a few inches. Her eyes widened with hope, but Kevin's leg remained sandwiched between the side of his face and the wall of the cab.

The doctor crawled through the opening. Dana handed his bag up through the widened gap space. He administered the IV and crawled out.

"He's asking for Dana."

"That's me," she said. "What should I tell him?"

"He seems to trust you, and he needs to know—if he's going to survive, we will have to amputate the leg. The IV is going to lengthen the golden hour, but we only have about forty-five minutes to get him out."

Dana crawled back inside. Although the opening was wider, it felt harder to navigate. The information she carried lagged low in her chest as she scraped her body through the sludge.

"I heard," Kevin said. "Don't let 'em take my leg."

"We're not giving up. I promise we're doing everything we can. We have a crane out there and six crews of firefighters working to get you out in one piece." The roar of equipment vibrated through the cab. "I gotta go out. We're trying to right this cab. I'll be right outside."

The crane's hook screeched and pulled and rocked the cab just a few inches. The concrete median followed, crumpling the roof and holding the semi in its cocoon.

"The crane is making it worse," Dana said.

"Hold up," Smitty shouted as he gave a hand signal to stop. "Righting the cab could crush him."

The crane came to a sudden stop along with the deafening shrill of the hook scraping against the cab.

The silence on scene was like swimming underwater as Dana wriggled back in.

"Don't let them take my leg. Sammy needs a dad with two legs."

"Time's up. Doc says it's your leg or your life. I wonder what Sammy would choose, a dad with one leg or no dad at all."

Kevin squeezed his eyes closed, and a tear rolled down his face. Dana gripped his hand.

"Long John Silver," he mumbled. "Sammy's afraid of pirates."

"I'll be close, right outside."

Dana backed out and the doctor belly slid through the cavity and added anesthesia to the IV. Kevin closed his eyes and slipped into unconsciousness. The doctor worked with precision, wielding his scalpel to get through skin and tendon. To cut through bone he'd brought a Gigli saw, a flexible wire designed for amputation, but after an unsuccessful effort he called to Dana, "I can't get the leverage I need in this tight space. I need a power saw that can cut through bone."

"I'll be right back," she said. She retrieved a reciprocating saw from the ladder truck, doused it with alcohol, and passed it through to the doctor. "Will this work?"

"It will. Keep your hand on the handle. I need it steady."

Dana grasped the butt of the saw. Its rhythmic pulse dulled inside Dana's head like sound waves in slow motion. She closed her eyes and imagined Sammy hitting a home run from the T-ball pedestal.

"I'm through. Should be able to get him out," came the doctor's voice. He handed the saw back through the opening.

Dana and Gabe extricated Kevin from the wreckage and loaded him into the back of the ambulance. Unconscious, he seemed so peaceful. Dana thought about the fragility of his peace, aware of the chaos soon to come.

Firefighters collected scattered equipment and returned it to its proper places on their respective rigs. Dana bent to retrieve the medical bag sitting next to the overturned semi and the deer carcass, muttering, "You sure caused a lot of trouble today." She started up the hill toward her ladder truck, still parked on the overpass, but turned back hearing Ruby call her name.

Ruby picked up a helmet from the grassy side of the freeway and held it up; on the back, reflective tape flashed behind Dana's scribbled last name. "Your helmet, Firefighter Strong."

Dana doubled back.

"You lived up to your name today," Ruby said, handing her the helmet.

"He begged me not to take the leg. I told him we wouldn't give up."

"We didn't. You didn't. He gets to keep his life."

"I'm not sure he'll see it that way."

Dana tucked the helmet under her arm. "What's up with you and Tyler?"

Ruby shrugged.

"That wink you shot him—friend wink or . . . ?"

"You were right, there is no brotherhood in tofu, but we may have had a connection over a Bloody Mary. He's okay. He was sweet when I had to do that damn rookie test again."

"You crushed it," Dana said. "That round fan is a bitch."

"It's not Fanny's fault. It's the fire department's obsession in making it clear: we don't belong here. Anyway, some of us are getting together tomorrow for breakfast. You should come. We need to make sure MFD hires more women."

"You mean the Women's Association?" Dana thought of the criticism she had overheard: *The Black firefighter association isn't enough? We need a special group for women? More shit to stir the lawsuit pot.* Dana knew she was one of few women steering clear of drama. "No thanks. I'm getting along good where I'm at."

CHAPTER 10

Jaws of Life: A powerful hydraulic tool that functions
as a cutter, spreader, or ram, used to extricate trapped
victims primarily from vehicles, aka **Hurst Tool.**

Dana

During her three days off after the freeway rescue, Dana woke each
morning without the help of her alarm clock. Her dreams just before
waking were becoming more vivid—more like nightmares. The loud
honking of the cartoonish speeding car smelled of diesel fuel, and
the semi rolled onto its side exactly as it had on the freeway.

She resented her promise to Lily to stay away from the card
club. On her last day off, while Lily was at work, she justified a compromise and watched poker on ESPN. Dana missed doing what she
was good at: seeing the cards, calculating the odds, and making the
right move. After a full day of armchair poker, she felt recharged and
ready for her next shift.

The next morning she reported to the fire station an hour early to inspect the truck tools. She checked the fuel level in the saws and pulled each starting cord, ensuring they would perform at the big one. She recalled the words drilled into them in rookie school: *you don't want to be the dumbass standing out on the front lawn of a house that's rollin', holding the empty saw you didn't check.*

She greased the springs on the extension ladders. She painted scratches on ceiling hooks with black spray paint. She wiped hydraulic fluid from the hose couplings on the Jaws of Life—the royal flush of tools. With a single finger on the trigger, a firefighter could pop off a smashed-in, jammed car door. She lifted the tool from its bracket. In spite of its massive power, Dana understood that failure is just one minute, one pound, or one step shy of the finish. *Just ask Kevin,* she thought.

She rested the Jaws on the floor next to the rig and positioned its gas-powered motor by its side. She pulled the cord. The machine spit out a cloud of smoke and then sputtered. "Come on," she said. She pulled the cord again; this time the machine offered no response at all.

Dana sat on the tailboard of the ladder truck and buried her face in her palms. She wondered how Kevin's little girl was adjusting to a dad with one leg. She thought about her own father. *Better than no dad at all.*

She stood up, adjusted the choke, and pulled again. The motor roared. She flipped the choke to off and the roar settled into a loud hum. Gas odor rose from the dissipating smoke, and she cradled her face in the crook of her arm.

"Maybe Kevin won't run again," she said through her sleeve, "but he will see his daughter sprint across home plate." She cut off the engine and returned the tool to its compartment.

Gabe yelled through the propped-open door leading from the kitchen to the apparatus floor, "Hey, Dana! Stand down. You're making the rest of us look bad."

Reggie added, "I just made a fresh pot. Come join us."

Dana took one last look for anything out of place and slammed the compartment door closed. The aroma of coffee is code for the end of routine tool checks, and the invitation to join the morning coffee ritual confirmed that Dana was back on the team.

Sharing the burden of rookie hazing and housework with Ryan, she felt she could relax. She was different from the other women—the only female to pass the physical test the first time, plus she knew how to go along to get along. The guys trusted her. It was just a matter of time before the target was off her back. A brand-new rookie was due to report to Station 10 next week to take her place as the scapegoat.

The engine crew and the truckies gathered around the long rectangular table in the kitchen, discussing who would do the shopping for dinner. She poured creamer into her cup, filling it halfway. Gabe raised his eyebrows.

"It's all about the color. I like it sweet," she said

Gabe and Reggie lifted their mugs in a toast and said, "We like it strong."

"Puts hair on your chest," Reggie added.

Gabe interjected, "Listen, Dana. We were talkin'." He waved his cup around the room, gesturing to the firefighters sitting around the table. "There's no private space in the station for rookies to study. You and the Leon-ess have your final written test next week and new rookies are comin'. Why not move the lockers upstairs around and make a little study room?"

Reggie added, "You could use lockers for the walls. Maybe put a desk in there and a couple chairs."

Dana searched the faces of all the men in the room, looking for dissent. She found nods of agreement and wide-eyed smiles. Smitty took a sip of his coffee from a mug with the inscription, *If at first you don't succeed, do what your captain told you to do the first time.*

Ryan emerged from the bathroom, pushing the mop bucket.

"We can do it together," Dana said, gesturing toward Ryan.

Ryan rested the mop handle against the wall and grabbed a cup.

"Ryan has noon watch," Smitty said. "The locker job is all yours."

Dana spent the afternoon moving the lockers from a single row lining the hallway into walls around a small study room. She arranged the lockers in order by shift and then rank, with the doors facing outward.

Standing inside the space, she imagined the furniture. So far all she had was one vinyl-covered school chair. She heard fumbling on the stairs. It was Gabe, carrying a small desk salvaged from the basement.

Gabe's cheeks flushed red. Dana glanced at a pile of *Hustler* magazine pages, featuring monthly cover models, on the chair. He quickly turned to leave.

Dana gathered the pages. "Looks like Wagrowski was a subscriber since, let's see here . . ." She flipped through covers. "Umm, forever? They fell off the top of his locker when I moved it." She shrugged and gritted her teeth to convince him she'd found them by accident.

"Huh. I thought those were supposed to be banned ever since—" He paused. "Well, you know."

Dana did know. Everyone knew about Patricia Peck, the first woman ever to be promoted to driver. She had sued the fire department after a firefighter taped a photo of her face over the face of a porn star and then hung it on the bulletin board. When Patricia tore it down, the battalion chief informed her that she needed to ask permission before removing publications from the official fire department board. The chief ended up transferred to another district. The remainder of Patricia's short career was spent in the back seat. Her official demotion came after not honking the horn when she passed through an intersection during a call. Everyone knew it was bullshit. She won her lawsuit and earned a reputation: the girl (the nicest of the terms) who ruined "good ole boy" fun. She left with an undisclosed wad of cash and became the official poster child warning women to never question the boys' club.

Gabe reached for the porn and said, "Wagz is an asshole. I'll throw 'em out."

"Naw, let's just put 'em back." Dana placed the porn back on Wagrowski's locker.

Gabe nodded and invited Dana to join a cribbage game. "It's five bucks to get in."

Dana didn't know cribbage, but the chance to gamble while chalking it up to work was a temptation she couldn't resist. After losing, she convinced the guys to switch to Texas Hold 'em. Dana pocketed thirty dollars before hitting the sack.

She didn't bother hiding under a blanket to remove her pants now. In the darkness of the dorm, she dropped her pants on the floor and slipped under the covers. She started to doze. The floor creaked. Shadows of durgans tiptoed to twin beds across the room. She rolled onto her side, felt for her pants on the floor, and stuffed them under her pillow.

After an unprecedented quiet night at Station 10, Dana woke feeling a slight panic, worried that she'd missed an emergency run. She checked for Ryan—sound asleep in the bed across from her.

Gabe shuffled through the dorm to the bathroom in his tighty-whities. The gray morning light surrounding the window shades illuminated his almost naked body. Dana covered her face with her sheet and whispered, "Some things you can't unsee."

She pulled her pants from under her pillow and wiggled them on under the covers before getting out of bed. In the hallway she ran her fingers along the wall of the new study room. She clicked open her locker. Seeing the photo of Lily, her poker winnings, and her reflection in the stick-up mirror on the door roiled her stomach with guilt. She grabbed her keys and slammed the door shut.

She took one more look at her makeshift room. *It's perfect*, she thought. Downstairs, her relief had stowed her gear neatly in her locker. Dana headed home.

She turned into her driveway hoping to find Lily home, but her car was gone. Dana went inside. Fresh coffee was brewing on the counter, and a note stuck to an empty mug read, *Miss you. See you tonight.*

————

Lying in bed that night, she told Lily about her locker room project and Gabe's skinny white legs. Lily snuggled close and draped an arm around her. Dana considered telling Lily about poker at the station. *Why ruin a peaceful moment?* she thought, and she drifted to sleep.

————

The next morning Dana loaded a swivel desk chair that had been sitting in the garage into her truck. It was a bit worn but comfortable, and it would fit in perfectly. She drove to work excited for the other shifts' reaction to her locker room.

In the station parking lot, Gabe's SUV and Reggie's truck were parked in their usual spaces. *They're early.* She glanced at the clock on her dash: 07:19. On her way through the station she passed the kitchen. She peeked her head in and smiled. Wagz and Joe from the offgoing shift sat at the table, reading the paper.

Joe kept his face buried in the crossword puzzle. Wagz looked up and pulled his black-framed glasses down his nose. "People shouldn't touch other people's stuff."

Dana raised her chin and squinted. *Is he talking about the lockers?*

"Everyone agreed. Even my captain said it was okay."

"People shouldn't touch other people's stuff," Wagz repeated.

Dana dismissed his lack of gratitude and climbed the steps to get her uniform from her locker. It was like her last shift had never happened. The lockers were arranged along the wall in a neat line. She walked the row, reading names written on masking tape. Her locker was missing. She checked her watch—07:30. *I'm okay. Thirty minutes to the eight-o'clock bell.*

She sprinted to the dorm and flipped on the light, ignoring the cussing of sleeping firefighters. No locker. She sped to the bathroom. No locker. Gabe stood at the sink, brushing his teeth.

"Looking for something?" he said

"Yeah, my locker's gone."

He spit a glob of white paste into the sink and smiled. "Did you touch someone else's stuff?"

The urgency she felt to find her locker flattened. She stared at Gabe, searching for her own misunderstanding. He bent over the sink and cupped a mouthful of water, swished it around, spit one more time, and said, "It's seven forty. Have you checked the basement? You gotta be in uniform by zero eight hundred."

Dana grabbed the railing as she raced down the stairs, trying to pull a few extra seconds. No locker. Panicking, she checked the first-floor bathroom. No locker. The air smelled of newly squeezed vanilla body lotion. Someone had removed the chair from her truck bed and set it next to the urinal. The August 1987 *Hustler* centerfold lay open on the seat with white lotion splattered across the face of Jessica Jensen, Miss Nude Universe.

Dana sprinted back to the second floor. Reggie stood at the top of the stairs. He glanced down the hallway toward the balcony door and then back at Dana. She hesitated, wondering if this was another setup. Reggie lightly tapped the end of the broken axe handle on his shoulder. Dana tracked the line it pointed down the hallway. She ran to the door and peered through the glass window. Her locker leaned against the railing overlooking the parking lot. She checked her watch: 07:55. She flung open the door, opened her locker, and grabbed a uniform shirt. She dressed as she sprinted down the stairs.

Through the rails of her gear locker, Dana was relieved to see her fire boots as she had left them the day before. Her bunker pants were rolled down around the ankles of her boots with the rubber loops jutting from the pants. She pulled her fire coat from the hook and pulled on the loops of her boots.

White paint splashed onto her wrist. Paint fumes escaped from her paint-filled boots. Dana knelt on the floor. Reggie came down the steps and lifted one boot with his axe handle. Dana wiped her face with her sleeve and said, "It's paint."

"Can't wear this to a fire," he said and dropped the boot in the trash.

Dana carried the other boot into the coop. "Captain—"

Sipping his coffee, Smitty glanced from her boot to the white splatter on her forearm. Dana waited for his eyes to meet hers.

"I'm reporting off sick."

He raised his mug. "Feel better," he said. "Bring your locker in before you go."

Dana dragged her locker inside and set it next to the others. She stopped in the bathroom and spotted Gabe's toothbrush still on the sink. She leaned into the hallway. Finding it deserted, she snatched the toothbrush and scrubbed the toilet bowl before returning it to the sink.

As she pulled her truck out of the lot, she laugh-slapped her steering wheel. "Never trust your toothbrush with the people you treat like shit," she said. Smiling, she adjusted her rearview mirror and saw paint smeared on her wrist. Her stomach squeezed, and vomit rushed to her throat. She held it there.

"Such assholes!" She pulled over, opened her door, and rubbed her wrist red. Flecks of dried white paint fell onto the street. She pulled the door closed and rested her arms on the steering wheel and her head on her arms. She thought of going home to an empty house to watch ESPN poker.

She had a better idea.

Dana turned onto the freeway entrance ramp. The squeeze in her stomach relaxed, and the tingle in her quads triggered her to drive faster. She passed the last of many billboards promising big wins ahead and turned into the casino parking lot, hoping to hit the jackpot of escape.

She patted her pants pocket. Not finding her wallet, she opened the center console, reached in, and fingered loose coins, thinking of her dad's pennies.

Each player took turns choosing the family card game. Dad mostly chose seven-card stud, deuces wild. Dana was five, and she chose the game no peekies.

She lost the last of her pennies to her dad and fell asleep to the sound of her parents arguing. "It's best she learns it from me," her dad said.

She woke hearing her mother at the door, kissing her father before he left for work. Dana bolted downstairs and sat on her dad's foot. It was a game they played when he went on work trips. This time the game was different. Instead of lifting Dana and rolling her to his face for a tummy raspberry, he reached into his pocket. He pulled out a fistful of pennies and threw them on the floor. She let go and hurried to collect the coins. Her mitts clenched around handfuls of pennies and a heart full of excitement, she looked up to show her dad, but he was gone.

Dana spotted her wallet on the passenger-side floor, reached for it, and noticed more paint splattered on the outside of her arm. "Fuckers." *I won't let them get to me.*

She dropped her wallet in the console with the loose change and drove home. As she pulled into the driveway, she was surprised to see Lily getting in her car.

"What's wrong? What are you doing home?" Lily said.

"What are you doing home?" Dana shot back, putting the truck in park.

"I told you. The high school choir is doing a sing-along tonight with the residents, so I'm going in later."

Dana did the one thing Lily had made her promise to never do again, under any circumstance. Dana lied. "I just don't feel well. I'm taking the day off."

"Honest? Last time you were sick, you insisted the best place to recover is the firehouse. You must be deathbed sick. Do you need me to stay home?" Lily reached through the window to touch Dana's cheek. "You don't feel warm." Lily leaned in closer and scrunched her face at the sour smell. "Buah, did you throw up?"

"No. Almost. Leftover pizza for breakfast was a bad idea. Go to work. I'm fine."

Lily opened her car door and shouted, "The granite guy is coming to measure for our new counter this morning. Should be here around ten thirty."

Dana went to the bathroom and brushed her teeth. Seeing her reflection, she scrunched up a wad of toilet paper and erased the last relic of paint from her arm. She leaned close to the mirror and exhaled, fogging the glass with her breath, and drew the centerline for a highway and the edge of a cliff. "Just don't fall off," she said, and ran her hand over her artwork, wiping the mirror clean.

CHAPTER 11

Dana

Dana pulled at the covers and reached for Lily, who was already up. She felt unusually groggy, thankful for the bliss of amnesia granted by dreamless sleep. Remembering that she should be waking up at the fire station, Dana caught her breath. *Damn, Dana,* she thought. *You couldn't just pull your locker from the balcony and stick it out.* She heard Lily downstairs rumbling through their almost remodeled kitchen. Dana sat up and yelled, "They're behind the toaster."

"The counter's gone. Where's the toaster?"

"On the microwave, honey."

First came the jingle of Lily finding keys and then her feet drumming up the stairs to the bedroom doorway. She checked her watch. "Shit. I'm late. How are you feeling? I gotta go. Rest today." She blew Dana a kiss, then rushed back down the steps and out the door.

Dana sat up on the edge of the bed and noticed Lily's lanyard with her work ID hanging from the bedside table. She grabbed it and rushed to the window, hoping to catch her. She knocked on the glass.

Lily got into her car. Dana slid the latch and opened the window. On the other side of the boulevard, she spotted Reggie's truck. *What's he doing there?* Lily backed down the driveway and sped around the corner.

Reggie opened his truck door, and his axe handle fell in the street. He picked it up, tucked it into his belt behind his back, and crossed to her driveway. He started up the walkway.

Dana ran downstairs and opened the door. "Yeah?"

Reggie took a step toward the open door. She pushed her hair behind her ear, crossed her arms, and stood her ground.

"All right," Reggie said, looking her in the eye. "I put the locker out there on the balcony. It was all in good fun. I swear I didn't know about the paint. I wouldn't do that. I wouldn't fuck—Shit. Sorry, I mean *screw*. I wouldn't screw with someone's fire gear. It isn't right."

Dana watched as he illustrated his good intentions with passionate hand gestures. She raised her arm to block the sun. "Is that it?" she said, slowly pushing the door closed.

Reggie pushed back, cracking the door open. "Wait. I want you to know. I know."

Dana peered through the crack and waited. His expression seemed contrite yet insistent. "I know what it's like," he said.

Dana let the door open a sliver more.

"I was in the first class of Black guys. It wasn't paint in my boots. The assholes spread broken glass in my bed. Scraped keys all along the side of my car. I'm not sayin' one is worse or better than the other. I'm sorry for the paint. The locker—well, all rookies get that kind of shit, even the white boys."

Dana thought of Ryan, drenched by a third water bucket, and softened.

"Truth is, we're glad y'all are here. You women are taking the heat instead of us Black guys. Now you're the low man on the totem pole."

Dana opened the door all the way. "You do know there is no low man on a totem pole. A totem pole's carved from one tree, and bottom and top are equal." She snorted a frustrated laugh. "I assumed firefighters were more heroic. I mean I thought I was signing up to rescue people. Thought I'd be standing up for the little guy—didn't know I'd be the little guy the so-called heroes crush."

"Ha. We get too much slack for running into burning buildings. Believing we're heroes is part of why we're assholes. Makes some believe they're invincible. I remember when I was you. You think you made it. You go in and put out the fire; hell, you saved that guy on the freeway. You're a hero too, part of the team. Feels important. You're making a difference working side-by-side with the good guys. Truth is, they're never gonna let you be one of the good guys. Never. A heroic Black man, and now with you here, a heroic woman—somehow, we make 'em feel smaller. You gotta be your own hero. That's how you can stand up for the little guy. Take care of you."

"What about paint in my boots? What about the not-so-white guys keeping me from doing my job?"

"I told you. I helped put the locker on the balcony," Reggie said. "But I wouldn't and I didn't touch your gear. You don't have to believe me, but I thought I'd do you a favor and come over here and school you. Watch your back." He turned to go.

"Wait," Dana said. "What's with the axe handle?"

He took a few steps toward Dana, looking left and right like he was about to tell a secret. "It's what they said they'd shove up my ass if I complained. Every day it was next to my locker. You know, a reminder. I went to paint tools—it was on the workbench. One day I found it under the covers in my bunk. Carried it with me ever since. It's my keep-your-enemies-close strategy."

Dana tried to picture her enemies. Her whole life she had been good at what she did and had more friends than most. For the first time she doubted her choice to become a firefighter. But Dana knew it was more than a choice. It was her all-in calling, and she wouldn't let bullies change that.

Reggie pulled an envelope from his back pocket, fat with dollar bills and heavy with change. "I almost forgot what I came over here for." Dana wondered what this had to do with an apology. "It wasn't up to me, but you've been assigned to getting the house supplies. I know you said you didn't want to do it. If you haven't figured it out yet, that was a mistake. Here's the bank." Reggie held out the envelope. "We need ketchup and mayonnaise. I usually get about a three-month supply. The newspaper bill is in here too. Most important, don't forget the coffee." The expression she had interpreted as apologetic transformed to resolve. He handed her his previous job.

Dana wrapped the lanyard for Lily's ID around the envelope and stood on the porch. Reggie waved at a car coming around the corner as he crossed the street to his truck. Lily pulled into the driveway.

"I forgot my ID. Who was that?" she said, joining Dana on the porch.

"He's the driver on my rig."

Lily's eyes moved from Dana's shoulders to her bare feet and back to meet her eyes. "Next time you meet with your coworker, you might wanna get out of your jammies first." She kissed Dana on the cheek.

Dana held out the ID. Lily lowered her head, and Dana slipped the lanyard around her neck. Lily opened the door to get back into her car and glanced at Reggie, who was standing in front of his truck. He offered a friendly wave. Lily shot Dana a suspicious glance, and Dana shrugged.

Lily said, "Don't forget, we have an appointment with the tile guys tonight. I need our normal back. This remodel is killing me."

Dana got dressed and counted the money for station supplies: $268.35. With an $18.00 newspaper bill, she had a $250 budget.

She drove to the grocery store, parked her Ranger in the Cub Foods parking lot, and grabbed her list from the center console. She commandeered a cart and headed for the condiment aisle.

Dana was careful to choose the right ketchup—"Has to be Heinz," she remembered the senior durgan saying. "Don't just get Miracle Whip, some people like real mayonnaise." She steered into the coffee aisle. The stock boy swept spilled coffee grounds from the floor.

"I'll be right out of your way, ma'am."

I can't believe he just called me ma'am. She waited for him to sweep the grounds into a dustpan. Seeing the broomstick, she thought of Reggie with his broken handle and his advice: *You'll never be a good guy. Keep your enemy close, and make sure you get the coffee. Go along to get along.*

Coffee grounds dotted a red plastic lid on a coffee can. She inhaled the caffeine, and her obedient fog lifted. "Fuck getting along."

Dana abandoned her cart in the aisle and returned to the parking lot. She drove to a swanky coffee shop in the posh Minneapolis neighborhood of Linden Hills and inquired about the most expensive coffee in the store.

"We have Blue Mountain, imported from Jamaica by way of Japan. It's a little more than eighty dollars a pound," the clerk said.

"I'll take three pounds."

Dana handed the house dues to the barista. The door chimed behind her as she left, like the ding of answering a trivia question correctly. Dana was sure she was doing the right thing. Next, she needed to make things right with Lily.

———

Driving to the suburbs for the backsplash appointment, Dana glanced from the freeway to Lily. It was time to come clean. She squeezed the wheel, searching for the right words, and blurted, "I didn't tell you because I didn't want you to worry."

"Tell me what? Are you gambling? I knew you should have stuck with those meetings."

Dana had been to three Gamblers Anonymous meetings before abandoning the mantra of "I'm Dana, and I'm a compulsive gambler." Talking about gambling with a bunch of gamblers, she reasoned, only made her want to accept what she couldn't change by immersing herself in it. At her last meeting she waited for the group prayer to finish before she was out the door and on her way to the casino, armed with the delusion that she had the wisdom to control her luck at the blackjack table.

That slip ended after she took the daily maximum from the ATM. She lost and wrote a check with insufficient funds. She didn't have her half of the mortgage, and she made up a story about being robbed in the GA parking lot. Lily didn't care about the money. She worried about Dana being hurt and insisted they call the police. Dana finally confessed.

It had taken a little over a year of Lily monitoring the bank accounts and Dana's abstinence from card playing before Lily started to trust her again.

"No. Not that. Not gambling. It's just, well, I wasn't sick yesterday. The guys hid my locker and messed with my fire gear. I can't believe I took it so hard. Reggie came over to smooth things over. I thought you'd worry about me. Sorry for not telling."

"I don't need you to protect me, Dana. Damn it. Geez. I just need you to tell me the truth. Is it that hard? What else are you lying about?"

After too much silence, Dana attempted to break the tension. "I have been lying about one other thing."

Lily jerked her head to face Dana.

"I spent way more on your birthday present than what we agreed."

"Not funny. This is different, Dana, and you know it. The one thing I can't stand is lying. I won't tolerate it."

Dana focused on the centerline of the freeway. The silence returned. Reaching the exit, she considered bringing it up again. *Sometimes it's better to let the conflict sink into the storehouse of a future argument.*

She bit the skin where flesh met fingernail on her thumb. "I think the reason I didn't tell you—I don't want to seem weak."

Lily said, "I'm thinking we should probably go with the subway tile."

Dana took another bite out of her thumb. "I don't want you to think I would let those guys get to me."

"I think white may be too stark with the marble countertop."

"I don't care about what the guys think. Hell, most of them don't think at all."

"And once the marble gets stained with a lemon or spaghetti sauce, the white will make the stain stand out."

Dana frowned and let out a little laugh. "It's funny. You're the one who really knows me. You'd think I'd be less scared to let you in."

Dana turned into the tile shop parking lot.

Lily opened the passenger door and said, "Let's go with gray tile. Gray will make the marble lines pop."

"I guess I just don't consider myself a sensitive person."

Still in her seat, Lily slammed her door closed. "Truly, Dana, you're just about the most sensitive person I've ever met."

Dana realized the damage she'd done to her thumb and buried the hand under her thigh. "Maybe we should go with the granite countertops and we won't have to worry about spaghetti stains."

On the way into the store, Lily put her arm around Dana and said, "Let's forget this one. But Dana, I mean it this time, no more lies. Not even fibs."

The next morning Dana showered and dressed in her uniform at home. She sacked the three pounds of coffee into her backpack, kissed Lily goodbye, and drove to the fire station. The lot was full of vehicles as firefighters came on shift. The apparatus floor was jam-packed with vehicles of firefighters going off shift. *Perfect,* she thought, *everyone's here.*

Ruby came in behind, carrying her fire bundle. "What are you doing here?" Dana asked.

"Workin' for Ryan."

"Did he owe you, or is this going into your favor bank?"

"He's taking my shift next Saturday. The Women's Association is holding a training session at the tower. Too bad you don't want to come. Imagine if you'd had a mentor just like you. Plus, it's fun."

"You wanna have some fun? Come on. Watch this."

Ruby dropped her stuff by the engine and followed Dana into the dining area. Wagz, Reggie, Gabe, and everyone—the ongoing and the offgoing shifts had gathered for a coffee clutch.

"Did you get supplies, Dana? We're down to our last pot," Wagz said.

Dana plunked the three-pound sack of coffee on the table with the $246 receipt and said, "House dues are going up."

Wagz checked the receipt. "Eighty-two bucks a pound! You gotta be shittin' me."

Reggie hid his grin behind his cup. Ruby's eyes widened in disbelief, or maybe awe, Dana wasn't sure.

Ruby made a quick exit to the apparatus floor, and Dana followed. They bent over together in laughter. "Hey, Ruby, you know what? I am free Saturday. You still need help with the new recruits?"

"Thought you weren't interested. You're all set, you said. Why the change of heart?" Ruby pulled her hair back and secured it in a ponytail.

Dana set her gear and new boots at the back of the truck. She thought for a moment about what was different. All she wanted to be was one of the good guys—maybe, instead, she might just have to be one of the good *girls*.

"Same heart," Dana said. "Different day. Now let's go get a cup of that swanky coffee."

CHAPTER 12

FMO: Fire motor operator, aka **driver**.

Ruby

Ruby searched under the couch at Station 7 on her hands and knees for her badged uniform shirt. She remembered taking it off during the morning house duties. *No sense getting my badge shirt dirty,* she had thought.

Peering under the recliner, she didn't see her shirt. She did see black shoes clicking across the floor.

"Not sure that's the best look for you," Bettina said.

"Have you seen my badge shirt? I left it right here this morning."

"You left your shirt out here? All day. Are you crazy?"

"Shit. No one's bucketed me in so long, I let my guard down."

"You scared 'em after breaking three of Hector's ribs on the river."

Double ribs plus one, Ruby thought. She took pleasure in knowing that Hector was out on IOD (injured on duty) due to her chest compressions. Instead of spending energy avoiding Hector, she became a bucket-dodging champion and the guys had given up.

Ruby pulled two Tupperware containers of ice from the freezer and recognized her badge—#515—protruding from one. She returned the other icebound shirt to the freezer. Ruby was happy to graduate from wet T-shirt contestant to just one of the crew caught with an unattended shirt.

Ruby ran hot water over her frozen shirt in the bathroom sink, melting away the ice. She unpinned her badge, wrung out the shirt, and threw it in the clothes dryer. The station lights flickered as Ruby slammed the dryer shut. She joined Bettina in the back seat of Engine 7, happy with Hector's replacement.

The monotone of the dispatcher reported a fire alarm at the Franklin high-rise building—again. At three times, the call to reset a faulty alarm at the same address on the same day was becoming routine—and annoying.

The ladder truck remained still like a ghost-town prop. Ruby didn't blame the ladder guys, in no hurry to respond and reset the alarm again. Truckies counted on the engine crew to get there first, check it out, and cancel them.

Tyler stowed his turnout gear in a side compartment. John stepped into his boots, last to get on the rig. He patted his lap and then his chest. Ruby and Bettina joined him in his mantra, "Spectacles, testicles, let's go."

Engine 7 sped out of the station with the siren wailing and lights flashing like they were on their way to the apocalypse. Responding code three to reset an alarm felt a little like opening the biggest gift under the tree and finding socks inside.

Arriving, John reported, "Engine 7 assuming command at Franklin high-rise. Multistory residential, nothing showing."

Tyler opened the high-rise bundle compartment and handed the captain's bundle to John. He heaved the heavier high-fire bundle, carried by the firefighter, onto Ruby's shoulder. John scanned the street for the ladder company. Sirens whooped in the distance.

Ruby and Bettina followed John inside the building and squeezed through residents gathered in the lobby. Bettina held the elevator while John checked the fire alarm panel to identify which floor tripped the alarm.

He keyed his radio. "Dispatch—incident commander on Franklin, alarm panel indicates the eighth floor."

Ruby, Bettina, and John got into the elevator. The radios clipped at the chest of their coats clicked—the tone of the ladder captain's voice, announcing their arrival, emphasized his irritation.

John inserted a key into the fire-service keyhole to hold the elevator, following protocol to wait for the truck crew and ride the elevator together. Ruby shifted her weight under the heavy load of the hose bundle. She knew John wouldn't embarrass the ladder captain by calling him on the radio. The high-fire bundle burned into Ruby's shoulder. She hopped it up and repositioned the nozzle. The handle found the gap between her tank and shoulder and dug in. She half smiled at John to hide her discomfort.

"Fuck 'em," John said, and pushed the button for the sixth floor, two floors below the fire floor. They would follow procedure and walk two flights, avoiding the possibility of meeting flames and toxic smoke on the other side of an opening elevator.

"The other shift responded to two false alarms at this building yesterday. It's bullshit," John said. "Ruby, you remember this building from our familiarization last month, right?" He didn't wait for her answer. She did remember.

"You two girls— Sorry, I mean ladies. Go to the floor and wait in the stairwell." He transferred his hose bundle to Bettina's shoulder. "Take a look down the hallway. Make sure it looks clear. Radio me so we don't all have to come back. I'm gonna check on the Ladder 3 princesses."

The elevator opened. Ruby and Bettina headed to the stairwell. Ruby held the door. "After you, girl," she said.

"Oh no. Ladies first." Bettina bowed her head. In stereo they said, "Dumbass," and started up the steps.

"Better than TWAT squad," Bettina said.

"I consider Tactical Water Attack Team a compliment."

Laughing, they trudged up the stairs to the seventh floor.

Bettina said, "Let's drop our bundles," and flopped her hose onto the landing.

Ruby nodded. "This is where we'd hook up to standpipe." She draped her bundle over the railing.

Ruby opened the door to the eighth-floor hallway. She smelled smoke, but the hall was clear. "Probably burned food," she said. "I'll be right back."

"Where the hell are you going?" asked Bettina. "John said to wait in the stairwell."

"This is our chance to buzz the tower."

Bettina raised an eyebrow. Ruby started down the hallway. She removed a glove to feel the apartment doors for heat. Close to the far end, she noticed smoke puffing from the doorjamb of apartment 830. She banged on the door. "Fire Department!"

She turned the handle. Locked. "Minneapolis Fire. Anyone home?"

No answer. Smoke seeped under the door. She turned and mule-kicked just below the doorknob. Nothing. She kicked it a second time and felt the latch give. On the third kick the door popped open. Black smoke escaped into the hallway, and the door slapped shut.

Ruby pulled her mask from her bag and called John on the radio. "Franklin Avenue IC, this is portable Engine 7, we have smoke in apartment eight three zero."

Bettina opened the stairway door and yelled down the corridor, now filling with smoke, "Ruby, did you find the apartment?"

"Hook up to the standpipe," Ruby shouted.

"Is it a fire? I mean, we're not supposed to lay a line to smoke. Is it burned food, or what?"

"It's not burned food. Hook up the line." Ruby buried her face in her mask.

John came on the radio. "Dispatch, this is the IC on Franklin. We have flames showing on the eighth floor. Give me a second alarm. Staging will be on the River Parkway and Franklin." Ruby heard him shout, "Shit, get your ass up—" before he let go of the transmit button, and she realized he was still outside with the ladder company. She kicked the door again. More smoke rushed into the hallway, and once again the door slammed shut. There was something, or someone, leaning against the door.

Ruby knew to wait for the hose line before trying to go into the apartment. Opening the door would feed the fire with oxygen. But the unknown mass blocking the door dared her to break protocol.

Ruby crouched low to the floor. She wedged the door open with her shoulder. Smoke had gathered at the ceiling and was slowly banking down. Ruby reached in to feel for whatever was keeping the door from opening. Blinded by descending smoke, she relied on her hands. She squeezed what felt like a limb and knew a person was slumped against the door.

She banged on the door. "Hey, can you move? I need to open the door to get you out."

No response.

She removed her glove to grasp the arm through the cracked door. The skin felt clammy—not clammy cold, but clammy hot and wet. Keeping her back against the edge of the door, she sandwiched through—and the door slapped shut.

She regloved, felt her way until she reached a naked male torso and wrapped her arms around him, like she had so many times with the dummy in rookie school. She lifted. Her gloves slipped across the slick expanse of his chest. It was like trying to grip a greased hog.

Her breath echoed inside her mask like Darth Vader with an accelerated heart rate. Ruby pulled in a deep breath to slow her pulse and gather energy. Then she repositioned the unconscious victim's arms above his head. She squeezed his fingers and leaned back, dragging him away from the door and into the room. She lost her grip, fell back, and re-clasped. Blocking the door open with her shoulder, she pulled him through the doorway and into the hall. As she dragged him slowly down the hallway, her breath once again grew amplified and accelerated. Reaching the door to the stairwell, she leaned and fell onto the landing where Bettina had connected the high-rise bundle to the standpipe.

The hose was tangled around Bettina's legs and waist and blocked the entire stairway. Ruby lifted her mask from her face just enough to make sure she was heard. "You didn't flake that shit out first?"

"Holy fuck," Bettina said when she saw the victim. She tried to untangle from the hose.

John and two truckies raced up the stairway and tripped on

Bettina's muddled mound of canvas. John keyed his radio and reported, "Be advised we have a victim. Engine 7, charge the standpipe." He pointed to the hose wrapped around Bettina with the antennae of his radio. "Fix that hose before you open the valve. Once that nest fills with water, it's impossible to unravel."

John and Ruby carried the victim down one flight to the elevator, where another firefighter waited with the medical equipment. Ruby kneeled inside the elevator, dropped her helmet to the floor, and placed two fingers on the victim's wrist and two on his neck, checking for a pulse. She leaned close to his face, listening for respirations. "Pulse is sixty. He's not breathing."

John pulled the valve mask from the medical bag and connected it to the oxygen tank tubing. The other firefighter handed Ruby an airway. She inserted the airway into his soot-covered mouth and held the mask to his face. John squeezed the bag.

By the third respiration the elevator had reached the ground floor and the victim had choked out a breath on his own, spitting out the airway. In the lobby medics were waiting to take over. John handed Ruby her helmet. She got in the elevator with him and pressed the button for the sixth floor.

John held out his hand to keep the door from closing. "Maybe take a break."

She checked the gauge on her harness. "I still got half a tank." Her adrenaline was speeding. No way would she miss putting water on that fire. John let the elevator close.

On the fire floor, Bettina had the hose spread out, charged, and ready to advance. The truck crew searched the apartment for more victims. John handed the nozzle to Ruby. "You found it, you knock it down," he said.

Ruby dragged the hose down the hallway and entered the apartment. A masked truckie reported, "Apartment's clear. We're opening windows."

John followed Ruby in. Bettina pulled slack, careful to keep the hose from catching in the doorway. Ruby opened the nozzle on a small kitchen fire. A ding signaling low air chirped. She closed the nozzle and turned to John, "Your air's low."

The burned-out kitchen was crowded with too many truckies, all wanting to be part of the action surrounding a real live rescue. Ruby couldn't blame them. The exhilaration of saving a life and returning to fight the fire was beyond anything she had ever felt.

"It's not me. It's you, Ru," John said. "You're almost out, better go down."

On her way out she checked her gauge. The needle pointed to zero. She inhaled the last of her air, and suddenly her mask was like a face-sucking alien.

She panicked and clawed at it. Instead of turning left toward the stairwell closest to the apartment, she followed the hose right, to the far end of the smoke-filled hallway. Short of the door, Ruby fell to her knees, pulled off her mask, and sucked in black air. She struggled to crawl toward the door and then felt a hand under each arm, guiding her to the stairwell.

"Go down and change your bottle," John instructed. Ruby stumbled down the steps. "And drink a Gatorade," he called after her. "Bettina can check for hot spots."

Ruby found the rehab rig, removed her tank, and slugged a can of red Gatorade. Through the radio she heard John say, "Fire under control." The ambulance squealed away from the scene. Ruby raised her can in a toast: *my first rescue.*

Rigs left the fireground one by one, returning to their firehouses to reheat dinner that had gone cold or restart the movie they had paused. Ruby's rig was last to leave. Tyler pulled away from the curb and turned to the back seat. "Hey, Ru, you got everything you need for the clutch tonight? We can stop on our way back if you need something."

Cooking dinner for eight firefighters made Ruby more anxious than a marshmallow at a Camp Fire Girls convention. Last time it was her turn to cook she'd secretly had Chinese food delivered to the back door during naptime. She clanked the pots and pans together and warmed it in the oven. The fire station sang with the aroma of egg foo young prepared by Ruby, posing as a gourmet chef. The problem was, takeout food is more expensive than home cooked. Hiding her homemade imposters was getting costly. But today she had a plan. "I'm set, Tyler, take us home."

"I'm starving," John said. "I can't wait to see what you make this time. Hmmm. Maybe Indian food. I love curry." He smirked at Tyler. The Indian restaurant was two blocks from the station. The pit in Ruby's stomach flipped; maybe her secret wasn't so secret.

At the station, Bettina and Ruby washed dirty hose. Ruby carried the clean hose to Tyler in the hose tower to be hoisted up to dry.

"How does it feel?" Tyler asked. "Rescuing that guy?"

"I admit, it felt a bit superhero-ish. And then I completely ran out of air and realized how superhuman I am."

Ruby draped the hose over the hook. Tyler hoisted it to the top of the tower.

"I'm super jealous you got to save that guy."

He secured the rope and turned, bumping into Ruby. She fell back. He caught her, pulled her close, and moved his lips to hers.

Ruby pushed him back. "That is not happening. What the fuck is with this hose tower?" She skipped from the hose tower and into the station.

In the shower stall, Ruby pulled a crumpled paper from the pocket of her uniform pants and set it on the bench. Scribbled in pencil was a jambalaya recipe she had jotted down while watching Food TV.

After showering, she pressed her hands over the recipe, ironing out the creases. She secured her wet hair into a ponytail and studied the recipe on her way to the kitchen. *Is there a difference between chopping onions and mincing garlic?* She shrugged and continued reading. "Cut chicken in symmetrical cubes and rub with creole spice." *Do I actually rub it?* She wasn't sure.

She would have to be creative with the sausage. Using chicken and shrimp was a reasonable compromise, but there was no way she would use pork. Squiggly pink tails would never see the bottom of her Dutch oven. Ruby buried the wrapper of the vegan spicy sausage in the trash. She seared the chicken, pinked the shrimp, and added the veggie sausage to the pan.

Tyler poked his head around the corner. "Smells delicious."

"That's half the battle," she said.

Ruby referenced the spice-stained recipe to determine the rice cooking time. She shook salt into her hand, squeezed a dash between her thumb and forefinger, and tossed it in the pan. The odor in the station was reminiscent of a New Orleans café.

The crew waited in line to scoop Ruby's masterpiece into bowls. Chairs scraped the floor. Durgans tucked in at the long rectangular table. Ruby expected the glorious three minutes of silence, typical at a fire station dinner.

Tyler broke the silence in just a few seconds. "Whew! That's got some kick!"

Two truckies slugged down entire cups of water. Ruby stuffed her hand into her pocket, feeling for the recipe. The battalion chief looked up from his bowl. He dabbed his red-flushed bald head with a napkin and said, "It's good, rookie. I like it hot." He took a long swig of milk.

Ruby retreated to the kitchen and fished the recipe from her pocket. Scanning the ingredients, she stopped at cayenne pepper and wiped off a spot of tomato, revealing a *t* for teaspoon. She crumpled the recipe. "A damn teaspoon. A quarter teaspoon of cayenne, not a quarter cup."

The scraping on the floor became the sound of chairs being pushed away from the table. Two guys threw their jambalaya in the trash, bowls included, saying, "Have fun digging those out. Looks like it's Taco Bell tonight."

"Trash is going to be heavy tonight," Bettina said. She popped a piece of the sausage in her mouth and shoveled the rice into the garbage.

Tyler took one more bite and joined Ruby in the kitchen. She rescued a discarded bowl from the trash. Tyler took the bowl from her. "You cooked. We clean."

"But no one ate. I messed it up."

"Exactly, you mess it up. We clean it up." He grabbed the last bowl from the trash can. The veggie sausage wrapper was stuck to the bottom. "What's this?" he said, holding up the label. "You lied."

"No. I, well, umm, I just didn't tell."

"Same thing," Tyler teased. "It's kind of brilliant, and to tell you the truth, the sausage was my favorite part. Thankfully Hector won't be back 'til next week. He would never let this go—even if you did break his ribs on the river."

Hector is coming back. Ruby's face flushed red. She quickly tied the trash bag and headed for the parking lot and the frigid evening air.

The door squeaked behind her. Tyler reached for the trash bag. She let go and leaned against his truck, staring at the concrete.

"You do know you're not the first firefighter to mess up dinner. You said it yourself. My tofu tastes like what? Umm, 'dirty socks,' I think you said."

"Wet socks," she corrected. "Was I wrong?" Ruby met his eyes, smiling.

"What's up with you and Hector anyway? I mean, I mention his name and you're gone. I don't get why you hate him."

Ruby looked into Tyler's eyes. "You're not paying attention."

He hurled the trash into the bin and stepped close to her. "I am, and you know what I see? I see an amazing woman who saved a guy today. Pretty much single handed. Do you know how many guys go through their entire career and never get an actual save in a fire? Don't let Hector pull you down. He's an underachieving Catman."

Ruby looked deeper into Tyler's eyes, searching for betrayal, longing for sincerity.

He reached for her hand, and she pulled away.

"I promise I won't try to kiss you again."

The gush spreading through her chest at his touch landed as a half-smile on her lips.

He pulled his keys from his pocket and unlocked his truck. "I have something for you." He removed a gold chain from the rear-view mirror. "This is a medallion of Saint Florian, protector of fire-fighters. They say he'll keep you safe."

He slipped the chain over Ruby's head, and the medallion clinked on the button of her shirt. "Spicy jambalaya is forgivable," he said. "You, Ruby Bell, you deserve a medal for what you did today."

Ruby pulled on the chain to study the figure of Saint Florian. The long red feather on the helmet resembled a ponytail. The saint looked more like a woman with soft features gently pouring water over a small flame.

"I'm calling her Saint Flora," she said. Tears filled her eyes like a swimming pool poured into a teacup. One spilled onto her cheek. Tyler reached out to wipe it.

She grabbed his wrist and threw it back. He looked unsure, maybe even hurt. She didn't care. She pushed him again, this time with two hands. Tyler fell back into the front seat of his truck. Ruby crawled up his thighs, pushed on his shoulders, and pinned him down. Her legs straddled his ribs. She felt him struggle to get up. She tore open her button-down shirt and pressed the skin splashing from her bra to his face and then sat up again. Saint Flora swayed like a pendulum from Ruby's neck. Tyler struggled beneath her.

"Are you sure you want to get up?" she whispered.

She felt him surrender and moved her mouth over his lips. She let his cool, soothing breath invade the hollow she had been pro-tecting. She grazed her tongue over his and moved her mouth to his ear. She asked once more, "Do you want to get up?"

He reached for her with his body. She pushed on his chest and loosened his belt.

The headlights of a vehicle pulling into the lot shined into the cab. Ruby ducked and lay flat on Tyler's chest. She covered his mouth with her hand and looked into his smiling eyes. They waited, motionless, as the driver got out and went into the station. Tyler fastened his belt. Ruby pulled her shirt over her shoulders and buttoned the two still intact.

Tyler held the door for Ruby. Inside, Hector stood next to the engine. Ruby glanced at Tyler and started for the coop.

"Hold on," Hector said. He pulled an orange kitten from behind his back and held it out to Ruby. The kitten meowed.

"Uh. No thanks."

"It's for the station. I mean for you while you're at the station." The ball of fur meowed again.

"The other shift can take care of her while you're off. I already asked 'em. You can name her if you want." The kitten screeched louder. "I was thinking maybe Siren?"

Tyler raised his brow. Ruby zipped her new medallion along the chain and said, "Sounds like you got a name for her. You don't need my help." She continued toward the coop. Hector followed.

"Maybe we could start over?"

"Start what over? We're past that. You made that impossible. Listen, we're not friends. I don't want an apology. Stay the fuck away from me." Hector turned to walk away. The kitten clawed its way to his shoulder, meowing and looking back at Ruby.

"On second thought, I will take the cat," Ruby said. She pulled the little orange fireball from Hector's shoulder and let its whiskers brush her face. The meowing kitten sounded more like a whine than a siren. "I think I'll call you Winnie," she said.

That night in the dorm, with the kitten cradled next to her, she removed the medallion from its chain and attached Saint Flora to

Winnie's collar. "Don't you worry. I'm not leaving you here. You're coming home with me."

PART
TWO

AROUND 2005

CHAPTER 13

Three Person: *The most junior firefighter on an engine,*
sitting behind the driver and partnered with the captain,
aka three man. The four person is typically more senior.

Six's: *Station 6 and in like fashion:*
twenty-eight's is Station 28.

Ruby

It took several years and three new cadet classes, but Ruby was officially no longer a rookie. At Ruby's new station assignment, the bromance was strong. Station 6 housed more rigs than the usual single engine and ladder truck. More rigs meant more guys to keep one another entertained.

She and John transferred together to six's while Tyler remained at seven's. They agreed it was best to keep work and personal lives separate.

Beating the eight-o'clock bell, Ruby opened the station journal on the coop desk and scrawled in her initials to confirm morning checks were complete. Her firefighting partner, Heath, sidled up next to her, hip bumped her, and playfully snatched the pen from her hand to sign his own initials.

John jogged down the steps from the men's locker room, wearing no shirt and with a towel draped around his neck. Station 6 was one of the few stations with separate bathrooms for women and men. In one motion he slipped the towel off and snapped it at Heath, who grabbed it and returned the snap. John retreated to his private captain quarters.

Ruby appreciated the attention they gave to one another. Even more, she appreciated the lack of attention they showed her. Ruby had learned that she was more successful at the fire department if she mastered the unexceptional.

A tall floor lamp stood next to the coop desk. Ruby couldn't resist the temptation. She ran her fingers along the tube, petted the red velvet shade, and cupped the crimson beads hanging from the fabric in her palm.

"You want it?" Heath said. "My wife hates it. It's been in my garage for years."

She imagined the bulb's warm glow next to her bed in the dorm. "Of course I do!" She lassoed the cord and carried the lamp down the hallway. She passed John and raised the lamp, flaunting her prize.

"I see Heath found a taker for the hooker lamp," he said.

Ruby hesitated and inspected the lamp, saying, "I guess. I'm thinking more retro than hooker. But I see your point."

Ruby set the lamp next to her bed and pulled the string. The red glow and the sparkling beads stirred a feeling of safety and warmth—something she missed working at the station with Tyler. Aligning herself closely with a male firefighter, especially one as popular as Tyler, had offered an unspoken protection. Everyone knew they were together. She felt untouchable. She didn't have to explain the bonus of not working at the same station as Hector.

She pulled the string again. The click from the station speaker, a splash of fluorescent light, and the whoop of a medical call proceeded the dispatcher: "One choking."

As a veteran firefighter, Ruby's adrenaline barely burped in response to a medical. She calmly walked to the engine, stepped on board, and slammed the rig door closed, taking her spot in the back seat next to Heath. The swirl of red lights ricocheted off the station walls, and the engine screamed out of the station.

Two blocks later the engine driver, Alex, slowed in front of the house. The parking brake hissed, and Ruby rushed up the walkway. A frenzied woman held the door open, pointed, and said, "It's my husband. He's right there."

Ruby wanted to say, *You mean that guy? The only other person here? The one with his jugular vein popping out? You mean the one who has his hands wrapped around his throat?* She approached the wiry, muscular, forty-plus male smelling of cigarette smoke. "Sir. Relax. I'm gonna give you the Heimlich."

She peeled off her fire coat and laid it on the floor. She stood behind him, planted her foot between his legs for balance, wrapped her arms around his torso, and found the sweet spot under his ribs. With just one abdominal thrust, a chunk of ham splattered on the wall—barely missing Heath as he stepped through the door.

"She got it," the wife said and then said it again.

John came through the doorway next. "Everything okay?"

"She got it," the wife said.

Alex recorded the man's information, including his refusal of an ambulance.

On the drive back to the station, Heath said to John, "I walked in—and boom. Pigs really can fly. That piece of ham shot across the room like a cannonball."

John turned to Ruby. "You didn't want to wait for us, huh?"

"I didn't know if I was gonna save him or not. But I figured if he was going to die—well, he'd rather go out with my chest up against his back than yours."

Laughter filled the cab. "You got me there," John said.

Mastering the unexceptional did require moments in the spotlight. But it would be on Ruby's terms and laced with humor. Rather than report sexual harassment and invite banishment, she decided her best defense was self-depreciation—in the right measure.

After backing Alex into the station, she replaced the lanyard in its holster and circled around to ready her gear. Alex jumped down from the driver's seat and shuffled toward Ruby at the back of the rig.

Alex was different from most of the guys. She considered him a friend and often wondered if his tendency to be inclusive of the women had to do with his own experience of being excluded as a Black man. Mostly, Alex was funny—witty funny. But the look on his face was the opposite of easygoing.

He seemed nervous and said, "I gotta tell you something. I don't want to, but I figure it's better you hear it from me."

"What are you waiting for? What?"

Alex buried his hands in his pockets with his head bowed and kicked at the dust on the floor. "I'm not sure how to tell you this, but there's a rumor going around. It's about us. It's that you and I are—"

"Shut up." Ruby pushed him and gave him a playful slap on the arm.

"No, I'm not joking."

"It's about time that came out. We've been doing it for how long?"

"It gets worse. You were wearing a thong and you climbed on top of me in the dorm. You told me I'm hot."

"That is so stupid."

Alex pulled his hands from his pockets and chuckled. "Thanks a lot."

"Now you're stupid. I meant everyone knows I'm with Tyler."

"Bettina warned me about the rumor this morning, and she's at seven's with Tyler. It won't take long for him to hear it."

"Don't be stupid. It's stupid. Bettina will tell him. It's obvious bullshit."

Hector, Ruby thought. *It's his mission to screw me over.* This wasn't the first rumor that had caused tension between her and Tyler. This rumor seemed especially ridiculous. Tyler would see through it, she was sure.

The phone rang. John yelled from the coop, "Ruby! Strap it on your back."

Ruby turned to Alex and said, "Don't worry about it. It really is stupid." She trotted to the phone, "Firefighter Bell."

Tyler inhaled, and Ruby felt a jealous vibration. "I didn't even know you owned a thong."

Like a flame chasing air in an oxygen-deprived cockloft, a rumor in the fire department quickly came full circle. Once the roof is open the flame spreads.

"Did you go through my drawers? It was gonna be a surprise."

The humor Ruby deployed for fire-department survival often spilled into her relationship with Tyler.

His tone softened to concern. "The bullshit never ends."

"I'm glad you're taking the bullshit by the horns by calling. I mean, Alex is cute and all—but hot? Hot is all you."

"It's supposed to snow tomorrow. Come over," he suggested and then borrowed her philosophy. "Hot is hotter with two."

The next morning Ruby pulled the chain on her new lamp next to her bed. The large red bead at the end came off in her hand. She held it to the light, amused by the beams that reflected on the floor like little flames. She was excited about her date with Tyler—and then she remembered she was hosting the Women's Association meeting at a neighborhood coffee shop. She threw off her wool blanket and dropped the bead into her duffel.

She expected Tyler to be disappointed when she called. She was unprepared for his anger. "The women's group again, Ru? When do I get a turn? Or do you only have time for Alex?"

Ruby was more surprised at her response. "Can you really blame me? Not only is he hot, but he doesn't need me to tell him he's hot." Ruby hung up. On her way out of the fire station she noticed a flyer on the union bulletin board. She pulled down the flyer and headed to the meeting.

CHAPTER 14

Paper Lip: *A fish with thin lips. Easy to unhook.*

Dana

Dana and Bettina set chairs in a circle at the coffee shop. They had learned that, for women to apply to a career advertised as *fireman,* women needed to see women firefighters. Dana was an obvious candidate, tall and hard-to-ignore strong. Bettina required imagination. Most unique about Bettina wasn't feminine or masculine qualities: she insisted on making the point that her attributes were human qualities. She was strong enough and didn't tiptoe around topics. When accused of being insensitive, Bettina was quick to correct: "Not being sensitive is not the same as being insensitive." And then she would be sure to add, "asshole."

Snow and chilling wind rushed into the shop with Ruby's arrival.

"I ordered you a latte," Dana said.

Ruby held up the flyer she'd ripped from the union bulletin board, "Wanna go?" she said, and sat across the circle from Dana.

"Hi. My name is Dana, and I'm addicted to recruiting women."

"Hi, Dana," Ruby and Bettina said in unison.

Ruby handed Dana the flyer announcing a fire department ice fishing tournament. "Seriously. We should all go," she said.

Dana took the flyer. "Wow, they're serving spaghetti, and the biggest walleye snags fifty bucks. How can I say no? I thought Tyler didn't like you hanging around"—she motioned air quotes—"'firemen' off shift."

"We're fighting. Let's go."

Bettina chimed in, "And you going to the biggest firefighter drunk fest of the year is going to help how?"

"C'mon. Let's go have some fun before our lives change forever." The promotional test for driver, or technically fire motor operator, was scheduled in a few weeks.

"My life is staying right where it is," Bettina said, "living the dream in the back seat as a firefighter and never, ever, frozen in an icehouse dangling a string through ice."

Dana handed the flyer to Ruby. "Too bad. I like Tyler."

"You date him, then."

"I think I'll stick with Lily. You two seem good together. Damn. Sorry. I'm a dumbass. Are you okay?"

A group of women approached the circle. One took off her ski hat, revealing a shaved head and a neck tattooed with the word *Unimpressed* in cursive. "Hi. Is this the meeting to become a firefighter?"

Bettina patted the seat of the chair next to her. "You're in the exact right place."

The next morning Dana pulled in front of Ruby's house. Ruby zipped up her parka, threw her duffel bag in the back of the pickup, and hopped in.

"Did you bring it?" Ruby said.

"I'm not sure why, but yeah, my swimsuit is packed right next to my long underwear and winter gloves."

"Trust me. We're never gonna look better than we do right now."

"Have you talked to Tyler?"

"He called. He's feeding Winnie while I'm gone."

"Have you made up, then?"

"I thought we were gonna have fun. I don't want to think about Tyler."

"Right. Let's go drill holes in the ice and freeze our asses off in a shack."

Two hours later Dana and Ruby arrived at the frozen expanse of Lake Mille Lacs.

"Holy shit," Dana said.

The lake resembled a shantytown, littered with tents and portable fish houses. Home Depot buckets, doubling as chairs for anglers, surrounded holes drilled into the ice. Fishing poles set on mounds of snow dropped expectant lines into the lake.

Ruby's eyes lit with excitement. "John said our house would be the eighth one in from this launch."

The ice crunched under Dana's truck tires as she slowly drove across the lake. "I think we're here."

She stopped next to a toilet bowl, decorated with fire department union stickers, set in front of a hole surrounded by what looked like a snow volcano. John came out from behind one shack, zipping up his pants. "Nice throne," Dana said, nodding toward the toilet.

"It's more comfortable than a bucket. Welcome to your ice palace. I set yours up next to my and Heath's place."

The outside of their shack looked more like a closet than a house. Inside they found twin bunk beds. After further investigation they discovered the bottom bunk could be converted into a small plywood table and a bench. On the floor in front of the bench was a plastic lid with a handle and a hole in the ice leading to open water.

"I call the top bunk," Dana said.

There was a whir and whoop and then a yell, "Fish on."

Dana and Ruby ran outside to see John reeling a ten-inch crappie from the lake.

"Check this out." He motioned for them to come closer. Along the way Ruby looked into the holes. The water was shallower than she had imagined, and at the bottom of each hole were random items—cheater glasses, a camera, a lighter.

John tugged on the line and lowered the fish back through the hole. "That paper lip is a little too small," he said.

"Paper lip?" Dana said.

Ruby answered, "A crappie has a thin mouth."

Dana did a double take. "Okay, fisher-girl."

"This has been the honey hole all day," John said. "I'm not sure if it's the hum of Heath's brand-new generator attracting the fish or the trinket in the hole."

Dana and Ruby leaned over the opening to see a retro glass ashtray.

After a full day of fishing neither Ruby nor Dana had gotten even a nibble. Firefighters gathered around the honey hole all day to watch John and Heath reel in fish after fish. It was catch and release for every fish but one. John's seven-pound walleye was currently the leader in the biggest-catch contest.

That evening, the group of thirty-plus durgans gathered at the local bar for a spaghetti dinner and a few too many shots of Wild Turkey. On the way back to the icehouse, Dana sat on the toilet in front of John's prized fishing hole and peed.

Ruby let out a hoot. "Now the honey hole's the right color."

Inside their shack, Dana climbed into the top bunk. Ruby crawled inside her sleeping bag. Outside zipped a whir, the unmistakable sound of fish on a line and cheering.

"Hey, Ru. Even if we don't catch any fish, this was fun. I don't mean to get sentimental, but I don't care about the fish. It's awesome to bond with these guys. And you."

Ruby threw off her sleeping bag. "Who's not catching any fish?" She dug in her duffel bag for the red bead from the hooker lamp. She attached it to their fishing line, dropped it into the hole, and replaced the cover. "Tomorrow we'll have the honey hole."

Later that night Ruby woke to a whir close to her ear. Before she wiped the sleep from her eyes, Dana's legs dropped from the top bunk and onto the floor. In one motion she lifted the cover and started reeling in the line, hand over hand. A giant fish surfaced and dove. It wasn't giving up easy. Dana held onto the line and reeled again, pulling like she was hauling a bucket from a well. The fish's tail splashed water into the shack. Dana jerked the line, reached into the hole, and wedged the fish on the underside of the ice.

Ruby screamed, "Don't you let that fish go. We need it."

Dana dropped the line and wrapped her hands around the fish. She leaned back on the icehouse floor and heaved the walleye from the lake onto her chest. They laughed and yelled and screamed. A loud pounding shook the door to their shack.

"Are you girls all right in there?"

Ruby put her finger to her lip in a *shhh*. The handle on the door started to turn. She grabbed her sleeping bag and threw it over the massive fish.

"Hurry up, kiss me," she said.

Dana stood wide-eyed.

"Come on. Let's start our own rumor. Kiss me."

The door slowly opened. Dana put her arm around the back of Ruby's neck, covered Ruby's mouth with her hand and dipped her back like the original movie poster from *Gone with the Wind*. Dana pressed her lips against her hand. Heath pushed the door open and spotted Dana and Ruby, apparently engaged in a passionate kiss. The door slammed closed, and the crunch of Heath's boots retreated across the ice. The two women threw their heads back in laughter.

The next morning Dana and Ruby donned their swimsuits, set a camera up on the union toilet, and took a photo with their winning fish.

CHAPTER 15

Red Helmet: Gear worn by the captain; sometimes used as a nickname for the person. In similar fashion, black helmet is for driver, yellow for firefighter, and white for chief.

Ruby

Tyler waited on the front steps at Ruby's house as she retrieved her duffel from Dana's truck bed and started up the walkway. Dana rolled her window down and called, "Hey, Ru. Grab Heath's gas can and extra cooler. I told him you'd bring them to the station tomorrow."

Ruby handed the duffel to Tyler and returned to Dana's truck for Heath's stuff. "Good luck," Dana whispered, and drove off.

Tyler followed Ruby around back to her garage and loaded the cooler and gas can into the trunk of her car.

"Miss me?" Ruby flirted. She leaned in to kiss him. She hoped to avoid a breakup conversation by distracting him with make-up sex.

"You know who missed you? The cat. She practically lived in the laundry basket, curled up in your pj's." Tyler grasped her arms, holding her at a distance. "We need to talk, Ru."

"We do. But not today, Tyler, okay? I need to study for the driver's test. It's next week, and I have no idea how to calculate friction loss."

Tyler followed her to the front of the house. "I don't know why you need to learn it. I carry a chart in my turnout pocket."

"Coming in?" Ruby asked.

"You need to study. But you're wasting your time. We both know you're not giving up fighting the fire to sit on the hydrant." He smirked.

Ruby opened her door and picked up a mewing Winnie. "I'll call you later?" she shouted from the doorway.

"I know about the kiss, Ru."

Ruby scrunched her face in confusion. "You mean Dana? Don't be stupid." She closed the door.

Ruby dropped her bag inside the door, fished her pj's from the laundry basket, and sat with Winnie on the couch. She flipped the FMO manual open to a chapter explaining the pump pressure for a high-rise. Sitting on the side table was a small stack of mail with a *Fire Engineering* magazine on top. The cover featured a strip mall engulfed in fire. Firefighters dotted the scene, raising ladders and aiming hoses. Men in white helmets pointed—mouths open, obviously shouting orders.

Ruby closed the FMO manual and studied the magazine cover, strategizing how to handle the disaster. She imagined wearing a white helmet and thought, *Chief is a stretch*. The captain's test was scheduled for the week after driver. *Maybe Tyler's right*, she thought. *I do look best in red*. She scratched Winnie's neck and rubbed the Saint Flora medallion, picturing her ponytail dangling from a red helmet. "Captain Bell feels right," she said to Winnie.

The next afternoon, Ruby parked inside the station, followed by Heath and then Alex. She opened her trunk and found Heath's gas can on its side, dripping gas onto the upholstery. She lifted the can, and fumes rose into the air.

"Your fuckin' gas can," Ruby said.

Heath inspected the trunk. "That isn't made to sit on its side."

"Thanks, Firefighter Mansplain. Now explain how I'm supposed to clean that spill."

"Relax, Ru. It's nothing a little ammonia can't fix," Alex suggested.

"You want me to pour a toxic chemical in my trunk, on top of gas?"

"Ruby, you don't gotta be so uptight." Heath winked at Alex.

"Yeah," Alex agreed. "I mean look at your shirt. You know that's not standard uniform."

Ruby pulled at her collar, buttoned right to the top.

Heath pointed to his own shirt. "It's supposed to be buttoned to the second button. You're not in the proper uniform. You should probably unbutton that top button."

"Definitely makes you seem uptight," Alex said.

"No. It makes you feel uptight." Ruby laughed.

Alex continued, "Really. You should unbutton that thing."

"Fine," she said and unbuttoned the top button with one hand.

"Whoa. Hey, why stop there?" Heath added.

"Take 'em all down," Alex teased.

Ruby slammed her trunk and spun around as Tyler charged toward them.

"Take 'em all down," he said.

"Listen, dude," Alex said. "Relax. We're just joking around."

"You tell my girlfriend to unbutton her shirt and think it's funny? How about don't say anything to Ruby that you wouldn't say to Heath. Better yet, if you wouldn't say it to me, don't say it to her."

"Guys, I got this," Ruby said.

Alex and Heath disappeared into the coop. Ruby reached for Tyler's hand. He pulled away.

Ruby started, "I know that looked bad. I get it. But I have to pick my battles. You have no idea. I can handle rumors. You know what wears me down? Finding energy, every day, all day, to explain why most of the shit men say to me is fucked up. And now I have to explain myself to you?"

"I saw it with my own eyes. What do you expect? How can you be so naïve? Go along with that shit, and people talk."

"I'm the one who's naïve? The protection you have just because you're a guy in the fucking fire-department brotherhood—imagine what I put up with. Actually, talk to Hector. Then come back and explain to me why I'm the one who's naïve."

"It's time you quit blaming everyone else for your problems. Most of all, you need to forget about Hector."

Ruby wanted to scream. She had kept her secret, fearing this reaction all along. Forget what Hector did. Report what Hector did. Each choice would either haunt her or label her. Ruby chose what she could control: secrets.

"Right now, Tyler, all I really want to forget about is you."

Ruby marched from the apparatus floor into the station. Alex stood on the other side of the door, holding a scrub brush and soap. "To clean your trunk out," he offered with a smile.

Ruby returned to her car. Tyler was gone. She opened the trunk and scrubbed the carpet. Like the gas odor, impossible to wash away, so is the ignorance of valuing woman less. Like gender somehow enables a person to fight a fire.

She grabbed the FMO manual from the front seat and filed it on the station bookshelf. She gathered copies of *Fire Engineering* from the shelves, retreated to the basement, and assumed the role of incident commander, practicing every scenario featured on the covers. *Let's see how naïve they think I am when they're following my orders.*

CHAPTER 16

Staging: *Designated place where fire rigs wait until
called in by police if the scene is not safe. Rigs also wait
in staging at a large fire or emergency scene, on deck
until mobilized by the incident commander.*

Dana

Dana parked curbside, on the departure level at the Minneapolis/
St. Paul airport. Lily lifted her backpack from between her legs and
said, "Sorry I can't be here for your big test."

Dana initiated the hazard lights and popped the hatchback.
Lily walked around, shifted a trash bag to the side, and heaved her
carry-on from the cargo space. Gesturing toward the trash bag,
she said, "Any chance you can drop that stuff at the Salvation Army
while I'm gone?"

"Right after I finish taking the driver's test. Have fun on your trip."

"Trip? Dana. You know I would be here if I could. It's work, not
a vacation."

Dana knew. Deep down she was more relieved than disappointed. With Lily out of town, she could leave dishes in the sink and miss
Lily's shout from the bedroom to come to bed. Dana was a night owl,

and Lily was like a robin hunting a worm before the sun rises. Dana was free to prepare for her big day on her own terms.

"I'm gonna miss you," Dana said.

Lily threw her backpack over her shoulder and gave Dana a peck on the lips. "Not that you'll need it, but good luck."

Dana wrapped her arms around Lily's waist and pulled her close for a lingering kiss. "That's what I call a good-luck kiss."

Lily dragged her carry-on through the automatic door and disappeared into a crowd of anxious travelers. Dana pulled away from the curb and headed for the freeway. She lowered her window and lifted her to chin to the sun. *Freedom*, she thought.

While she drove, she reviewed the steps for putting the fire engine into pump. *Set the brake. Shift to neutral. Throw the lever into pump. Shift to drive. Listen for the pump to engage. Make sure the speedometer needle jumps.*

Water pressure for a four-story building using an inch and three-quarter hose: one hundred fifty pounds to the door, and then I add five pounds for each floor—that makes one seventy. "Wait," she said. "One sixty-five? Do I count the ground floor?"

A car passed on the right, belching out a drawn-out honk. The passenger stretched his hand out the window, flipped her off, swerved back into Dana's lane, and slowed. Dana hit the brakes and read his bumper sticker: *One good Turn deserves a drowning on the River* and two cards—a seven and a deuce—the worst starting hand in poker.

Dana yelled, "Good luck with those odds, dipshits!" The thought of meeting guys like that at the poker table, entitled and counting only on luck, tempted her to follow them to the card club and teach them a lesson.

She rested her arm on the steering wheel and glanced at her watch. 09:40. The next tournament at the Running Aces Card Club started in twenty minutes. *I could make it.* She felt a tingle on the inside of her thighs.

The guys exited the freeway. *I'm sure there will be plenty of dip-shits at the tournament wanting to give their money away.*

And then she said, "Go home, Dana. You need to study."

Position the fire truck at the fire front, extend the outriggers. Raise the aerial ladder below the window. Dana looked at her watch. 09:46. Lily will never know. She imagined her hand lightly tapping the poker table. The tingle in her thighs intensified. She pulled her wallet from the center console and counted her cash. If she was going to gamble, she couldn't leave the evidence of an ATM with-drawal. Seventy-eight dollars was more than enough. *It's a sign*, she thought.

The neon sign on the freeway flashing chicken-wing discounts and poker jackpots prompted Dana's mantra: "You are lucky. You are a winner. It's better to fold a winning hand than call with a losing one. You are lucky. Not that you need luck. You are a—you are *the* winner."

She exited the freeway. The traffic light turned green. *Another good omen.* Dana pulled into the card club lot, removed her debit and credit cards from her wallet, and locked them in the glove box. Creating the necessity to return to the car for more money provid-ed a come-to-your-senses gap.

"One poker tournament and then home to study," she said, rein-forcing her intention.

As she opened the door to the card club, the click of stacking poker chips was like inhaling the first hit of crack. The swish pattern on the carpet spun like a whirlpool, swirling her into a sea of gamblers. At the poker table Dana was free to think of one thing only—the cards in her hand. The suited security guard at the podium said, "Welcome back."

Dana paid the thirty-five-dollar tournament entry fee and took her place at the table. She leaned forward in her swivel chair and ran her hand over the purple felted table. "Did these used to be green?" she asked the dealer.

He took Dana's entry receipt and placed a stack of chips in front of her. "Haven't seen you in a while."

"Been busy," Dana said. *And I promised my girlfriend.*

———

Two hours later, at the first break, Dana was well ahead of the chip average. She was dealt winning cards hand after hand. With no need to bluff, she became the one to beat. Her confidence soared along with her justification. *I'm good at this. I need to relax before my test. Lily should support me in what I do so well.*

She passed the snack bar on her way to the women's restroom and resisted the temptation to change her luck with appetizers. In the restroom, above the paper towel dispenser, she noticed an eight-by-ten poster: *Gambling Problem? Call the hotline.*

Dana knew where the number led. The voice on the other end of the line couldn't possibly understand the desperation she felt in dialing that number. The desperation of hitting bottom—even if the hotline listener had been there, he wasn't there now. Dana knew, the bottom is the one place you make sure you forget.

She leaned close to the mirror and said, "Today, you can't lose."

Returning to the table, Dana was dealt two aces. Three players acted before her. The first called; the second folded. The one to Dana's right removed the mirrored sunglasses perched on his ball cap and covered his eyes. *He's gonna make a move.* He resembled Tom Cruise in *Top Gun*, so confident, with no idea he was about to lose his wingman.

He leaned back in his chair and sucked on a straw. At the slurp of an empty cup, he returned the cup to its holder, leaned forward, and shoved his entire stack of chips into the middle. "I'm all in."

With a larger stack of chips and the best starting hand in poker, Dana snap called.

The remaining players folded their cards in turn like dominoes. Top Gun turned toward Dana. Seeing her confidence reflected in his mirrored lenses almost made her feel sorry for him.

The dealer tapped the table and said, "Flip 'em."

The phone in Dana's sweatshirt pocket vibrated. She slid the phone from her pocket and saw Lily's face. Guilt weakened her confidence. She pushed the phone deep inside her pocket, worried that, somehow, Lily knew.

Top Gun flipped his cards—pocket eights. She thought of Lily's face on her phone, head tilted slightly to the side and no smile as if to say, "I wonder what you're not telling me." She peeked at her aces and recovered. The odds were in her favor. Dana flipped her cards.

"Whoa," one player said, dropping a half-eaten chicken wing from his mouth.

Top Gun picked up his empty cup and chopped at chipped ice with the straw. The dealer clicked the burn card from the deck and turned over the first three cards for the flop. In the window, right on top, an eight. One player gasped. Another sucked his teeth and said, "Figures, best hand loses again."

"I folded an ace," another player confessed. Dana dealt him a fuck-you look.

The dealer fanned out the three cards. Hiding beneath the eight was the case ace. Dana tripled up. Her heart pounded. She rarely showed emotion at the poker table, but this time she whispered an enthusiastic, "Yes!"

The turn card was an inconsequential two of hearts. The dealer tapped the table and flipped the final river card, the nail in Top Gun's coffin. She saw the card before it landed. The only eight left in the deck gave Top Gun quads. Dana's stack shrunk by two-thirds. Her phone vibrated. She ignored the buzzing. *Damn you, Lily.*

"That's poker," the player who'd folded an ace said.

She pushed her chair from the table and stood while the dealer counted the chips from her stack and slid them over to Top Gun.

"Nice hand," she said.

"Sorry," Top Gun said.

She crossed her arms. "All in with eights?"

"You seemed to like my shove a few minutes ago."

She knew he was right. After the bad beat, Dana's chips continued to disappear into the felt until finally, she was dealt a pocket pair—eights.

Dana pushed her remaining chip stack forward. "I'm all in."

The dealer didn't need to turn over the river. Her opponent had a straight on the turn. Dana was drawing dead. She walked through the card club toward the exit. She passed a row of blackjack tables and heard the dealer say, "Dealer busts. Pay the table." She fingered the forty-three dollars in her pocket. She could see the door.

Dana bellied up to a ten-dollar blackjack table. Four hands later she had three bucks. She went to the snack bar, ordered nachos, and helped herself to a complimentary ginger ale.

She dragged her feet across the parking lot, thinking of Lily. *This is exactly why I shouldn't go to these places. No way can I tell her. Not only am I a loser, I gotta lie.* She backed out of her parking spot and drove to the exit at the front of the lot. The space next to handicapped was open.

"It's a sign."

She pulled into the space and opened the glove box for her cash card. She couldn't walk fast enough. If the security camera were to play it back, it would look more like a sprint than a walk. She didn't bother acknowledging the security guard. Dana beelined to the ATM machine and withdrew her daily limit—five hundred.

Eleven hours later, after another trip to the parking lot for the credit card, Dana was down twelve hundred dollars. At one minute to midnight Dana sat by the ATM, waiting for the clock to tick to the next day. *If I win it back, Lily will never know.* She withdrew five hundred more.

Dana pulled Lily's car into the garage at 06:30, with $1700 of unexplainable debt and two hours to prepare for the driver's test.

During the serpentine portion of the exam, Dana hit two cones going forward. Backing she missed them all. She pumped at the right pressure and positioned the rig perfectly to raise the extension ladder to the window. *Two crushed cones should land me somewhere in the middle of the pack.* Dana went home and slept.

When she woke, she was unsure if it was seven at night or seven in the morning. She ran to the window and pulled the curtain. "It's night." She resisted the compulsion to return to the casino to win her money back. Dana knew she would have to come clean when the credit card bill arrived. She practiced her confession in the mirror. "Lily, I messed up. You know I love you." She leaned in, looked deep into her eyes, and said, "Dipshit."

Dana was more scared than repentant. *I know*, Dana thought, *I won't tell. It's technically not lying.* She began to concoct a plan.

Over the next few weeks Dana rushed to the mailbox to intercept the credit card bill. She signed up to work overtime to cover her losses, but being at the firehouse and away from the mailbox skyrocketed her anxiety.

Working overtime at Station 12, Dana paced the apparatus floor. She was relieved by medical tones distracting her from worry. "Engine 12 to a shooting at the Carter Paper Company, 1517 Chestnut Street."

The engine raced through the streets. The captain turned the radio volume to its max. "Police reporting the scene is not safe. Shooter remains at large."

The FMO parked the engine on the hill above the address in staging, waiting for the all-clear from police. A Lucky Clover delivery truck passed and turned toward the paper company. The captain got on the radio: "Possible delivery truck arriving on scene."

Seconds passed like minutes. The radio clicked. "Engine 12,

police reporting scene is still not safe. Shooter location is unknown. Remain in staging."

A man ran up the hill toward the engine and pointed down the hill. "I think the delivery guy is shooting people. I heard shots and ran."

"Shit. It can't be the delivery guy. He just passed us," Dana said.

The dispatcher's voice vibrated from the radio. "Engine 12, police have not located the shooter. Scene is not safe. They are requesting your assistance for multiple victims."

Getting called in during an active shooting meant serious injuries. After the Columbine school shooting, protocols for an active shooter changed for first responders. Before Columbine, firefighters waited outside until the suspect was in custody. After Columbine, firefighters were trained to go in, protected by bullet-proofed police officers wearing helmets and shields and arranged in a four-person diamond pattern. The strategy: grab and go. It was up to the fire captain to decide if the risk was reasonable.

The captain asked the crew, "What do you wanna do?"

Dana didn't hesitate. "I say we go."

The driver echoed, "Let's go."

Dana carried the med bag. Two officers met them at the sidewalk. Dana assumed that the officers in regular uniforms, with no helmets or shields, wore bulletproof vests. *A diamond has four sides*, she thought. The crew followed the two-officer escort into the building. The radio clipped at the cop's shoulder squawked with panicked voices.

"Scene is not secure! Scene not secure."

On the loading dock, two men lay facedown. The captain checked the pulse of one. Dana checked the other. The four-leaf-clover patch on his sleeve was soaked with blood. Dana and the captain exchanged nods, confirming neither was alive. With no time to process, Dana's only thought was that the delivery driver had been speeding toward his last trip. They followed the police inside the building.

A man dressed in slacks and a button-down shirt lay in the entryway. He reached out to Dana, his hand dripping blood. He didn't speak. All she needed to know she saw in his eyes. He was terrified. She knelt and held his hand. "We're going to get you out of here. Relax."

Like Dana had given him permission, he slumped and rested his head on the ground. The paramedics came in behind, carrying a canvas stretcher. She gestured to his pants, soaked with blood by the groin. "He needs to go now," Dana said.

They carried him out, and two new medics entered. The fire captain waved, directing the medics to follow him and the police downstairs to the basement. Dana continued searching the first floor. A woman hid under her desk in her fabric-paneled cubicle. "Help me," she pleaded.

Unsure of the shooter's location, Dana put her finger to her lips.

Commanding voices shouted from the basement, "Police! Drop your weapon!" Next came the pop of one gunshot. The radio chirped, "Shooter down! I repeat, the shooter is down."

With the shooter neutralized, Dana and the medics checked the remaining cubicles. A man sitting on a desk chair lifted his slumped head and said, "He's shooting everybody. He worked here. He shot everyone." Blood dripped from his head.

"We're gonna get you outta here," a medic said.

The man stood up and stumbled. Dana guided him onto the

stretcher and followed to help load him into the ambulance. The woman who had been hiding under her desk clutched onto the arm of the officer who walked her out. A crowd of bystanders was gawking and taking photos. Dana marched to the crowd and slapped a camera from one bystander's hands. "Show's over."

She returned to the ambulance and placed an oxygen mask on the victim. His hair was matted with blood. She had separated his hair to inspect the wound when a phone rang. The ringing stopped. Dana set up an IV bag and handed the tube to the paramedic. The phone rang and stopped and rang again. On the next ring the phone fell from the patient's pocket. Dana picked it up. The screen flashed a photo of a young woman with two little girls on her lap. The ringing stopped. She placed the phone on the cot next to him.

The ambulance arrived at the emergency room entrance. Dana checked for respirations. He was no longer breathing. The phone started ringing. Dana squeezed the air bag alongside the medics steering the stretcher into the trauma bay. With her patient in the care of an orchestrated frenzy, Dana exited the trauma bay and peered through the window. The medical team lowered their masks. He was gone.

Engine 12 met Dana on the street outside Hennepin County Medical Center. At the station the crew sat in front of the TV with bowls of ice cream and the intention to forget. The station door clicked and scraped across the floor. Steve, a former firefighter turned clinical social worker and the head of firefighter employee assistance, interrupted their retreat.

"Hey guys. Tough call today. Everyone all right?" he said.

"We're fine," said the captain.

Dana gave him a thumbs-up over her shoulder and buried her face in the bowl of ice cream.

"Thought I'd check in. Be safe out there." The door clicked and he was gone.

"Bullshit," the engine driver said.

Dana snorted and turned up the volume.

Since her gambling relapse, Dana's first waking thought had been her pocket aces losing—and Lily. This morning, waking at the fire station, she saw the wide eyes of a shooting victim. She rubbed her eyes but couldn't shake the smiling faces of two kids on a phone screen never to be answered again.

Dana knew what it felt like to be a kid whose dad wasn't coming home.

The officer had knocked on the door, and her mother had fallen to her knees. The screams escaped on a snowy morning at the edge of a cliff had simply been postponed. Saved for the day her mother would scream alone.

The last time she'd seen him, she was clutching his leg and sitting on top of his shiny black shoe. She could still see his hand leaving his pocket and the pennies scattering. The excitement she had felt dashing for them was now colored with resentment. The station wagon's signal blinked and disappeared around the corner.

Dana didn't need philosophy to convince her money didn't bring happiness. For Dana, money was all about losing.

She hid the pennies in a tin box under the basement steps, tucked inside the square hole of a cement block. Cupping the palm full of coins in the dim light of the cellar made her feel close to her dad. One day, when she tiptoed down the steps to count them, the tin box lay open on the floor. She checked inside the cinder block. The pennies were gone.

Footsteps drummed down the wooden stairs. It was her older brother Troy. He ducked under the steps and gasped in surprise. Dana stared in disbelief. Troy glanced at the empty tin, and Dana knew.

"Did you take Dad's pennies?"

"No. How was I supposed to know whose pennies those were?"

"They weren't yours! I was saving 'em for Dad."

"Dad isn't coming home."

"Yes, he is."

"Dana. Dad is dead and he's not coming. Not ever."

Dana pushed past Troy. "I'm telling Mom what you said. I'm telling."

Dana ran up the steps. Her mother was waiting. She wrapped her arms around Dana and squeezed her tight, and in spite of the sadness Dana felt safe, just as she had felt on that snowy morning.

One more clutch onto Dad's leg wasn't in the cards. A "senseless accident," the police officer on the doorstep had said. Dad had dropped his newspaper in the street while crossing and he leaned down to pick it up. The approaching car never saw him.

When Dana got home, Lily's car was in the driveway. She hurried inside. The credit card bill sat on top of a mail pile on the kitchen table.

"Do you have something to tell me?"

"I'm not perfect. I messed up."

"Dana, geez, can I count on you for anything?" She threw the trash bag of donation items at Dana's feet. "I thought you were going to drop this at the Salvation Army. Two weeks later I find it still in the trunk."

Dana glanced at the table and saw that the credit card bill was sealed.

"Sorry. I'll take it today."

"You're right you will."

Lily left for work, and Dana got to work. She steamed open the envelope with an iron. She scanned down the column, searching for cash advances. She photocopied the statement, cut out the zero for an overdue balance, and pasted it over the seven-hundred-dollar cash advance. She adjusted the totals and photocopied a new statement showing a zero cash advance. The paper grade wasn't perfect, but Lily wasn't one for details. Dana admired her work, a little too proud of her deception.

"Now I need to get my money back."

She returned the bill to the pile. Under it was an envelope from the City of Minneapolis. She ripped it open.

Thank you for your interest in the position of Fire Motor Operator, blah, blah blah. She scrolled to the bottom. *Your rank: # 6.* She left the letter on the table, got in her truck, and drove to the card club.

Six hours later, Dana sat alone at the poker table with all the chips. First place had earned her a little more than five grand. She sped into the driveway, only to see Lily's car already there. Dana tucked the cash in her jacket pocket. Inside, she quietly hung her jacket in the closet.

Lily shouted from the TV room, "Dana, is that you?"

Dana shouted back, "No. It's an intruder who happens to have a key to the house. Hand over the jewels."

Lily turned off the TV and met Dana in the kitchen. "Well intruder, I don't have jewels, but how about I give you this bag of clothes and household wares." She held up the bag of Salvation Army items. "Where were you?"

"Shit. I forgot again. Um. I was at the library."

"The library?" Lily gave Dana a sideways look. She held up the City of Minneapolis letter. "It's Friday night. Let's celebrate, number six. How many drivers are getting promoted?"

"All twenty-two of us who took the test. We have more wannabes than the fire department has positions. No interviews. They'll make it official in a few weeks. No need to celebrate."

"What is up with you? You've been kind of off since I came home from my work trip. Have you been gambling?"

Dana stuttered. "What? Gambling. No."

"Promise?"

"I promise, and you're right. Let's go out."

The next morning Dana slept in. She savored the Saturday mornings when neither she nor Lily had to work. When she did wake, Lily the worm chaser was already up and Dana could smell the coffee. "Lily?" There was no answer. Dana checked the driveway. Her car was gone. *Perfect,* Dana thought, *I can hide that cash.*

She opened the mudroom closet to get her jacket. When she didn't see it, she checked the hall closet. She heard Lily's car pulling in the driveway and met her on the walkway. Lily waved the Salvation Army donation slip. "I donated a few of our jackets. We have so many."

Dana's heart sank. "You didn't even ask. You gave my jacket and didn't ask."

Lily pushed past Dana and went inside. Dana followed. "Lily. That was my jacket. Why would you do that?"

Lily pulled the wad of poker cash from her bag. "Is this what you're so worried about, Dana?"

"I was saving. Ahh, umm."

Lily threw the cash on the floor. "Take your money and go. I can't do this anymore."

"It's a slip, just a slip."

"This isn't about a slip. You think this is about gambling? I know you have a problem, but Dana, I told you. No more lies. Go, or I will."

Dana swooped up her truck keys. She crouched and gathered the cash scattered on the floor, "You do know," Dana said. "Gambling and lies. They're the same thing."

She opened her truck door and climbed in, but then just sat in the driveway. She fanned the fat stack of twenties with her thumb. The money she had believed would save her, like the tin box of pennies, ruined everything. Dana considered going back to convince Lily that this would be the last time. But she knew it wasn't true. She slammed her door and drove away.

CHAPTER 17

Ruby

Ruby would have welcomed Dana as a temporary roommate with no strings attached. But taking the captain's test was an "everything is better with two" situation. She had proposed a deal. Dana agreed to take the test, and Ruby agreed to let Dana crash in her guest bedroom.

Now Ruby was the last of nineteen fire-captain hopefuls sequestered for the day. Dana had left the holding room three candidates earlier to perform the practical part of the exam. When finished, each applicant exited through a separate door, ensuring no contact and no possibility of information sharing.

Ruby wiped the moisture from her palm onto the thigh of her neatly pressed uniform pants and opened the door to the testing room. The tap of her shoes echoed across the room as she approached a vintage rectangular table and a plastic Jetsons-like chair. She untucked the chair and sat in front of a forty-two-inch TV screen held by ceiling brackets. She placed a blank sheet of paper on the table in front of her, scribbled a few notes, and lined up colored markers. "Ready," she said to the chief.

The chief turned to the panel of evaluators sitting on an elevated platform to Ruby's left and nodded. Ruby knew no one on the panel, and no one on the panel had ever met Ruby. The fire department hired an outside company to judge the candidates to ensure neutrality.

Ruby felt confident but nervous. She knew it didn't matter what scenario flashed on the screen. She knew she could handle every catastrophe pictured on the cover of *Fire Engineering* magazine over the last two years. Plus, she had real-life experience. Due to a captain shortage, Ruby had been riding out of grade in the captain's seat. She couldn't remember the last time she'd sat in the back of a fire engine. It wasn't the scenario rattling her. It was the serious faces of the panel. Being on stage for this group of testers felt like ringing the doorbell at Heaven's gate on Judgment Day.

Ruby tugged her collar to hide the heartbeat thumping the fabric of her uniform. She turned to her jury and found friendly smiles.

The TV screen lit up white. First came the dispatcher's voice: "Initial assignment, Engine 5, Engine 7, Ladder 2, and Chief 3 to a possible structure fire, 2929 Bloomington Avenue South." She mapped out the scene with a red marker, recording the responding rig numbers and cross streets.

She looked up from her outline. On the TV screen, smoke poured from the upper-floor windows of a two-story home. Ruby had prepared for a warehouse fire, a river rescue, an explosion. *A single-family home is kid's play.* She opened her mouth to report her arrival, but no words came. The smoke turned from gray to black and swirled toward the roofline. The scenario on the screen would continue to unfold based on Ruby's action or failure to act. The smiles on the panel deflated and their eyes narrowed, surrounded by wrinkles of concern.

The tick of the second hand on the wall clock echoed in her head, and the scratch of the chief's pencil recording who knows what amplified. *How can I be frozen and sweating?* She covered her face with her notes. At the top of her diagram she spied the symbol she had drawn before anything else: S3

"Strength to the power of three," she whispered behind the page. Ruby found her voice.

"Dispatch, Engine 5 has arrived at 2929 Bloomington Avenue South. We have black turbulent smoke showing from the second floor, alpha side. Engine 5 will be laying a tank line through the front door for an interior attack. Give me a first alarm."

Once she broke her paralysis, she moved through the test collecting every point like coins in a video game. Set up a command post: check. Create an area for staging: check. Establish a collapse zone: check. What the hell, she even called in the duty deputy for environmental concerns. An extra point could move her up a spot on the list, and Ruby wanted to leave no advantage in the ruins of the virtual fireground. She knew when the screen went dark and the chief winked that she'd done well.

Ruby gathered her markers and smiled at the panel. She heard Dana's laughter on the other side of the door. She threw open the door and stepped into a hallway crowded with those who had gone before her.

"I rocked that test," Ruby said.

"I bombed it," Dana said. "I forgot to set up the command post."

"I didn't find the victim," said another captain hopeful.

Dana and Ruby looked at each other, "What victim?" they said in stereo.

"Fuck it," Dana said. "I'll be way better at driving than commanding. I know I did just enough on the FMO test last week to get me in the driver's seat. The captain gig, it's all you, Ru."

"Are you saying I'm bossy? Everyone knows the one steering the rig is the one in charge."

Ruby's laugh thundered above the rest. The emotion of a once-in-a-lifetime performance needed a release. The role she hadn't even thought about a month ago had become her obsession—and her focus on the bigger prize had paid off. The only thing missing was Tyler. After she told him she wanted to forget him, he hadn't called. Maybe he was trying to make it easier on her. The problem was, the longer he was gone, the more she couldn't stop thinking about him.

Dana and Ruby walked together across the parking lot to Ruby's car. "Maybe I should drive," Dana said. "You should probably get used to riding shotgun."

Ruby threw Dana the keys. Dana slammed her door and buried her face in the crook of her arm. "What is that smell?"

"I know. Heath's fucking gas can. The warmer the weather, the stronger the smell. I can't get rid of it."

"It's not that bad, Ru. I like the smell of gas. It reminds me of when I was a kid. My brothers and I had contests after the rain. We'd squirt lighter fluid on puddles and light it. They'd squirt fluid in a circle. Not me, I'd squirt the whole can in one great big blob. My fire lasted longest every time."

"Okay, future *Firefighter* Strong."

"I knew it would go out once the fumes burned off."

The next day, riding out of grade on Engine 16, Ruby obsessed over the virtual fire scenario details. She covered the desk in the captain's room with blank papers. On each sheet she drew a different room to analyze her decisions. *I should have sent a rescue team to the basement right away.*

She sketched a stick figure in the kitchen where other candidates had found a victim. *Was there smoke coming from the cellar stairwell?* She swirled a thin gray line at the cellar door in the shape of a question mark. She squinted, trying to recall her decisions. *I went upstairs. I followed the smoke. Never follow the smoke, or is it never lay a line to smoke?* "Shit," she said and threw her marker on the desk.

Joe, the driver, yelled from the apparatus floor, "Hey, Ruby, you're letting this riding-in-charge thing go to your head."

She looked at the wall clock—09:15. She was late for Saturday super clean. For a made captain, paperwork might take precedence over rig cleaning. A firefighter riding out of grade who skips Saturday duties is a slacker.

Ruby picked up her red pen and scribbled flames over the drawing. Joining Joe and Willa on the floor, she reached into the soapy mop bucket and pulled out a sponge.

The red phone rang, and Joe slapped Willa on the shoulder. "Back to you and me."

Ruby splashed the sponge into the bucket and dried her hands on her shirt. "Sorry, someone has to be in charge."

Out of breath, Ruby picked up the phone on the third ring. "Station 16, Acting Captain Ruby Bell."

"Hey, Ruby, Assistant Chief Hall. I wanted to let you know the test results are in, and you finished on top."

Ruby's stomach flipped with surprise. "On top? How close to the top?"

"The top. You're number one."

Ruby thought she'd done well, but number one was an ego blast. The red ink flames scribbled over her stick-figure victim didn't matter. She crumbled her artwork and shot it into the trash like the winning basket in the final seconds of the game. *I'm number one? I am number one.* She knew she deserved to be captain, but ranking number one would convince everyone. *They'll all want to be me.*

Ruby skipped back to her crew.

"No thanks to you, rig's clean," Joe teased. "After Willa finishes the tools, call me for the final rinse. What'd the chief want? I hope it's not training this afternoon. I was out late last night."

"No training. Plenty of time for your one-to-three nap."

Willa held a ceiling hook like a rifle, inspecting her work with one eye closed. Ruby looked into the one open eye, and a smile blazed across her face at the gush of being ranked number one.

"Perfect," Willa said. "This tool is ready for the big one. Happy looks good on you. What's with the grin?"

Ruby looked away. Willa was a flirt. She wouldn't be like other captains, unable to draw the line between supervisor and friendship. The even thicker line of romance was out of the question. She thought of Tyler. Her smile dropped.

"I'm happy to see you did such a great job on that hook." She handed Willa an axe. "Touch up this next. After we rinse the rig, we'll get lunch."

Ruby handed Willa the axe, and Willa grazed her fingers, saying, "Mmm, you are one tall glass of water."

Ruby pulled back her hand. "Do people actually say that? First of all, I'm not tall. The bigger disqualifier: I'm not gay."

"We're all on a continuum." Willa laughed and placed the axe on the worktable.

"It's never happening either way. I took the captain's test. Boundaries."

Willa raised her left hand and placed it at the line of her eyebrow in a half-hearted salute.

"Wrong hand, soldier," Ruby corrected.

Willa clicked her heels and saluted with her right hand, then drew her hand across her face, completing the salute. "Can't blame a girl for tryin'."

The newly washed fire engine reflected the sun as Joe pulled out of the station. Ruby clicked her seat belt. "I'm buying lunch. Whatever you guys want."

"Did you win the lottery?"

Joe looked over his shoulder. "Willa, if she won the lottery, she'd be driving her convertible into the garage at her beach house. Not sitting shotgun on a fire engine."

"I might stick it out a bit longer. I mean, I am number one on the captain's list."

Joe tapped on the air horn and said, "Congratu-fuckin-lations. Right you're buying lunch."

"Number one," Willa echoed. "I guess no one's gonna accuse the department of fixing the test this time." Ruby turned to the back seat. Willa looked into her eyes and winked. Surprised at the wave of heat she felt, Ruby looked away.

"I still have the interview. I go downtown Monday morning."

The monitor on the dash lit up—possible dryer fire. Ruby keyed the radio and answered, "Dispatch, Engine 16. We're en route."

While red lights and siren are the protocol for every 911 response, Joe maintained the speed limit. Lint on fire inside the metal container of a dryer would most likely be out before they got there. Arriving at the address, Ruby reported light smoke showing from the basement window.

"Grab the pump can, Willa."

Willa did so and followed Ruby into the home through the side door, closest to the basement.

"Doesn't smell like a dryer to me," Ruby said. "Something real is on fire."

She opened the door to the basement. A cloud of thick black smoke rushed up from the stairwell. She turned and sucked the clear air behind her.

"Dispatch, this is the IC on Bryant, we have a heavy smoke in the basement. Complete the assignment for a first alarm."

Ruby readied her mask. Willa smiled. "Shame to cover up that pretty face."

"C'mon, Willa. Focus."

"I'll get the tank line."

Hearing the crackle of fire from the basement, Ruby secured her mask and took the pump can Willa had left. She wanted to see the layout of the basement before the smoke banked down, choking out visibility.

At the bottom of the stairs were a washer and dryer on the right. She opened the cold, empty dryer. When she slammed it shut, the crumbling cement wall released a puff of dust. She studied the floor plan. To the left, a rack of winter coats partitioned off a narrow hallway running from under the stairs to the length of the basement. The ceiling was reinforced with four wooden columns. On the right, VHS tapes spilled onto wood pallets. The heat intensified; Ruby searched for the bashful flame. Chirping sirens let her know reinforcements had arrived.

Smoke spread across the ceiling and, with nowhere else to go, crept toward the floor, stealing the light. Ruby crouched for a last look and to orient her position in the basement. A hot flash of light drew her attention. Down the narrow hallway, behind the rack of coats and under the stairs, a small, flickering flame danced on a blackened pallet.

"There you are," she said. "So little to be causing such big trouble."

The flame responded with a bright flash. The underside of the wooden steps was burned to a black char, letting Ruby know the fire had been burning a while.

She keyed her radio. "Dispatch, this is the incident commander on Bryant. Have the first arriving truck crew bring in the junior extension ladder. The basement stairway is compromised."

She emptied the five gallons of water from the pump can onto the little fire. It rebelled, its fiery fingers encircling the beam and lighting coattails on fire.

"I got the line, and I'm coming down," she heard Willa yell from above.

"Wait for the truckies!" Ruby ordered. "I don't trust the stairs."

Ruby heard a crack. Blackened embers rained from above. Willa's leg punctured a hole through the step. A large chunk of wood fell to the ground at Ruby's feet. Another crack and Willa's second leg broke through. Slowly the nozzle dropped, dangling between Willa's feet and Ruby's helmet.

Ruby reached for the line. Willa's legs pumped, running in midair with flames licking at her boots. Ruby opened the nozzle and soaked Willa's turnout pants for protection before directing the water stream to the flaming coats. The wide palm of the fiery hand stretched open before the flaming fingers balled into a fist and surrendered.

She closed the nozzle and looked up. Willa's feet floated upward, disappearing into the smoky black sky above Ruby's head. The junior extension ladder dropped in front of her, providing an egress. Ruby stepped from a puddle of ash onto the ladder and quickly climbed, anxious to check on Willa.

Outside, Ruby searched the fireground for the rehab rig, hoping to find Willa sucking down a Gatorade and changing her air bottle. When she didn't see her, she scanned the street for the ambulance. The medics were casually standing outside their rig. No frantic energy of an injured firefighter being treated.

"Hey, hot stuff," Willa said, coming up behind her. "Why don't you go change your bottle and meet me inside? I'll be checking for hot spots."

Willa headed back into the house to start overhaul. Furious, Ruby dropped her SCBA on the ground and followed Willa back into the basement. Ruby climbed down the ladder to where Willa poked through debris with her hook. Ruby grabbed the collar of Willa's fire coat and pushed her against the crumbling basement wall.

Willa apologized, "I know, I shoulda checked the steps before I—"

Ruby pushed the helmet from Willa's head and kissed her hard. Tasting ash on her mouth, she softened. She grabbed her gloved hand and tugged, dropping the glove to the floor. She moved her face close to Willa's ear and held her breath, interlacing their fingers. Ruby squeezed her hand and let her breath go. She moved back over her lips, and Willa's tongue reached for her. Ruby leaned away and shoved her into the wall.

"You scared the shit out of me. Pick up the hose. This fire's out."

Ruby self-quarantined for the rest of the shift, hiding out in the captain's room. Was it Willa's unending flattery? Or was it the stress of feeling completely out of control as fire lapped at Willa's flailing legs that drove Ruby to that kiss? She didn't know why, but she didn't have the energy to field another rumor, or the time. Tomorrow was her interview.

Ruby trotted down the steps outside city hall. Her interview had been unremarkable, with the anticipated questions. She was sure she had the right answers. On the sidewalk she met Trent, ranked number two after the virtual fire scenario, on his way in for his interview.

"How was it?" he asked. "Did you have to tie knots?"

"Can you believe it? They gave me the square knot." She squeezed his large bicep. "Easy peasy, big guns, squeezy."

She dreaded going back to Station 16 the next day. She ignored three calls from Willa over the weekend. Living together at the fire station for twenty-four hours made Willa tough to avoid.

Ruby parked next to Willa's SUV in the lot. She scanned the apparatus floor, relieved to see she was alone. She put her gear next to the engine and climbed on the rig to check her mask.

Willa bounded into the back seat. "Miss me?"

"Listen, Willa."

"You don't have say it. I know. You're a captain, and a straight one at that. No worries. It was the literal heat of the moment. It is comforting to know that losing me was so terrifying, you had to throw me against the wall and show me you cared."

"I'm sorry about that. I shouldn't have given you the wrong idea."

"That kiss? I cannot find one wrong idea there. And don't worry, this won't end up in Ruby's Chronicles of the Thong gossip. I'm keeping it between you and me." Willa winked and covered her face with her mask.

After checking her equipment, Ruby drove her car into the station. Today, she would get rid of that gas odor once and for all. She emptied everything out. After taking out the boxes and papers and shoes and books and socks and gloves and tools and even a crowbar, she scrubbed it down—this time with vinegar. The gas smell remained. She ripped out the carpet lining the trunk.

At the sound of the red phone, Ruby slammed her trunk closed.

Joe yelled from the coop. "Ruby! Strap it on your back."

She rushed to the phone, hoping this was the call. "Acting Captain Bell."

"Hi, Ruby. Assistant Chief Hall. Bad news. We won't be promoting you to captain this time. We're passing you over."

She heard the chief suck in air like he was getting ready to say more. She pushed the phone close to her ear, making sure she heard right.

"You scored sixty-nine points on the interview, and you need seventy to pass."

The interview questions flashed through her mind. *I tied the knot. I outlined the incident command system. I didn't find the victim. No. That wasn't part of the interview.* Ruby's mind raced—her words froze.

"Let's see here." She heard the rustle of paper. "You got zero points for education."

Zero points for education? I graduated college. I took the leadership and incident command classes. I even took the driver's course. How can I get no points?

"Chief. I'm one of the few candidates who has a bachelor's degree."

"It says here that it was in adolescent psychology. It's not relevant."

Ruby had mostly followed the fire department platinum rule to never challenge authority. She covered the handset and muted her voice to say, "Fuck you!"

S to the power of— Fuck sweet, she thought. "Chief, this is bullshit. I took the captain classes. No points for that? I took the FMO class too."

"Ruby, everyone took the captain's classes. I don't think you stressed how your education relates to the fire service. You'll stay on the list. The good news is, we'll be making more captains in six months and you'll still be at the top of that list."

Ruby slammed down the red phone. She lifted the handset and slammed it again when the outside line rang.

"What?" she answered.

After a pause Dana said, "I think the correct way to answer the phone is Fire Station Sixteen, Captain Number One."

"I don't like to brag," Ruby said.

"Since when? I have some gossip. Number two, aka Trent, was called downtown today. He messed up his knot. Poor sap got the running bowline. Here's the thing: they made him a captain anyway. The chief—I'm not talking about the training chief. I mean Chief Gallo. *The* chief of the department called Trent into his office and said he can see how obviously committed Trent is to the job by his physique. Chief had him tie the bowline 'til he got it right. After like seven tries he got it, and the chief handed him his captain bars right then and there."

Ruby looked into the mirror and flexed her bicep. "They passed me over."

"That is bullshit! I told you not to be number one."

"He said they'd make me captain next time. I'll stay at the top of the list, but I don't think I'll interview again. Fuck 'em. They're missing out."

"You can't let the ha-has get to you. You think they care about missing out? They don't think they're missing out. You are interviewing again. If you don't, they beat you. You're not hurting anyone but you. Besides, when you do make captain, I'm drivin' for you."

"It's official? You made driver?"

"I wasn't stupid enough to be number one. Remember when Meg was number one on her test? Passed over. Nina, number one. Passed over. I know how to keep a low profile. I'm good with number six. I get paid the same as number four, three, two, and yup—same as number one."

Ruby hung up the phone and dragged her feet to her car. She threw the torn carpet in the trash and opened her trunk. The odor, like the discrimination in the fire department, suffocated the air around her. Tired of the fight, Ruby surrendered and slammed her trunk closed.

CHAPTER 18

Tramping: Traveling to a different station than normally assigned. Minneapolis hosts four or five districts and nineteen to twenty fire stations.

Ruby

After three more months of tramping to half of the city's twenty fire stations as an out-of-grade captain, Ruby had a date for her second-chance interview. Dana was working, and Ruby planned to drive home, change into sweats, and study all day for the next day's challenge.

She packed her gear into her oversized red duffel bag. The yellow letters of *Firefighter* stenciled on the side, which had once filled her with pride, now felt like a taunt. Being passed over meant one thing. She wasn't good enough to officially wear the bars, but the shortage of officers made her good enough to play the role.

On her drive home she passed a vacant lot where a convenience store had once thrived. She recalled the fire she had fought and lost when it burned to the ground. "Good save," she said. She rolled up the window—a thin layer to shield her from the memory. The window sealed, and the gas odor returned.

A few blocks later, exhausted and dizzy from the lingering gas vapors, she ran a stop sign. She swerved, barely missing honking cars, before turning down the alley to her garage.

She parked inside and popped the trunk. *What will it take to kill these gas odors?* She glanced at the shelves lining the garage behind high piles of her stuff, boxed up to make room for Dana's furniture.

She recalled Dana's story of burning gas vapors on puddles and mused, "I wonder."

She pushed aside a box marked *Storage* to get to another labeled *Goodwill*. She ripped off the packing tape and rummaged through an assortment of candles to find the one Tyler had given her on their first Christmas together. She held it to her nose and breathed in gingerbread, recalling his attempt at romance.

"There's nothing sexier than making love on Christmas next to a fire. Let's light it," he had said.

"No, it's too pretty. I'm saving it."

Tyler fastened one button on his shirt, making as if to leave. Ruby tugged at the tail and said, "Where do you think you're going? I'm not gonna light—let's see here"—she turned the candle over to read its label—"Cookie Kisses. But that doesn't mean we can't fuck."

Now Ruby dug to the bottom of the box and found a lighter. She placed the candle in the open trunk and lit it. If she couldn't wash the fumes away, she would burn them off.

The flicker of the candle grew, consuming the vapors.

"Cookie Kisses saves the day," she said, seeing the end of her gas-fume misery. The flame on the candle dimmed. Satisfied that the fumes were gone, Ruby leaned in and blew.

Vapors scattered. Flames flared as if annoyed, igniting a piece of cardboard wedged inside the wheel well.

Ruby felt cavalier, unthreatened by a small piece of cardboard. She picked up a carpet remnant from the garage floor and beat the flame. Frayed threads caught fire. Heat scorched her arm. She dropped the carpet and slammed the trunk, cutting off the air.

As the fire intensified, so did Ruby's doubt. The car glowed blue inside. She knew she had only a moment to save what mattered. She pushed the Goodwill box to the side, rescued a box marked *Save*, and retreated to her front lawn to call 911.

The first siren chirped and then silenced. Red and white strobe lights permeated the smoke as the rig slowly rolled down the narrow alley. Ruby waited. Engine 7 stopped with a jerk before reaching her garage.

Hector hopped off the rig and prepared the tank line for attack. Flames shot through the roof. Tyler engaged the pump. He pulled the lever on the fire panel, releasing water into the hose. The hose stiffened, and Hector pulled back on the handle. Air inside the hose hissed, and water shot into the air. He closed the nozzle, dropped it on the muddy ground, and pulled his gloves from his hip pocket.

Seeing the hose splayed over the muddy alley, Ruby recalled Hector's words in the dim light of the hose tower more than five years ago. *Double hot*, he'd said.

Hector retrieved the nozzle and stomped through puddles toward Ruby's garage.

Ruby's seven-year-old, mud-covered legs skipped to keep up. Her mother held her hand, pulling her behind. Her mom's other hand clenched a wad of muddied clothes.

Her mother marched up the green-painted steps of Stan's screened-in porch. Ruby followed. Stan, wearing his typical white T-shirt, sprang from his cot like he'd been caught sleeping on the job. Ruby hid behind her mom.

Her mother threw the pile of clothes at his feet. "Who do you think you are, rolling my daughter in mud? You can wash these! And stay away from my kids."

Stan quickly gathered the muddy clothes. The cigarettes rolled in his short-sleeve shirt slipped to the floor. He seemed timid. Ruby wasn't afraid anymore. She moved from behind her mom and stuck out her tongue at Stan.

On the walk home, Ruby's mom stopped and crouched in front of her. Taking Ruby's face in her hands, she said, "Ru. Did that man hurt you?"

Ruby saw anger and fear in her mother's eyes. She looked away, afraid to tell and afraid to keep a secret.

"You know you can tell me anything. You're a sweet girl, Ruby. But you have to be strong, and more than anything you have to be smart. If you're not, assholes like that will hurt you."

That was the only time Ruby had heard her mother swear. When her mother sat her down at the table that night with a pencil and paper and instructed her to write the words *strong* and *smart* using capital *S*'s until the page was full, Ruby didn't feel punished or blamed. Even at a young age, Ruby understood her mother was preparing her for the double s in *asshole*.

Ruby ripped open the box she'd rescued and threw a pinecone fire engine, made by schoolkids on a visit to the station, on the grass. She dug for a card made by a little girl. It featured a handprint with each finger decorated with a face and a fire helmet. Connected by the palm, the five firefighters were handling the hose line together. Scribbled in red crayon under the firefighter representing Ruby—the only firefighter with a ponytail hanging from her shiny yellow helmet, were the words *My Hero*.

Like her garage roof giving in to the flames, Ruby could no longer contain her rage. She ran at Hector, lowered her shoulder, and pushed him from behind, sending him to the ground. "Stay away from my stuff. You asshole!"

She snatched the nozzle and pulled back the handle, aiming at her garage. The fire, inspired by a flicker of bad judgment, stood its ground. Flames fueled by overstuffed boxes and wooden support posts reached into the sky.

Ladder 3 blasted its air horn, announcing its arrival at the end of the alley. Dana and Bettina marched down the alley alongside two more truckies, axes and hooks in hand.

Tyler depressed the pump lever, cutting off Ruby's water. She looked over her shoulder to serve Tyler a "what the fuck?" expression. Durgans standing side by side in a line stared at Ruby holding the uncharged nozzle. Dana stepped from the line.

She grasped the nozzle and whispered in Ruby's ear, "I'll take it from here. Don't let 'em get to you."

Ruby tried to speak. She glanced at Hector brushing mud from his coat. "He—"

"I know," Dana said. "Me too. Double hot, hot dogs, right? I gave him a double swift knee to his double-small nuts for both of us."

Ruby let go of the nozzle. Dana lowered her face shield and nodded to Tyler. He pulled the lever, and the water returned. Flames fanned out like a red sun. Rising smoke painted black clouds against the blue sky. Dana directed the water stream on the flames, forcing the fiery sun to set and reducing the black puffs to wisps of gray.

Ruby's blackened car was a shadow in the rubble of glowing ash and burnt support posts. She tucked the handprint drawing into the box and stood on her deck.

Dana uncoupled the nozzle from the hose and rested it on the engine tailboard before joining Ruby on her deck. She removed her helmet and gestured toward the pile of ashen rubble. "I guess I'll be parking on the street."

"Why didn't you tell me?"

"You know the definition of insanity, right?" She didn't wait for Ruby to answer. "It's women reporting the same shit at the fire department over and over, expecting to get justice this time."

Ruby thought about the women, isolated and transferred to less-than-desirable stations. About Patricia Peck, who lost her fire career and got an EMT gig in a nearby suburb—another victim of the insanity.

Dana continued, "Same reason you didn't tell me. We can't let those assholes ruin us. We just want to do our fucking job and not deal with that shit. Problem is, when we don't deal with it, we burn our garage down."

"I tried your light-the-gas-on-the-puddle trick. I'm guessing my fire burned longer than any of yours."

"Key component is the water, Ru."

Ruby considered her thought process. "I have my captain interview tomorrow. This won't look good."

"Well, you did fight your own garage fire, and without fire gear. That seems pretty badass to me."

Ladder 3 tapped the air horn.

"I think that's for you," Ruby said.

"Good luck tomorrow. Try not to let 'em know you're the smartest person in the room."

Ruby looked at the curls of smoke rising from her flattened garage. "I don't think that'll be too hard."

Dana headed to the ladder truck. Ruby searched the alley for Tyler and found him standing by the engine. He threw his helmet in the cab and approached Ruby. With a nod toward the garage he said, "I got your smoke signal and came right over."

"I thought about texting but didn't want to be unoriginal."

"Dana told me it was you who started the fake rumor at the ice fishing tourney."

"I didn't expect you to believe it."

"I'm sorry, Ru. I've been an idiot. I'm not sure why Hector's been hobbling around, but I have noticed him avoiding Dana."

"She's not someone you want on your bad side. Why do you think I kissed her in the icehouse?"

"Wait. That kiss?"

"You're right, you are an idiot."

Tyler bowed in deference. Ruby envied his freedom to be sweet.

"I don't know what happened between you and Hector, but whatever it was I'm sure he deserved to eat some mud." Tyler turned to go.

Ruby would no longer keep a secret.

"Hector hurt me. That day in the hose tower. The day you made me tofu. I don't want to talk about it, but I can't keep pretending."

Tyler's eyes flashed anger. "Fuck."

"Please don't say you're mad at me."

"You? Why would I be mad at you? I'm mad at myself. Fuckin' fire department. We're supposed to be the good guys. He's not getting away with this."

"You still don't see. He *is* getting away with it. If I report him—"

"We. *We* report him."

"There is no we. It's me they won't trust. Me, who climbed on top of Alex with a thong."

"That's a bullshit rumor."

"Truth doesn't matter. I complain, and the second I walk through the doors of a firehouse, the joking stops and the whispers get really loud."

"Okay, so you don't report it. He's still not getting away with it."

Tyler stormed toward the rig where Hector was having a smoke. Hector lifted his chin to nod. Tyler returned the nod and, without breaking stride, balled his fist and with one punch knocked Hector to the ground.

The arson investigator pulled into the opposite end of the alley. His headlights shined on Hector like a spotlight. The investigator stopped short of the garage and flicked on his red strobe. Hector shielded his eyes as he struggled to stand.

"Lover's quarrel?"

"Misunderstanding," Hector said. He swung the engine door open and stepped onto the rig. He glanced at Ruby watching from her deck and massaged his chest.

Not quite a kick in the balls, she thought, recalling her chest compressions. *Effective nonetheless.*

The investigator retrieved his fire boots from the back of his SUV. He assessed the burned-down garage and then hiked across the lawn to Ruby, still sitting on her steps. He pulled out a pack of smokes and offered one to her. She shook her head no.

"What happened, Ruby?"

She shrugged. "I guess I will take one of those." She pulled a long drag, turning the tip bright red.

"Seriously, what happened?"

She took one more drag and flicked the cigarette to the ground.

"Heath's fucking gas can. Check the trunk. I have a feeling there's a stubborn puddle of gas still hiding in there."

She watched as the investigator stepped over a charred beam into the ruin and snapped a photo of the vehicle. He picked up her soot-covered crowbar and pried open the trunk.

She picked up the box she had rescued and went inside her house.

The next morning Ruby's only thought was her interview. Dressed in her class-A uniform, she straightened her tie in the bathroom mirror. She thought about earning zero points for education after the first interview and practiced a modified response.

"I have a degree in adolescent psychology, and if that doesn't prepare me to lead a bunch of men who constantly reminisce about catching the winning touchdown in high school, nothing will."

Winnie jumped up onto the vanity and meowed.

"Too sarcastic? You're probably right." She scratched the cat behind the ear and traced her collar to the Saint Flora medallion. "I might need this more than you, just for today."

She removed the medallion and threaded it onto the chain around her own neck. She placed her formal bell cap on her head and leaned in close. "S to the power of three," she whispered, and then added, "Just don't be too *smart*."

She adjusted her cap. "I took the captain classes, where I learned the value of communication in leadership. I took the driver classes because the leader of a fire company should understand the responsibilities of everyone on her crew."

Ruby slid her keys from the hook and pushed the garage door opener.

"Shit. I don't have a car."

She raced to the kitchen and pulled a drawer so hard it fell off the rails. She knelt on the floor, throwing takeout menus and coupons to the side. At the bottom of the drawer she found a bus schedule and ran her finger down the page for arrival times. *Bus 11A can get me there five minutes early.* She checked the departure time: 8:38. She checked her watch: 8:43. She crumpled the schedule, threw her head back, and screamed. Then she paced. "Think," she said.

A honking horn grew progressively louder until it was blasting directly in front of her house. She ran to the window and lifted the blinds.

Dana honked again as she stopped. An unsecured dresser in her truck bed slid into an upside-down swivel chair, causing it to spin. Ruby ran to the door and flung it open.

Dana leaned across the cab and opened the passenger door.

"Looks like you're all dressed up with somewhere to go, and no way to get there. Need a lift?"

"I forgot I don't have a car."

"I didn't. That's why you need me. Never light gas on fire unless it's on top of a water puddle, and even if you burn up your own car the day before an interview, there's no excuse for being late."

As they arrived at city hall, Dana said, "Go knock their bugles off."

"I thought I did the first time."

"Nope, last time you knocked their socks off. Keep it simple. Don't blow it with your college-educated smarty pants IQ."

"You're a good friend, Dana."

Ruby jogged up the steps. Her shoes beat a familiar rhythm on the wide marble stairs. Her adrenaline-charged red cheeks showed up on cue. She was prepared for every leadership, technical, and tactical question they could throw at her.

Entering the office, she faced a panel of three chiefs in white shirts. The bugles pinned at the collars inspired her smile. *Time to knock some bugles off.*

"Mornin', chiefs."

Chief Hall sat in the middle. "We have one question."

Ruby's mouth went dry as she realized she had just one shot. One question stood between her and a promotion to captain. She thought of Dana's argument for interviewing again: *The difference in pay between firefighter and captain is the same difference as riding a bike and driving a Porsche. Don't let your pride force you to pedal for your entire career.*

Ruby knew Dana was right. But not about the money. True, she did need a new car, but mostly she wouldn't let pride stop her from getting the promotion she deserved.

Chief Hall cleared his throat. "Which knot would you use to raise an axe up the side of a building?"

Ruby stared in disbelief. *That's it? Is this a trick question?* In spite of her anger at the formality of a dumbed-down interview, Ruby chose *sweet.* "It's a clove hitch with a half hitch, Chief."

He handed her a rope and an axe. "Let's see how it's done."

To tie one of the simplest knots used on the fireground, Ruby wrapped the rope close to the axe head and tied a clove hitch. She followed the axe handle with the rope to the end and flipped a loop, creating a half hitch.

She lifted the rope above her head. When the head of the axe reached eye level, she noticed she had tucked the rope over instead of under, a rookie mistake. The axe slipped through the rope and fell to the floor with a thud; with it, Ruby felt her promotion slip away.

The chiefs sat silent. Ruby quickly gathered the axe and rope—a tangled mess. *Knock their bugles off, not their socks.* She tied the rope in six granny knots along the handle and held it up again. This time the axe held.

"You know what they say," the chief said. "If you can't tie a good knot, tie a lot of bad ones." He placed a captain badge and bars on the table. "You've been assigned to—" He lifted his glasses to reference his paper. "Report to Station 5 for your first shift. Congratulations, Captain Bell."

Two days later Ruby pinned her badge on her chest and the captain bars on her shirt collar. She tucked Saint Flora inside her uniform. On her first day as captain, a little extra protection wouldn't hurt.

Dana drove Ruby to Station 5. Ruby hopped out and retrieved her gear bag from the truck bed and ran her hand along the word *Firefighter* on the side of the bag. No longer a taunt but a proud part of her history.

"Show 'em who's boss, Captain Bell," Dana said.

Ruby's stomach flipped with her new title. Ruby didn't need to *show 'em who's boss*. As captain, they would know. She deserved respect.

She was relieved to be assigned to Station 5 with just one rig. Fewer people meant less testosterone. She went to the coop and checked the lineup taped to the wall.

Captain: R. Bell
FMO: Sick
Firefighter: Sick
Firefighter: Sick

"What the hell?" Ruby said.

The offgoing captain shuffled out of the restroom in his Crocs. "They reported off. My guys can't hold over. Strange, they all have doctor appointments. The chief called. Engine 5 is shut down for the day. You're supposed to report to Station 8."

"I don't have a car."

CHAPTER 19

PTS: *Post-traumatic stress. Dropping the D for disorder, and thus the stigma, identifies it as a normal reaction, characterized by anxiety, for people who have experienced one or more traumatic events.*

Dana

Since breaking up with Lily almost four weeks ago, Dana had realized that being with Lily meant giving up the one thing she needed to forget. Thoughts of amputated legs and gunshot wounds to the head remained vivid and difficult to shake. Only at the poker table did Dana find calm in her chaos by seeing nothing but the cards in her hand.

After a full day at the card club, Dana was looking forward to chilling with her roommate. As she pulled up at Ruby's house, though, she spotted Lily's Volvo parked in front. Dana considered returning to the casino. Instead, she sneaked in through the back door leading to the kitchen, hoping Lily had had a change of heart. *Maybe she's ready to accept me as I am.*

Ruby stood at the counter, opening a bottle of wine. She shrugged and whispered, "She said she wanted to wait."

Dana poured a glass of red wine, grabbed a beer from the fridge, and went to the living room. Lily sat on the couch, snuggled up with Winnie. Dana handed her the wine and took a swig from her beer.

"We should get a pet," Dana said. "I've always wanted a fish."

Winnie jumped from the couch, making room for Dana, who sat and reached for Lily's hand. Lily reached for her wine. "Where were you today?"

Dana took a long drink of beer. The most effective way for her to avoid lying to Lily was by not talking. *Besides*, Dana thought, *does she really want to start out with a fight?*

Lily pulled an envelope from her pocket. "I didn't realize it was getting bad again." She slipped the credit card statement from the envelope. "You lost seven hundred dollars and doctored the bill?"

"I didn't want you to worry. I knew I'd win it back."

"Dana, I don't even know who you are. This is beyond lying. This is—"

Dana interrupted. "I lost seventeen hundred. The credit card bill doesn't include the money I took from my checking account. Anyway, I paid the credit card bill."

"The money. You always go to the money. By the time you figure out what you lost has nothing to do with your bank account, it'll be too late." Lily stood to leave.

"I told you the truth. It's seventeen hundred." A casino chip fell from her pocket.

Lily snatched the chip from the carpet. "This is all the truth I need to see." She dropped the chip in her wine, tipped the glass over, and stormed out the door.

Dana bolted for the kitchen. Ruby met her halfway with a roll of paper towels.

"Sorry, Ru. Damn, this stuff stains."

"I guess this means you won't be getting those fish."

Dana threw a balled-up paper towel at her. "You were listening?"

"I didn't exactly need to hold a glass up to the wall. Dana, are you sure you're making the right move?"

Dana thought about the nights of lying in her bed and finding the bliss that comes one second before falling into a deep sleep—and then being jerked awake by her breath catching on a feeling she couldn't explain, hot and filled with doom. The feeling that something is wrong, but nothing actually is. Then the flashes of babies not breathing, a stab wound to the face, shiny black shoes crossing the street and a car coming too fast. The pictures changed, but the feeling stayed the same until she could imagine holding two cards—usually pocket kings, but it didn't matter so long as the cards flipped slowly on the felt at the poker table. In her thoughts she controlled her fate. As she raked in the chips like a hero, sleep returned.

"I feel like it's my only move."

Dana wasn't choosing poker over Lily. Dana just wanted to feel better.

CHAPTER 20

Aerial Ladder: Heavy steel ladder mounted on a fire
truck. It can be mechanically extended to 100 feet,
approximately ten floors of a building.

Ruby

Ruby hiked up the waist of her pink plaid pajama pants and carried
a bowl of popcorn to the living room. Dana twisted the caps off two
beers, set them on the side table, and maneuvered the coffee table
to cover the wine-stained carpet.

"Covering it up doesn't mean it's not there," Ruby said.

"So philosophical."

"I'm pretty sure you said you were going to get that cleaned."

Dana handed Ruby a beer and lifted her bottle. "A toast."

Ruby raised her bottle. "To girls' night. Popcorn and a movie."

"To getting rid of the one thing you hate most."

Ruby sipped her beer. "And that would be?"

"Hector retired."

Ruby tipped back her head and poured what was left of her beer
down her throat. The effect of the alcohol didn't disappoint. She felt
almost giddy.

Dana continued, "Everyone expected him to stick it out until mandatory retirement at sixty-five, and he's out the door at fifty-nine. I heard it's his heart."

"Damn right it's his heart. It's made of dogs' anal sacs."

Dana raised her beer higher. "Diseased rat guts."

Ruby clinked her empty bottle with Dana and said, "Grab the videos from my bag. I'm gonna grab another beer."

Ruby returned to the living room, and Dana held up two DVDs. "Leg strength or cardio?"

Considering the amount of time they had left to prepare the women recruits before the next firefighter entrance exam, Ruby pointed with her fresh beer bottle to the *Cardio for Firefighters* DVD. "Most of the recruits are at peak strength. We need to make sure they can carry those muscles to the end of the course."

Dana loaded the DVD. Then a spotlight flashed through the living room window like a strobe at a dance party. Dana peeked through the window past the curtain. The air horn of a ladder truck pulsed two blasts. "I think this one's for you."

Ruby threw open the door, still carrying her bowl of popcorn. "Who the hell?" she said, and proceeded to the sidewalk.

Dana followed. A hook-and-ladder truck, its extension ladder raised twenty feet in the air, filled the street. The silhouette of a firefighter hung from the ladder.

Tyler wore his fire pants, his helmet, and a white dress shirt with a black bow tie. The rig speakers crackled, followed by a pause, and then blaring rock music filled the starlit sky. Neighbors peeked from their windows while others watched from their porches. Tyler held onto a ladder rung with one hand and a leg locked through a lower rung as he danced over the street to the Melissa Etheridge song "I'm the Only One." He shouted along with the music more than he sang, promising to walk across the fire for Ruby.

Ruby said, "He's so stupid," not taking her eyes off him.

Dana leaned over and shouted in her ear, "He does know he's serenading you with the lesbian national anthem?"

"You gay girls don't get all the good stuff. Rock is rock."

By the time the chorus repeated, the sidewalk was crowded with neighbors. Tyler motioned with his index finger for Ruby to come to him.

"Go rescue him before he wakes up the next block too."

Ruby clutched her bowl of popcorn like a security blanket.

"Ruby, go! Before I switch teams and go myself."

Ruby tried to find a word beginning with s that meant "happy." She looked up at Tyler swaying from the ladder. "Sexy," she said. She placed her bowl of popcorn at the bottom of the ladder and climbed up to him. Tyler wrapped Ruby in one arm, pulled her close, and kissed her.

"I think you may just be one of the good guys," Ruby said.

The lights and music stopped. Through the loudspeaker the captain announced, "Romance is over. We have a call."

Below, Dana cleared the street, shouting, "Okay, everyone, show's over. Sweet dreams."

Ruby hurried down the ladder with Tyler right behind her. He handed her the bowl of popcorn and hopped into the driver's seat. He tapped the horn. The ladder truck's red lights swirled, and the siren faded as it disappeared down the street.

Dana stopped next to Ruby on the sidewalk and looked into the popcorn bowl.

"Looks like it's your turn to decide on a right move."

Ruby pulled a diamond ring from the bowl. A popcorn kernel was wedged inside. She dropped it back in the bowl and followed Dana into the house. Dana went to the kitchen for a fresh beer.

Ruby sat on the couch with Winnie, who batted at the medallion hanging from Ruby's chain.

"You're right," Ruby said. "I did promise to give this back."

She attached Saint Flora to Winnie's collar. Then she retrieved the ring from the bowl, ate the popcorn kernel from the center, and strung it on the collar with the medallion.

Dana flopped down next to Ruby and scratched Winnie behind the ear.

"I see Winnie accepted your proposal."

"Can you blame her?"

"Are you sure? I wouldn't want you to miss out."

"They don't think they're missing out. Isn't that what you said?"

"I didn't mean Tyler. He's one of the good guys."

"I know. He is really sweet, but sometimes, when I think about how he stood by—you know, when I was just another female infiltrating the station. Was he one of the good guys then? What's changed?"

"I know you're right. Fear makes some people mean. But sometimes it takes getting to know the people you resent. People can change. Look at me. People meet me and like me—as long as they don't know I'm gay. I admit sometimes I tiptoe around, incognito-like. Once I'm sure they won't be able to resist my charming personality, I attach my U-Haul to the back of my truck, put on my flannel shirt and Birkenstocks, and reveal my true identity."

Ruby slapped Dana's arm, laughing. She removed the ring from Winnie's collar and tried it on.

"Maybe a change is exactly what I need."

PART
THREE

AROUND 2010

CHAPTER 21

Brazil

For Brazil, a chance meeting had nothing to do with luck and everything to do with divine intervention. Preparing for a morning run through her South Minneapolis neighborhood, she dropped to one knee, bowed her head to tie her sneakers, and said a simple prayer. *Jesus, I'm not asking for a miracle, just a nudge in the right direction.*

After the recent split with her husband, Brazil and her two boys lived with her mother. Although she appreciated her mother's hospitality, living in her childhood home now that she had children of her own wasn't the happily ever after she had planned. She started out on her run, focusing only on the steady rhythm of her stride.

Something flashed in the distance as she jogged toward the one-mile mark. Intrigued, she quickened her pace. The beacon was a badge pinned on a woman's uniform, reflecting the rising July sun in front of a fire station. The badge flashed and dimmed as the fire-fighter maneuvered the largest wrench Brazil had ever seen over the top of a fire hydrant. The firefighter put one finger in the air, motioning Brazil to wait.

Direction from a person in uniform can cause even the most focused person to follow orders. Brazil stopped, and water gushed across the sidewalk from the hydrant.

The uniformed woman spoke. "Testing the hydrant."

Brazil wondered if she had asked for an explanation. The firefighter continued, "Hi, I'm Jasmine. I've noticed you running past the station. The fire department is accepting applications. You should apply."

The woman turned the wrench in the opposite direction, shutting off the water.

"I'm studying to be a nurse," Brazil said. "I don't know anything about fighting fires."

"A nurse? You'd be great. You seem fit. You could totally do the firefighting part. Most of our responses are medical."

Behind the firefighter, Brazil spotted three more firefighters standing in the open doorway of the huge garage. The massive red trucks made the men appear almost small. The trio clenched cigars—one in his teeth, the others between fingers. Although she couldn't hear words, their hand gestures indicated a critique of the woman's work.

"What about that?" Brazil asked.

"I'm making sure the hydrant is good, flushing out debris."

"I can see what you're doing." Brazil raised her chin toward the cigar-puffing crew, "I mean that. It looks like you're doin' all the work. I'm not so sure this is for me." Brazil readjusted the lace on her running shoe and continued her run.

Jasmine chased her long enough to hand Brazil a recruitment

flyer. "Think about it. It's only two to three shifts a week, and we get great benefits. Believe me, I get what you see in those guys. The fire department isn't a lot different than the rest of the world. We can't let them keep the great jobs all to themselves."

Brazil stuffed the flyer in her waistband. She had started to jog away when Jasmine shouted, "We have lots of down time. You can get paid while you study for that nursing degree."

Brazil slowed her run to a walk when she reached the neighborhood park. She passed a trash can, pulled the flyer from the back of her sweatpants, and tossed it. The flyer dropped to the ground. Brazil leaned to retrieve it and read, *Paid training. Women and minorities encouraged to apply.* She folded the flyer back into her waistband and started home.

———

That night she tucked her boys in for bed and settled in with *Anatomy 101.* Her bookmark was a tuition bill for the fall semester. Brazil wondered if, maybe, meeting not only her first female firefighter but a *Black* female firefighter was God's way of saying, "Trust in a little help from your friends." The next morning Brazil filled out the application.

One week later she got a phone call. "Hi. I'm Ruby from the Minnesota Women's Firefighter Association. I see you've applied. We offer free training sessions on weekends to help applicants prepare for the firefighter test. Interested?"

Obvious divine intervention. "See you Saturday," Brazil said.

———

After two bus rides, Brazil arrived a block from the training tower in Northeast Minneapolis. She crossed the bridge spanning the Mississippi and passed through the gates of the training ground. The sound of the river disappeared into the roar of portable engines and the screech of metal on metal. The long, paved road, bordered with a chain-link fence and a strip of overgrown grass, opened to a field littered with half a dozen crushed or burned-out vehicles. Men dressed in fire gear operated heavy tools, cutting through metal and forcing car doors from their hinges.

In the distance a four-story concrete tower rose from the pavement. She approached it and realized that the trainees surrounding it, chopping railroad ties, hoisting ladders, and occasionally slapping one another on the back for a job well done, were all women.

A tall woman sporting spiky blond hair and an oversized rubber fire coat greeted her. "Hi. I'm Jessie. You must be Brazil. Ruby hoped you'd be here today. She asked me to help you feel at home."

"Are you a firefighter?"

"Not yet. I'm taking the next test, same as you. I've been training with the Women's Association for a couple months." Jessie cupped her mouth like she was sharing a secret. "They call me their star student—truth is, it's all about leverage." Jessie winked. "Come on, I'll show you around." Jessie handed her a coat, a helmet, and gloves.

Brazil followed Jessie through the course, listening to her tips on how to tackle the obstacles. "Try this one first," she said, and led Brazil to an extension ladder encased in a metal bracket fastened to the side of the tower. "You can't just grab the rope and yank it. It'll slip through your gloves. You need to grip the rope so it bites the back of your glove. Keep the thumb of one hand at eye level." Jessie pulled the rope to demonstrate. "With your other hand, reach up and grab. Squat as you pull. Legs mean leverage."

Brazil squatted and pulled, fully extending the ladder. "This is actually easier than I expected," she said, smiling.

"Right?" Jessie encouraged. "Now let it down easy, hand over hand. If it slides through your gloves you gotta start over."

Brazil loosened her fingers, and her confident smile dropped with the rope zipping through her gloves. The ladder rattled against the bracket and crashed to the ground. Brazil squeezed her eyes closed, ducked, and ran from the building.

Jessie laughed. "That's what the bracket is there for—to keep it from falling on you. It's not about speed here. It's control. Come on. I'll show you how to drag the charged hose line."

Throughout the day Brazil improved. She lowered the ladder slowly and without a crash. She advanced the hose, pulled the rope to simulate starting a saw, and practiced on a chopping machine. She waited in line, watching women struggle with the dummy lift.

The 6-foot, 175-pound dummy was a Frankensteined figure with a patched fire coat draped over its shoulders and one foot, wrapped in duct tape, dangling from tattered fire pants. Its blurred facial features created a sense of anonymity. Brazil noticed that the rope cinched around its neck was knotted into a noose. *A white guy with a noose around his neck—I guess it's about as likely as a fire training tower surrounded only by women.* Firefighter hopefuls struggling to lift the dummy resorted to using the noose. Women cheered one another dragging it along the pavement and across the finish line.

Brazil reached the front of the line and grasped the rope just as a leader—who turned out to be Ruby—stepped out of the tower and addressed the trainees.

"You can drag it for now, but you will have to pick it up on test day."

One of the women in line protested, "I thought we could drag it."

"You could on the last entrance exam, but the powers that be have changed it. You will have to carry the dummy. The good news is, this is the first test where everyone finishing the course in under six minutes earns the same number of points. That means women will be ranked and woven through the rookie class instead of clumped at the bottom. No more reach downs."

Brazil tugged on her coat and squatted beside the dummy. She forced its rigid arms above its head and pushed its shoulders, raising it to a seated position. She wrapped her arms around the rubber fire coat and lifted. The dummy seemed anchored to the cement. Brazil adjusted her grip and lifted again. The plastic coat hiked up past the dummy's ears, and Brazil slid to the ground.

"Is this some kind of joke?" she said, and sat up back-to-back with the dummy.

"Okay, Brazil. Grab the rope and drag it. Get a feel for the weight." Ruby said.

Brazil stood and grasped the rope. She pulled, but her gloves slid along the rope. The smell of others wearing the same coat before her reminded her she wasn't alone. *Not one of us can lift it. It would take a miracle to lift this monster.* Brazil dropped the noose.

"Jessie, show 'em how it's done," Ruby said.

Jessie crouched behind the dummy, folded its head into its lap, and lifted it like it was a box of pillows. Brazil tried to imagine matching Jessie's strength. She closed her eyes to call on her only hope—prayer. *If this truly is where I'm supposed to be, you're going to have to figure it out for me because I cannot lift that dummy.*

It was almost as if Jessie heard Brazil's prayer. "I couldn't lift Frankie at first either. Don't worry, you'll get there."

Brazil glanced at her watch. Her mom had committed to four hours of babysitting, and her mother was clear: *Be where you say you will, when you said you would.* She thanked Jessie for her help and promised to return next Saturday.

As a single mom, Brazil couldn't justify paying for a gym membership, but she was innovative. She recognized resources all around her that would provide everything she needed to build strength. She tied weights to the end of a rope and slung it over a tree. Hoisting them simulated raising and lowering the extension ladder.

Her boys followed her to the side of the garage to help retrieve a discarded sheet of plywood buried in weeds. She drilled two holes in the end and laced a rope through, creating a sled.

"Climb on and hold on tight," she told Bentley and Emmett. The boys raced to the board and flopped on.

She wrapped the rope around her body, leaned forward, and pulled them down their driveway, strengthening her quads.

"Faster," Emmett squealed. "Run, Mommy, run!"

"Run like your butt is on fire," five-year-old Bentley echoed.

Brazil's muscles hardened and her cardio increased. Her best time on the practice test clocked at five minutes and forty-eight seconds.

If she could match that on test day, she would earn the full hundred points for the physical portion of the entrance exam.

The association rewarded her hard work by paying for a temporary membership to the YWCA. Encouraged and humbled by their support, she took full advantage of the exercise equipment and the free daycare provided by the gym.

Ruby had mentioned that Black women made up less than 2 percent of Minneapolis firefighters, and they were counting on Brazil to stoke the fire of change. That expectation felt more like a red flag than a checkered flag, but she began to believe she was part of something important.

Brazil concentrated on conquering the only thing holding her back—she was still dragging the dummy. With the test date approaching, she reminded God, "Fifteen more days. I can't lift it alone."

The next morning, Brazil jogged from the bus stop over the bridge and down the familiar road to the tower. Jessie met her halfway, excited and speaking fast.

"I've been trying to teach you to lift the dummy the same way I lift it, and then it hit me. You're shorter than me, and I'm stronger than you."

"Thanks for the pep talk."

"No, I mean it hit me when I was reading this article about Wonder Woman and Superman. It was a big debate between comic geeks, but in the end—she can kick Superman's butt if she uses her magic lasso."

"First of all, why would superheroes fight, and more importantly, if you have one of those magic lassos, can I borrow it?"

"You got jokes. Nope. You don't need magic. What you need is to use what you already have. You need to put those short, powerful legs to work."

Jessie demonstrated the technique she had worked out for Brazil. She pushed the dummy's head up from behind and supported it on her thigh. She wriggled her body close to the dummy, wedging her thigh under the dummy's back. She wrapped her arms around its chest like always, clasped her hands in front and pushed with her legs. Jessie stood and so did the dummy. "Once you get him up, take a step backward and don't stop 'til you cross the finish."

Brazil crouched next to the dummy and rested its head on her thigh. The head alone felt like a medicine ball. She pressed her chest against the dummy's back, breathing in the sweat-infused odor of a rubber fire coat. She wrapped her arms around the wide torso and grabbed her wrist with her opposite hand.

"Son of a daddy," she said, struggling to stand.

It was like she was pushing her legs through the concrete, but she stood, surprised. She took a step back and let the momentum take her back five more before dropping Frankie on the pavement. Gathering women cheered and clapped. Brazil placed one foot on the dummy's chest and raised her fist in the air. *Thank you, Jesus, for this spiky-haired star student.*

After mastering the dummy, Brazil continued to cut her time. On test day she crossed the finish line at five minutes, twenty-three seconds, earning the full hundred points. Jessie finished in just under four minutes—earning the same score.

———————

Two weeks later, as Brazil made peanut butter sandwiches for her boys, the clang of the closing mailbox sent Bentley running to the door. He returned with a pile of letters including an envelope from the City of Minneapolis. *Two thousand applicants*, she thought, *Not likely I'm in the top fifty*. She finished making the sandwiches before opening the letter. She scanned to the bottom of the page.

Your Rank: 38.

Her eyes widened with a flash of unexpected excitement. She returned the letter to the envelope and imagined wearing a badge reflecting the sunlight. Then she remembered the men smoking cigars and critiquing Jasmine, and Ruby's hope that Brazil would stoke the fire of change.

I guess it's bonfire season because here I come. Brazil was determined to provide for her sons, and she could do that working with superheroes like Jessie.

CHAPTER 22

MMPI: *Psychological test. Nonphysical firefighter entrance test. Psychological and/or personality tests gauge mental fitness and "right fit" for a firefighter.*

Jessie

Jessie found her dream job and her dream girl on the same day. As she edged past a woman standing in front of the coffee-shop bulletin board, holding a notecard and searching for a spot to pin it, Jessie was drawn to a Women's Association poster taking up half of the board. The women on it looked like champions, standing confidently, wearing fire gear like armor with axes tucked in their belts like swords. They seemed to be saying, *I dare you to make a difference.*

Jessie knew how it felt to be a champion. The story of her birth had always made her feel like she was meant for something big. It was her dad who retold the story most, bragging about how the doctor held her by her feet and slapped her behind. Instead of crying, Baby Jessie blinked, glanced at her mother, and smiled. The euphoria in her mother's voice—"Do you promise me? It's a girl?"—

had impressed Jessie with her first emotion: accomplishment. Success for Jessie simply meant being as she was born—a girl.

The woman reached over Jessie and pinned her ad, "Seeking Female Roommate," on the helmet of a firefighter. Jessie was about to correct her until she realized, *This woman is gorgeous.*

"I'm Kim," the woman said. "I noticed your eyes glued to the poster and figured pinning it there might attract exactly who I'm looking for."

Is she flirting with me?

During the many dates that followed their coffee-shop encounter, Kim heard the passion in Jessie's voice as she described touring MFD stations to learn about truck tools and fire engines. Jessie recounted how the most joking firefighter became serious when the red phone rang, sprinting to answer like responding to a fire alarm. All joking squelched, the firefighter picked up the receiver and formally answered with location, rank, and name.

After that, whenever Kim called, Jessie answered by mimicking firefighters, adjusting for her location: "Drug store parking lot, soon-to-be firefighter Jeroncyk." When Jessie accepted Kim's invitation to move in, she was surprised by the newly installed red phone on the kitchen counter.

"Practice for your future," Kim suggested.

On Jessie's final trip, moving her stuff from her apartment to Kim's place, she stopped at the coffee shop. She ripped down Kim's advertisement for a roommate and took a long last look at the women on the poster, the kind of women who would never let a little brother down.

———

Four days short of one year after Jessie's birth, her little brother Tag was born. Their mother had hoped Jessie would get a little sister for a playmate. They would be so close in age. But when Tag was born, his mother couldn't hide her disappointment. The doctor held him high and slapped his bottom. Tag wailed with terror.

Jessie adored Tag. Adoration was her first strategy to protect him. As her father praised her, Jessie did the same for Tag. But their father longed for a son as fearless as Jessie, and compensating for his longing wasn't easy.

Later Jessie would blame herself, believing her coddling had contributed to the shame at the core of Tag's personality. After they lost Tag—and to make up for whatever it was she'd missed—Jessie pushed harder to be the best.

The Thursday before the physical test, Jessie ran the 113 steps at Minnehaha Falls carrying a backpack filled with 65 pounds of rocks—her usual workout. She'd never done anything half-assed. *Focus. Don't miss the details. Dig deep.* Her tenacity had made her a star athlete, breaking records at her high school and earning one of the few scholarships granted to women at her university. Now, as the sweat dripped down her calves, she daydreamed of the tattoo she would get once she graduated rookie school: the firefighter's Maltese cross, inked on the deltoid of her right arm. In the center would be two common firefighting tools, a fire axe intersected with a pike pole. But first she had to pass the entrance exam.

Team sports had proved to her that helping others made her better, so she had quickly become the ambassador for the new re-

THE FIRE SHE FIGHTS

cruits at Ruby's training program. Teaching Brazil to use her legs to lift the dummy had shaved twenty-two seconds from Jessie's own time. She was proud to be part of the reason more women could carry the dummy across the finish line.

On the Saturday before the physical test, Jessie attended her final practice session. She was surprised to see a handful of men getting pointers at the tower. She soon learned that the men paid to join the Women's Association, granting them the opportunity to attend the final weekend of practice.

"We use the money to pay for women's gym memberships," Ruby explained. Jessie was especially surprised to see PJ, who she recognized from the trainees' barbeque the week before.

"I took the test five years ago," she'd overheard him say, waving his bottle of Bud Light in front of his face. "I was ranked fifty-ninth and didn't make it 'cause I don't have tits."

Jessie looked PJ over as she waited for her turn to chop railroad ties. His fire coat was open, and when he raised the axe above his head, the pink of his stomach spilled over his gray gym shorts. *Having tits is probably why you didn't make it*, she thought.

After warming up with chopping practice, Jessie headed for timed practice of the full test. She lifted a sweaty turnout coat from the pavement, donned an air tank, tightened the strap on her helmet, and imagined her brother's face. She whispered, "This one's for you, Tag."

Jessie focused on the thumb of the woman keeping time. Instead of starting on "Go," she moved with the push of the stopwatch button. She pulled the extension ladder rope. The bell chirped. She lowered it hand over hand, careful not to let it slip, yet not so careful as to waste precious seconds. She hurried to the fire engine, slid the hose bundle from the compartment onto her shoulder, and climbed the stairs to the fourth floor, touching every step as required.

"Drop the bundle on the floor inside the painted yellow square," the timer instructed.

Jessie dropped the hose and continued through the doorway to a flat roof. She slipped her foot into the handle of the target saw for leverage and pulled the rope of the saw eight times. Next, she was sure to slam the hammer square on the chopping simulator, ringing the bell in twenty-eight chops. She paused, looking over the parapet and slightly lifting her helmet, allowing the breeze to cool the sweat on her brow.

Returning to the yellow square, she hoisted the bundle back onto her shoulder. She hit every step on the way down, eliminating the possibility of a two-second penalty. She dropped the bundle at the bottom of the steps and lifted a charged hose line from the ground.

She knew not to grab the nozzle. She lifted the hose six feet back and wrapped the nozzle behind her. She leaned forward, using her weight to set her in motion, and trudged back into the tower, head down, leaning so far forward she could have kissed the floor. When her helmet bumped into the corner, she knew she had enough slack to pull the hose to the opposite side of the tower.

"You're good." The timer's words felt more like a compliment than a decree.

Jessie dropped the nozzle and climbed the stairs one flight. The dummy waited at the entrance of a waist-high maze made of plywood. She lifted its silicone head and folded it into its lap. She squatted behind and wedged her hands under the arms of the rubber coat. Cheek to cheek, the strong smell of rubber ensured her she had the best position.

She wrapped her arms around its waist, leaned back, and focused her power into her legs. The burn in her quads nudged her to take the same advice she had given Brazil. She took one step back and then another, gaining speed, moving backward through the maze. She crossed the painted yellow finish line. But she wasn't done.

"Go," the timer said.

Jessie planted a kiss on the plastic hair of the dummy and dropped it to the floor. She descended the steps to the final task and easily hung the fan on the door.

"That was awesome. Four minutes, twenty-three seconds," the timekeeper said, looking down at her stopwatch. "I'm Dana." She stretched out her open palm.

Jessie slapped Dana's hand. "Thanks," she said and bent, resting her hands on her knees. She caught her breath and waved off the cup of Gatorade offered. With the test only three days away, it was reward enough to be one minute, thirty-six seconds under the cutoff time. Jessie was sure she would earn the full hundred points.

"You should probably take that tank off and drink the Gatorade," Dana advised. "We don't want to lose our—what do they call you?— our *star student* to pride." Dana lifted the tank from Jessie's shoulders. Jessie accepted the drink and relaxed against the wall.

"You're Dana. Ruby said you'd be here. She brags about you a lot."

"I'm gonna give you some advice I wish I'd had when I started," Dana said.

Anxious for a tip from anyone Ruby admired, Jessie stood. "Yeah? I think I could get my chops down to twenty-four with a little more force."

Dana shook her head. "Physical strength will only get you so far. You have it, and it's good. People will try to convince you strength is the only quality of a firefighter. To be a good firefighter you need a heart like Ruby. To make it in the fire station you need crocodile skin."

———————

In the few days leading up to the test Jessie rested her muscles and read about crocodiles. She ate healthy, feeding her body exactly what it needed to perform. On test day, Jessie hung the fan on the top of the door at a full thirty seconds under her best time. Jessie was sure she was in.

The psychological and personality tests the week before had felt more like fun than a test. Asked to choose between skydiving and waterskiing, she checked the box for skydiving. *Either seems like an adventure, but jumping out of a plane seems more courageous than being pulled behind a boat in the water,* she reasoned. When asked, "Do you secretly hope a clever thief gets away with the loot?" she changed her answer twice and finally settled on "Who doesn't?"

———————

Two weeks later, when the letter arrived in her mailbox, she didn't wait the five minutes for Kim to get home. She tore open the envelope. Their golden retriever, Blaze, followed her through the kitchen.

"Ready, Blazer? I don't have to be number one. Even if I'm twenty-nine, it's good enough."

She went out onto the deck and ripped the letter from the envelope. Jessie scanned to the bottom of the page to find her rank.

That was the first time Jessie passed out.

CHAPTER 23

Firefighter Combat Challenge: *An international, touring, five-event physical challenge in which firefighters compete for speed.*

Jessie

Blaze was barking. Jessie heard whines and the scratch of pacing toenails and then Kim's voice.

"Blazer, what's wrong, boy?"

Jessie sat up, blood dripping from a gash on her chin, as Kim followed Blaze through the open deck door.

Kim dropped her keys and crouched at Jessie's side. "You're bleeding."

Jessie swept up the letter. "One hundred twenty-four. I didn't make it."

"You need stitches," Kim said. She went inside to dial 911 on the red phone.

"Wait," Jessie said. "I'm okay. Just drive me to urgent care."

Inside the hospital elevator, Jessie leaned close to the mirrored door to examine the butterfly bandage on her chin. She held her hand out to Kim, who grasped her fingers. Jessie turned her palm up and said, "Keys. I can drive us home."

Kim followed Jessie through the parking garage to their car. "I guess the fact you fainted is a secret. The doctor can't help you if you don't give her all the information."

"It's weird. I saw 'number one hundred twenty-four' and then black. Even if they hire two classes, two whole classes"—she held up two fingers to accentuate her point—"it only gets them to number sixty. I worked my ass off. I can't believe I didn't make it."

"It has to be the psych test," Kim said. "They got this one wrong, Jess. You're made for that job."

———

Jessie consoled herself over the following weeks with dates with the rocky steps at Minnehaha Falls. She added five pounds to her backpack, as if increasing physical pain would change her fate.

Working her nine-to-five job at the woman's shelter, she researched the best answers for the psychological test instead of reviewing case files. She tossed in bed at night, trying to shake her fear of having the wrong personality. *It's obvious. I should want a thief to be punished, stupid. Is waterskiing really that courageous?* Rolling over, she pulled the covers off Kim.

"You're perfect, honey. Go to sleep," Kim said.

"I'm going to El Paso to compete in the Firefighter Combat Challenge."

Kim turned on the light and sat up. "Combat? What are you talking about? El Paso in Texas?"

Jessie slid a pamphlet from under her pillow and handed it to Kim. "The Women's Association is paying for the plane tickets. A few women are going as spectators. They asked me to go, and they want me to enter the challenge. They think I have a chance to make an impression."

"On who? Shouldn't you be focusing on the psych questions? I mean, Jess, you have the physical part mastered. It doesn't make sense. Who are you impressing?"

"Nobody. I don't know. Me, I guess. I need to do this. I feel like I'm right on the edge, and if I don't step off, I'll be stuck forever. I'm one step away from what I want more than anything."

"Maybe it's time to take a step back from the ledge. Life is short, Jess. Maybe focus on what you have right here."

Jessie switched off the light and pulled up the covers. "Life is only short for happy people," she said.

She thought of her brother and the torment that had made her life feel longer than most.

They lived in the last house on the edge of town. The backyard was lined with trees and opened to a cornfield. Beyond the field, the town changed to country, marked by the first farmhouse. Jessie shared the duties of her paper route with Tag. He woke first to retrieve the bundle of newspapers dropped off every morning next to an abandoned round barn.

Hearing the screen door slam, Jessie sat up in bed and peeked out the window. Tag raced down the road, pulling his red Radio Flyer wagon. She dressed and waited for him on the stoop. When he didn't return, she assumed he had gotten distracted again, playing with barn cats. She approached the round barn, but the papers were still bundled with string and the wagon stood empty on the roadside. A brown cat crouched near the barn door, hiding in a patch of wild daisies.

"Tag! You know you're not supposed to be in that barn."

Jessie marched toward the entrance. Three older boys, pushing one another and laughing, rushed out of the barn.

"Homo," she heard one say.

"Cocksucker," said another. "What a pussy."

The tallest of the three shouted, "Your little brother's a fag."

The boys broke open the newspaper bundle and scattered them across the road.

Jessie ran into the barn. Tag sat on a haybale next to a pitchfork jutting from the hay. He wiped his tears on his sleeve.

"I didn't want to," Tag said. "They made me. If I didn't suck it, he said he would stab me with that pitchfork."

Jessie pulled the pitchfork from the hay, set it down, and sat next to her little brother.

"It's okay, Tag. It doesn't mean anything."

"It means I'm queer. He called me his bitch. Please, Jessie, don't tell Dad."

"I won't. I promise."

Jessie would regret keeping that promise. While sticks and stones may break bones, names can truly hurt you.

———

A week later Jessie loaded her backpack with weight, intending to drive to the falls, but drove downtown instead. She parked at a meter in front of city hall and sprinted up the steps to MFD head-quarters. In the waiting room she noticed a photo of Ruby and Dana in rookie school. They were surrounded by a sea of men in blue shirts. Flames shooting from a simulated tanker fire erupted behind them. Jessie knew she belonged on the wall and she would do what-ever it took to get there.

She approached the woman sitting behind the chest-high count-er and said, "Hi. I'm here to see Chief Gallo."

"What time's your appointment?"

Jessie glanced at the wall clock. It was 8:47. Was this going to be like trying to see the wizard? "I don't have one. I took the last firefighter test and I—"

The chief emerged from his office, the first door beyond the sen-try's desk. Inspired by the bugles on his collar, imagining the bravery it took for him to earn them, she shouted, "Chief Gallo. I'm Jessie Jeroncyk, and I took the last firefighter exam."

She didn't hesitate when he motioned for her to come. She stood in his office, where black-charred fire helmets lined the wall.

"You took the test. How did you do?"

"One twenty-four," she said, staring out the window.

"I didn't ask you for your rank. How did you do? What was your time?"

"A little under four minutes, but I've been practicing and I'm closer to three."

"You're the one. Most of the men can't beat that time."

"We all get the same credit as long as—" She stopped talking, realizing he knew the requirement. "There is nothing I want more than to be a firefighter. No, not just a firefighter, Chief. I want to be a Minneapolis firefighter."

The woman from the lobby interrupted, "Chief, your nine o'clock is here."

He nodded toward the charred helmets. "It takes more than strength and speed."

Jessie studied the helmets and realized that the face shields had melted.

She met the chief's eyes. "I see what it takes, and I have it."

"Good to meet you, Jessie. Good luck."

Jessie met Brazil at the airport for their flight to El Paso. "Congrats, number thirty-eight," she said, trying to hide her envy.

"If you're mad, I wouldn't blame you."

"Naw. You deserve it. You not making it wouldn't help me. One hundred and twenty-four is a long way from thirty-eight." She bumped Brazil with her shoulder, "Why would I be mad at you? I am completely jealous, but mad? At you? Never."

When they landed, Jessie beelined to check the arrivals board. Dana's flight was scheduled to arrive soon. Ruby and Tyler would arrive early the next morning. After this quick stop in Texas for the combat challenge, they would continue to Sanibel Island for their honeymoon.

"Where's the fire?" Brazil said when she caught up to Jessie.

"Dana's flight is canceled. She said she'd be here. I can't do this without her."

"Someone's got a crush."

"What? I do not. I respect everything about her in a mentor sort of platonic way." Jessie smiled. "Just because I worship the ground she floats above doesn't mean I have a crush."

Brazil's ringtone belted out the tune of Lady Gaga's "Bad Romance."

"Is it Dana?" Jessie asked.

Brazil pushed mute on her phone and said, "Calm down. It's my ex-husband. He's"—she gestured air quotes—"babysitting the boys."

Jessie motioned that she was going to the restroom. When she returned Brazil was off the phone. "Let's go to the hotel."

"I think we should wait," Jessie said.

"Oh, did I mention? Dana called. She'll be here in a few hours, and she wants us to meet her at the Italian Kitchen for dinner."

Brazil nudged Jessie's shoulder. Jessie tripped and regained her balance.

"Is that a skip? Are you skipping?" Brazil teased.

Jessie returned the shove. "Let's go get our bags and the car."

At the rental car counter, the agent pointed to the fire department logo on Jessie's gear bag. "You two here for the combat event? That's cool. Lady firemen. I can respect that. We're out of compact cars." He handed her keys and said, "Your car is in space G5."

They looked at each other and rolled their eyes. When they reached space G5, though, Brazil ran her hand across the hood of a red Mustang convertible.

"Are you kiddin' me? This is money!"

Jessie put the top down and drove toward the Holiday Inn. *Finally*, she thought, *I'm on the road to happy*, and she pressed the gas pedal to the floor.

Jessie had time to unpack and nap for a bit before Brazil knocked on the door.

"Let's go. We don't want to be late to meet your not-crush." Brazil stepped in and picked up a book from the bed. "*A Crocodile's Life*?" She shot Jessie a confused glance.

"Dana told me if I want to make it into the fire department, I need crocodile skin. I get why you think I have a crush. But it's not Dana; it's what she represents. She's a textbook woman firefighter, and if she says I need crocodile skin, I believe her."

Jessie checked her look in the mirror. She pushed back her short blonde hair and traced the fading scar on her chin. *Time to put one hundred twenty-four in my rear view.*

They rode to the restaurant with the top down and waited for Dana. After too many complimentary breadsticks, they gave up and ordered.

At last Dana followed the waiter to the table. With a mouth full of breadsticks Jessie mumbled, "She's here."

The waiter set lasagna in front of Brazil and a salad for Jessie.

Dana said, "That looks like something a sparrow would eat. Bring her your biggest plate of spaghetti. We have high hopes for this girl tomorrow. You need carbs."

Jessie nodded to the hesitant waiter.

"I'll have the chicken parmesan," Dana said, and swigged down her full glass of water. "You'll never guess who I ran into at the airport. Here's a hint." She mimicked playing a bugle.

"Dolly Parton?" Jessie guessed.

Dana gave her a "what the fuck?" look.

"Well, we are in Texas."

"Dolly Parton is from Tennessee," Brazil said,

"Exactly, and no, I didn't see Dolly. I did see the chief."

"Theeeee chief?" said Brazil.

"In the flesh. Can you believe Chief Gallo is here with the assistant chief for a fire conference? I told him you were competing and suggested they stop by."

"Great," Jessie mumbled. She reached for another breadstick. "I need all the carbs I can get."

"I wonder if crocodiles eat carbs," Brazil teased.

"Private joke?" Dana said.

"She thinks she needs crocodile skin to be a firefighter. I'm sure you meant thick skin."

"I did. And she does. You need it too, maybe a lot more. The fire department prides itself on tradition without change. Part of that tradition is keeping someone holding the short end of the stick. It's hard on the women. Before us, it was hard on the Black guys. Being Black and a woman, I imagine you know a lot about thick skin."

Brazil swallowed a mouthful of lasagna and said, "And as a lesbian, I'm sure you have a closet full of short sticks."

———

The next morning Jessie and Brazil drove to the competition together. Jessie recognized the fire combat female world record holder standing by the spectator stand. She had recently come out of retirement to compete in her last event, in honor of a friend who had died in the line of duty, and broken her own world record. Jessie gathered her courage and approached her hero.

"Hi, I'm Jessie. I follow your career, and basically"—she paused—"I idolize you."

The woman stepped back. "Idolize?" she said. "I'm a human being. Worship should be reserved for God alone."

Before she could respond, Dana had her hand around Jessie's shoulder and led her away from the bleachers. "Did you just tell a Mormon you worship her?"

"I didn't know."

"You need to focus. The only idol you need to pray to today is the combat fire challenge goddess. Look what I found." Dana held up a shiny penny. "It was heads up in the parking lot. It's good luck." She handed Jessie the penny. Jessie rubbed it between her fingers and dropped it in her fire pants pocket.

"The fastest woman here can do this course in two minutes and forty-four seconds. You got your work cut out for you. Think you can do it faster?"

Jessie nodded, and she believed it. She had told Kim she would make an impression. While she couldn't fix what she got wrong on the psych test, she could prove the fire department was crazy for passing her up.

"I'll be sitting in the bleachers with Ruby and Tyler. Ruby wanted me to mention—lots of competitors are losing seconds hoisting the weight up the side of the tower. The rope is slipping through their gloves. Not sure how to fix it, but if you can think of something, you might shave some time."

The loudspeaker crackled. "Firefighter Jessie Jeroncyk from the Minneapolis Fire Department is our last competitor. Jessie will be competing in her first combat challenge."

The firefighter part wasn't true, but Jessie hoped the power of believing would lead her to the certainty of knowing. As she approached the starting line, Brazil skipped out to her with a water bottle.

Jessie shook her head.

"It's not for drinking. Hold out your gloves."

Brazil soaked Jessie's gloves and said, "This will fix your grip. How do you think I finally lowered the ladder without crashing it?"

Jessie clipped the regulator to her face piece and glanced at the large neon start clock displaying the temperature—ninety-three degrees. *For you, Tag.* She crouched at the starting line, tightened her helmet strap, and focused on the clock countdown. *Two . . . one!* A siren whooped, signaling the start. The cheering crowd faded into the background.

Jessie threw the hose bundle over her shoulder and attacked the stairs. She didn't need to think about it; she knew to take one step at a time. The metal stairs shook under her boots. She reached the first landing and stepped again. *Control your breathing. Grab the railing, pull, and step. Same at the next landing, pull and step.*

At the top, she reached over the rail for the rope and pulled. *Hand over hand.* Her wet gloves were like glue. Her back muscles burned. She reached and pulled, reached and pulled. The weight popped over the rail. Jessie turned to descend the stairs.

One step, two steps, hit every step. Breathe. She gathered energy, giving her muscles a rest all the way down. Next was the chopping simulator, the Keiser Force Machine.

She lifted the mallet and straddled the I-beam. She swung down between her legs, striking the steel beam. She slammed and stepped backward and slammed and stepped—forcing the beam to glide, inch by inch, the required five feet.

Jessie sprinted to the hose stretched on the pavement. She lifted it a few feet back from the nozzle—*lean and step and drag*—lowered her shoulder, and crashed through a swinging door. On the other side she pulled back on the nozzle handle, aiming the stream at a target. The target fell, and she dropped the hose on the ground.

She moved to the final challenge: Frankie. Without its tattered clothes the dummy appeared fancy, but she knew the 175 pounds would be the same. Jessie crouched and put the dummy in a seated position. She wrapped her arms around its torso and pushed with her legs. She leaned back and stepped. Her quads burned. *You can't stop now.* Take a step. Jessie started to run backward. Her breath accelerated, echoing inside her mask.

She crossed the finish line at two minutes, eighteen seconds, catapulting to first place.

She threw off her helmet and mask. Looking into the cheering crowd, her vision blurred. She made out Dana, standing with her fist in the air. Tyler and Ruby appeared as one shadow surrounded by silver light in a celebratory kiss. Her head swirled like a tumbleweed caught in a hot tornado. *Breathe.*

Dana came up behind her, slid off the tank, and peeled off her turnout coat. "Did you keep the liner of your coat in? You're supposed to take that out." She handed her a cup of water in a paper cone.

Jessie pulled off her boots and collapsed to her knees. The chief came from the stands to congratulate her. She dropped the cup and vomited in her boot. The chief did a quick 180 and shouted from the sideline, "Nice work, Jessie Jeroncyk."

Her idol, the fire challenge champion and Mormon, cupped

Jessie on the shoulder. "I can't believe this was your first challenge. That was phenomenal."

"I puked in my boot."

"Never be ashamed of giving it all you got. You—you are a ball of fire."

Jessie offered a closed-mouth smile. Inside she was bursting like flames on a freeway. Her debut as an almost-firefighter *had* made an impression.

She gathered her coat and the vomit-filled boot and carried them to Brazil on the sideline.

Brazil took the coat. "If you wanted the chief to notice you, that sure was a great finale. Puke aside, you're a superstar."

Jessie held out the boot, and Brazil said, "Yeah, that one's all you."

Jessie collected her first-place medal, tossed her gear into the trunk of the Mustang, and put the top down. She and Brazil cruised down the hot streets of El Paso. The warm breeze and the title of fire challenge champion helped Jessie forget she wasn't a real firefighter.

"Wait. Stop. Did you not see that?" Brazil said.

Jessie pulled over.

"You gotta turn around right now."

Jessie checked her rearview mirror and made a U-turn.

"Here, stop here," Brazil said.

Jessie slammed on the brakes. Brazil pointed at the street sign. "Is that perfect?"

Jessie smiled. She handed Brazil her camera, grabbed her medal from the dash, and put it around her neck before she hopped out of the convertible. Instead of sliding down a fire pole, she shimmied up the street sign pole on Dana Boulevard. Brazil snapped a photo of Jessie with her medal and her mentor, smiling as big as the state of Texas.

———————

When Jessie arrived home the next day, Kim was waiting.

"There's a message for you on the answering machine."

Jessie kissed Kim on the lips. "I won the challenge."

"Of course you did. Listen to the message."

She pushed play on the machine sitting next to the red phone.

"Jessie Jeroncyk. This is human resources from the Minneapolis Fire Department. We have an unexpected opening in the cadet class, and you're next on the list."

Jessie took the crocodile book from her bag and flipped it open to read, "The sensitive bumps on a crocodile's skin alert her to faint ripples in the water." She called Brazil and then Dana to share the news, thankful for the ripples they had stirred in her swamp.

CHAPTER 24

Rookie School: Three-month paid firefighting training.
Training includes national EMT certification, hazardous
materials, firefighting skills, and rescue.

Brazil

Jessie pulled to the curb in front of Brazil's house behind the school bus. Brazil hugged Bentley and walked him to the bus and then blew a kiss to Emmett, standing at the front door with Grandma. Emmett covered his face with his open palm, turned his shoulder like he was about to fling a Frisbee, and released a kiss into the air.

Brazil tossed her backpack through the open passenger window of Jessie's Pontiac and got in. She opened her notebook. In exchange for rides to rookie school, she was helping Jessie with the academic side of firefighting.

"Before you drive off, let's go over the fire tetrahedron. What three things does a fire need to ignite?"

"I don't know how you do it," Jessie said.

Brazil clicked her seat belt into the buckle. "Well, when the training captains mention important details in class, I write them down in this little thing called a notebook. I like to call it taking notes."

"Smart-ass. I know why you ace the tests and why you tie perfect knots. You're practically a genius. I wanna know where you learned to be a great mom. Or did you take notes on that somewhere?"

"It's my mom. She shows up when I need her, and I do the same for my boys. I know I can count on her."

Jessie nodded. "Right. Power of believing."

"I didn't say *believe*. I said *know*. *Believe* is for the stuff we can't see. My mom and me—honestly, it did take some believing before we got to knowing. We're here now. Okay, what are the three ingredients?"

"Um the tetrahedron, it's—" She drew a triangle in the air, identifying the elements as she drew. "Oxygen, then heat, and umm, then of course you need fuel." She underlined fuel at the bottom of the triangle, knowing she was right. "Can we go to class?"

"Let's do it," Brazil said, "and even though this will not be on the test, since the old-school fire chiefs resist change like a two-year-old with a messy diaper—ignition requires another ingredient, a chemical reaction. It makes sense because the tetrahedron is more than a triangle. It's a pyramid with four sides."

Unsatisfied with simply knowing how to perform a skill, Brazil had challenged the training captains with questions, wanting to understand the why. She had been reminded more than once to respect the chain of command, but she was undeterred. And, thanks to Brazil's critical mind, Jessie knew the answer to most every potential test question *and* the reason it mattered.

That morning they were scheduled to take their final hazardous materials and firefighting written test. In the afternoon a representative from the National Registry would conduct the EMT exam. As Jessie pulled through the gate at the training tower, Brazil thought of the many times she had walked this road. At each training session she became stronger and faster, but always a step behind Jessie. In the classroom she waited for others to catch up to her.

On the way into class Jessie said, "I couldn't have done this without you—all of it. When I failed, you came with me to Texas. And now I wouldn't have made it through Haz Mat without you."

"I didn't get here alone. You never did get me that magic lasso, but I'm here. Just don't forget about me once we get out of the classroom and into the tower."

"Never. I look forward to chopping through your railroad tie right after I smash mine to toothpicks."

The cadets were assigned seats in alphabetical order at rectangular tables. Jessie sat in the middle of the second row. Brazil sat on the end of the fifth row. The test sheets were issued along with a no-talking warning.

Twenty minutes later Brazil was finished. The room was silent. She sat at her desk and reviewed her test once more before disturbing the silence with the scrape of her chair. Brazil approached the chief, sitting at his desk in the front of class.

"Do you have a question?" he said.

"Nope. All done."

"You can go for lunch. Be back here by thirteen fifteen."

Brazil returned to her chair, grabbed her backpack, and turned to Jessie. She gestured a thumbs-up and pointed toward the door, letting Jessie know she'd be waiting.

As Brazil opened the door, another chair scraped the floor. It was Louis. She waited by the door, thinking they would leave together. He spoke to the chief but didn't have his test in hand. She saw him point at a flip chart by the door, leaning against the wall. The tetrahedron from yesterday's lesson was in full view. The chief quickly rolled a handful of sheets from behind the chart and covered the information. Brazil went outside and waited.

Twenty minutes later, Jessie and several classmates burst from the classroom.

"Aced it," Jessie said, and gave Brazil a fist bump.

"I couldn't remember the odor for phosgene if my life depended on it," PJ said.

"*Hay*," Louis teased, "didn't you say you would name your dog Phosgene someday?"

Jessie joined in, "*Hay*, I remember that same promise. I wonder if *hay* will keep his word and name his dog after a toxic chemical."

Brazil chimed in, "*Hay*, is someone mowing the lawn? Or did a phosgene bomb just go off?"

"Shit," PJ said. "It smells like hay. Oh well. It's one question. I know I got the name of the rope for the life safety right. Kevlar."

Brazil raised one eyebrow and said, "*Knot*. And that's with a *K*, knucklehead, like the rope. *K* as in kernmantle."

"Kevlar starts with a *K*," PJ shot back.

"We only have thirty-five minutes, and I'm starved. Let's go eat," Jessie said.

After lunch they piled into the classroom. The EMT representative instructed the cadets to fill in the circles using the provided number-two pencil. "After completing the test, hand it to the gentleman at the back of the room. The training chief expects you back in this room at sixteen thirty to get the results of the firefighting test you took earlier."

Brazil finished first again, but she waited in her seat for her classmates to finish. *Humility isn't being less than someone else, it's knowing I finished first and sitting in this chair like I'm last.* She smiled.

———————

Right on time, the training chief circulated the room with a stack of tests. Jessie held hers up for Brazil to see: 88. PJ let out a whoop, happy with his score of 70.

"Congratulations," said the chief. "We had a few squeakers, but you made it. Go home and get some rest. The real training starts tomorrow."

Brazil raised her hand. "Um, Chief. I didn't get mine."

"Class is dismissed. Brazil, you can stay right there."

The cadets filed out of the room. Brazil stayed seated.

The chief held up her test. "Impressive, except for the fact that you got some answers from the flip chart. That isn't the worst of it. You also pointed out the chart to the rest of the class on your way out."

First, Brazil felt afraid. Was she about to be dismissed? Next, she felt angry. *All that I risked getting here. God opened this door—I will not let a lie slam it shut.*

She went on the offense. "I don't mind you believing that the worst thing I did was share an advantage with my teammates. What I do mind is that you left the temptation of the answers for all to see in the front of the class and then blame me for your mistake."

Brazil expected to be disciplined but was surprised when the chief chuckled. "I'll tell you what. How about you take the test again? If you cheated, we'll know."

Twenty minutes later, Brazil exited the classroom. Jessie was waiting.

"What the hell?" Jessie whispered.

"Judas Iscariot! They think I cheated," she said, not softly at all. "I got a ninety-eight. Highest grade in the class with a wide margin. He accused me of getting answers from the flip chart. Then he said I pointed it out to the whole class."

"You're the smartest person here. I got your back."

"Forget it. It doesn't matter. I had to take the whole thing over. He graded it while I stood by his desk."

"And?"

"Do you doubt me?"

"What? I totally believe you didn't cheat."

"Believe or know, Jess?"

"Am I the bad guy here?"

Brazil held up her retake test with the score of 100 written on the top of the page. As they walked to the car, Jessie asked, "What'd you get wrong on the first test?"

Brazil smiled. "Chemical odors aren't exactly my strong suit."

"Phosgene?"

"Thanks, PJ."

CHAPTER 25

Jessie

Jessie was paired with PJ again for the confined-space exercise. She lined the inside of her mask with dark paper. The maze they would navigate resembled a pitched roof covered by shingles, set on the ground instead of topping a building. The shingles provided darkness and hid the course from rookies waiting their turn. Jessie peeked through the entrance of the makeshift rafters, knowing the boards would have been rearranged into a different pattern from the day before.

She thought about PJ's excuse for not getting into the fire department on his first try—no tits. She hoped his tits wouldn't keep him from getting through the smaller openings in the maze.

They donned their darkened masks, turned on their air, and entered the maze.

Jessie traced the first wooden frame with her gloved hands,

gauging if she and PJ could fit through. "PJ, it's this way. Grab my tank and follow me."

She felt the weight of his arm on her tank and was hopeful they would finally finish with an acceptable time. When she reached the end of the course, where the space widened before the exit, she knew they had made it.

"We're home free. This way."

PJ was no longer holding her tank. She listened for his amplified breathing. Silence.

"Damn it, PJ. Where the hell are you?" Silence.

She doubled back through the maze. In a loud whisper, she called his name and called again. She held her breath to silence her own breathing and still heard nothing. Feeling her way back, she at last bumped into the large mass of PJ wedged in one of the small openings.

"Dumbass. Our time is running out. If you make us fail—I swear. Push yourself back and then come around the side."

"I can't do it. I'm stuck." His voice was clear, without the obstructed echo of breath inhaled into a mask.

"Did you take your mask off? You could see me looking for you the whole time, and you didn't say shit. You know your tank is gonna be full. They'll know you were off air." She felt for his mask and found it dangling at his side. "Here's your mask. Put it on. Let's take your tank off and put it through first."

She heard him shuffling to press his face piece to his chin. The sound of his breathing returned. He slipped the harness off his shoulders and handed it to Jessie. She pulled it through the hole, staying close to ensure the air hose wouldn't pull his mask from his face. Once his body was through, she handed him his tank. Jessie guided him through the maze, pushing from behind this time to be sure she wouldn't lose him.

"We're at the end. Crawl through. I'm right behind you."

The training captain stood at the exit with his stopwatch. "Looks like we have a new record here. This should make the books for the slowest fucking time in history."

He grabbed the control module on PJ's harness to check his remaining air. "Good job, PJ, you still have half your tank. That's efficient breathing." He wrapped his hand around the module on Jessie's harness, pulling the screen close to his face. "Less than a quarter. You need to be more efficient in there. Pace your breathing and quit slowing your partner down."

Jessie looked at PJ, waiting for him to confess. The ring of sweat around his head and the black hair stuck to his scalp gave the impression of a dark halo. With his helmet in one hand and his face piece in the other, he nodded, agreeing with the captain.

Jessie lowered her tank to the floor. "I'll work on it." She walked by PJ, shoulder bumped him, and cough-cursed, "Asshole."

Next the recruits were separated into teams. Each team was assigned a railroad tie and one axe. The team chopping through the railroad tie fastest would be excused from the two-mile run after class.

"The idea here is to break through the wood," the captain explained. "Our axes are dull for a reason. We don't want our blade to stick in the wood. We want to smash it to pieces. An axe stuck in a roof with smoke trapped in the cockloft becomes a falling hazard.

It's all about ventilation. On my whistle, each team member takes twelve chops and then goes to the end of the line. Make a hole."

Jessie rushed to the front to chop first for her team. Growing up on a farm, she had been chopping all her life. She knew she would finally impress the captain.

The whistle shrieked, and Jessie raised her axe. She slid her hand down the handle, creating the most efficient fulcrum. She squatted with each chop, driving the axe into the railroad tie. Splinters flew into the air. Her awareness of choppers beside her dulled. She recalled teaching her little brother to split wood. *Up slow, down quick with force.* Distracted by her thoughts, she lost count. The cadet on deck forced the axe from her hand.

"What the hell, Jess. You're at fifteen. You have a team. Cap'n said twelve chops."

Jessie dragged her feet to the back of the line and never returned to the front. Her team busted through the railroad tie, and together they let out a victory whoop. She watched Brazil swing at her railroad tie. After her final chop, not much had changed. Her teammate took the axe, and in four chops he busted through.

Jessie headed to the curb with her team to sit and drink Gatorade while the rest of the class lined up for the two-mile run.

"Where do ya think you're going?" the captain said.

"We won," three of them said in unison.

"You chopped through first, but you didn't win. You forgot about teamwork, and Jessie's extra chops gets you disqualified."

The stare of her team was like being a bug under a magnifying glass on a sunny day. She peeled off her turnout coat and started to run.

The captain blew his whistle. "Jessie, you're not running. You like chopping so much, you can grab your buddy Brazil and a couple axes. I expect you both to chop through a railroad tie before the rest of class gets back."

The class jogged off. Jessie handed Brazil an axe.

"Sorry."

"It's not you they're after," Brazil said. "It's me they don't want. Dana was right."

"They don't know you. Let's make getting rid of either of us impossible. Hold your axe like this." Jessie put one hand close to the head and the other at the bottom end of the handle. "When you bring it down, don't let it drop. Bring your hands together at the end of the handle and drive it through. Smash it like your kid is on the other side and the only way to get to him is through this railroad tie."

"How do you know so much about chopping—and kids?"

"I had a little brother."

Brazil and Jessie chopped side by side. Wood chips spit into the air. The thud of their axes sounded like friendship—the kind thunder offers just before lightning strikes. The wooden ties split apart in tandem. Together they dropped their axes and jogged to the finish line to join their classmates.

Two weeks from graduation, Jessie and PJ stood at the maze entrance and again lined their face pieces with paper before ducking into the maze. When they reached the first narrow opening, they discovered a two-by-four suspended twelve inches above the floor and plywood at chest level. They would have to step over the board and then crawl under the plywood.

"You go first. Over then under," Jessie said. "I'll follow you."

PJ stepped over the first board and approached the plywood. He tried to go over instead of under. Jessie heard his breath quicken and then stop.

"You better be dead and not pulled your mask off again. Are you trying to fuck us over? Or, I guess more likely, fuck me over when you finish with a full tank."

Jessie squeezed past PJ and continued through the course without him. She heard him hurrying behind her. She moved faster. She neared the exit and listened. Hearing nothing, she thought, *I'm sure he's in a corner, unable to find his way through bright daylight.* Jessie exited the maze.

"I'll be shit kicked," the captain said. "Quite an improvement. Best time yet."

Jessie stood at the exit and looked back inside the maze. There was no sign of PJ. The captain went to the exit and bent to look inside. "Where's your partner?"

"He. Umm."

"Did you leave your partner?"

Jessie sniffed and then snorted. She knew the number-one sin is to leave your partner on the fireground.

"You never leave your partner. We have a buddy system for a reason." He paused. "And it's a damn good reason—it keeps you from getting injured or, worse, killed. Grab a bundle, put it on your shoulder, and run the tower steps. When you're done, do it again."

On her way to the tower she heard the captain scrutinizing PJ. "Did you get lost? Or could you just not keep up with her?"

PJ's explanation disappeared under the sound of Jessie's feet hitting the steps. She knew it was wrong to leave PJ, but waiting for him and getting blamed for his inadequacies felt more wrong. She dropped the bundle at the bottom of the steps. On her way back to the classroom she noticed a red Suburban parked in the spot reserved for the chief of the department.

She opened the door to the classroom slowly. All eyes went from the chief to her and then back to the chief.

"Hi, Jessie. Have a seat," he said.

"Hi, Chief Gallo."

Jessie felt the class staring. Someone whispered, "Do they know each other?"

"I'm not sure if you're aware," the chief said, "but we have a celebrity in the room. Not only did this person win a national fire combat competition, but this person also has the fifth-fastest time for the entire Minneapolis Fire Department."

The cadets looked around the room, sizing one another up and wondering who it could be. Jessie knew he was talking about her. Being a bug under a magnifying glass was getting too familiar.

"Jessie. Come on up here." He looked out over the class. "Where's my other girl? Brazil. Girls, come on up here." They shuffled to the front. The chief opened his arms. "Can I get a group hug?"

Jessie and Brazil locked widened eyes before surrendering to the chief's outstretched arms. Released, Jessie dropped her head and dragged her feet to her chair. Passing PJ's desk, he said, "Hey, where's my hug?" The guys seated nearby chuckled.

The training captain thanked the chief for stopping by and instructed the cadets, "Gear up for your last chance to prove you can find your way through small spaces in the dark. Tomorrow we move on to the auditorium raise."

The cadets lined up outside again with their partners and their gear.

"We're switching it up for the final run-through. Count off for new partners."

PJ's new partner was Louis. Jessie was stoked. She knew—and so did PJ—Louis wouldn't take the hit for PJ. But seeing the panic in his eyes, she almost felt sorry for him.

The captain stood at the end of the course, congratulating two cadets for efficient use of air. Louis and PJ were up next. PJ covered his face with his darkened mask. Jessie noticed his regulator wasn't hooked into his face piece.

"Don't forget you actually have to hook up to your air," Jessie said.

"Gimme a minute, we're not up yet."

Jessie decided to do Louis a favor and snapped PJ's regulator into the receiving port of his mask. She listened for his first breath of air, letting her know he wouldn't cheat. She heard him inhale—and then nothing.

PJ panicked. He clawed at his face piece. He pulled the straps and turned in circles. Jessie realized his tank was closed. She reached to turn on his bottle, but he shoved her and she stumbled back. The captain hurried to the commotion. PJ sank to his knees. Louis knelt next to PJ and turned the knob on his harness. Air rushed into his face piece. PJ sucked in a breath that whistled like a victim of an asthma attack.

PJ recovered and ripped the mask from his face. He stood. The captain grabbed the collar of his fire coat and threw him against the wall. Then he ordered him out of the room and followed, slamming the door behind them.

Jessie shrugged and said, "How was I supposed to know he didn't have his bottle turned on?" She clipped her own regulator to the mask and said to her new partner, "Ready?"

PJ never returned to class. The only explanation given was a general speech about claustrophobia and firefighters, emphasized with a cliché: oil and water don't mix.

———————

At rookie school graduation Jessie and Brazil stood side by side at city hall in front of the mayor and their families. When the chief pinned the shiny silver badge on Jessie's shirt, the heart under the badge swelled. Her mission accomplished, she whispered, "A long life of doing nothing—obliterated."

CHAPTER 26

Firefighter Accountability Magnet: A four-by-two-inch magnetic panel identifying name and rank of the working firefighter by color, displayed on the back of the driver's seat. Referenced for firefighter accountability on an emergency scene.

Brazil

Brazil's first assignment landed her in the back seat of Ladder 4. By default, the next youngest firefighter in the station, Bettina, steered the back of the rig in the till.

Brazil sat behind the driver, going over her grocery list for dinner. "What do you guys think about tacos?" she said.

Gordy—short for Gordon—sat shotgun as captain. "My mom told me to never marry a Mexican. They're lazy," he said.

Is he calling me lazy? Brazil studied the magnetic accountability board on the seatback in front of her. The color outlining the firefighter's last name matched the crewmember's helmet: red for captain, black for driver, and yellow for firefighter. "Martin," she whispered, reading the captain's name. His deep brown eyes and medium-hued skin were dark for a white guy and light for a Black man. But a name like Gordon Martin sounded pretty un-Mexican to her.

She ran her thumb over the back of her hand and wondered, *Does he think I'm Mexican?* She read her own name on the yellow magnet. Considering her mother's crystal-blue eyes, Brazil conceded, *A Black woman named McFadden isn't exactly typical.*

A good dinner at the right price was more important right now than Gordon Martin's lineage. She had learned while preparing her first meal at Station 4 not to use mushrooms or onions. Two guys complained they couldn't eat them. "It feels like fungus snot in my mouth," one had said of the mushrooms.

"Onions? I'm a single guy. I need to keep my breath make-out ready," said the other.

The first dinner she had prepared at the station, pork chops in sweet potato gravy, was where she learned that charging six bucks per person broke the eleventh commandment: *Thou shall not charge firefighters more than five dollars per meal.*

She should have gotten the hint from a large print of *The Last Supper* hanging in the dining room. Someone had drawn a cartoon speech bubble over Jesus's head like he was announcing the cost for the meal, "$5.75." Above the head of the disciple on Jesus's right was another speech bubble with "Each?" scribbled inside. If Jesus could be questioned, no one was beyond reproach.

For Brazil, her turn to cook meant a break from meatloaf and mashed potatoes, or pot roast surrounded by carrots and chunks of potato slathered in fat—they called it juice. Worst of all had been the meat surprise hidden inside a ball of undercooked dough—and the bigger surprise in the middle of the night, when the emergency tones woke her from a dead sleep and, instead of heading for the toilet, she had to climb on the rig and respond to someone else's emergency.

Brazil would have opted out of the tradition of eating in the clutch, but she had been warned in rookie school that not taking part would be a mistake. The camaraderie of sharing a meal coupled with the math—more people equals a lower price—made sense. But accommodating both fellowship and economics was becoming arduous.

Chicken tacos were a safe bet. She could offer onions and any other resisted ingredient on the side. More importantly, it kept the price under five bucks while satisfying her need for something healthy.

FMO Damien pulled the rig to the curb by the grocery store. Brazil waited on the sidewalk as Bettina, at five feet, three inches tall, made the leap from tailboard to the ground.

Inside the store, Bettina pushed the cart. Brazil threw tortillas into the basket and said, "Is Captain Martin part Mexican?"

"Not sure. I do know he's one hundred percent asshole."

"Harsh."

"Actually, I'm being kind. Us chicks need to stick together."

"So how are we chicks? Is it the peeping or the cute yellow fuzz?"

"If we call ourselves chicks, we're taking back our power."

Brazil had never felt powerful describing herself with terms others used to demean her. She missed Jessie, who was working on a different shift at a different station. Bettina was more of an acquaintance than a friend, but despite their differences, another woman in the firehouse was Brazil's saving grace.

They checked out. As Bettina pushed the cart filled with taco fixins across the parking lot, the radio clipped to Brazil's belt alerted them to an incoming call.

"Ladder 4 to an unknown medical, possible intoxication. Broadway and Lowry. Respond in the alley behind the grocery store."

Bettina and Brazil quickly loaded the groceries in the cab.

"It's right around the corner," Damien said.

Bettina climbed into the till and tapped the horn. Damien maneuvered a three-quarter turn from the curb. Gordy didn't bother with the siren but flicked on the lights. They circled to enter the alley just as a large garbage truck pulled out. Gordy pressed his foot pedal to the floor, sounding a deafening blast; Damien swerved left, just missing the truck.

"Do red flashing lights mean nothing, idiot!" Damien yelled.

Behind the store in the alley, a tall Native American man paced, seemingly unaware of the arriving ladder truck, repeating, "She's gone. She's gone."

The crew dismounted the rig and approached. Brazil buried her face in the crook of her arm. Damien did the same and whispered, "Whoa, shower much?"

The man turned to walk away. The back of his pants appeared wet and soiled.

Gordy said, "Hey, you, Totem-Pole Shit-Um-Pants. Who's gone?"

Still pacing, the man looked to the sky and shouted, "Whoever took her, give her back!"

"Hey, Chief!" Gordy said louder. "Who'd you lose?"

The man stopped and stared at Gordy, pointing at him with a brown paper bag. Brazil wondered if he was responding to the racial slur or if he had to think about Gordy's question.

"We were walking right next to each other, and now she's gone."

Gordy snatched the bag away and unsleeved an almost-empty bottle of vodka. "Ever think maybe she left you? You drink this whole bottle yourself?"

"She would never leave me," he said, and snatched back the bottle.

Bettina said, "Sir, let's start from the beginning. First, what's your name?"

"My name is Thomas."

Damien pulled out his pad and scribbled.

Bettina continued, "Where were you two coming from?"

"It's our anniversary. We had a drink on the railroad tracks."

"Could she have gone home?"

He spun around and stumbled, still pointing. He stopped when his finger indicated a tarp set up as a lean-to on the other side of the tracks. He squinted.

"Nope, she's not home." He staggered. "She's gone." He started to cry.

Brazil walked down the alley and ran her hand across the outside of a dumpster on the edge of the tar. It was clean, almost new; the garbage truck they had almost collided with must have dropped off the new bin. She went around it and stepped onto the grassy patch between the tar and the railroad tracks.

Then she heard a soft cry and turned back. She stepped up to peer into the dumpster. Empty. Another whimper. Brazil lay on her stomach to look underneath. Nothing. She pushed up to stand and heard the cry again.

Brazil pulled her flashlight, dropped down, and wedged her

shoulder against the dumpster's wheel. The light flashed on an open manhole.

"Is someone there?"

"I fell down. I'm lost," came a voice.

"She's here," Brazil called.

Gordy rolled the dumpster onto the gravel, and the crew gathered around the gaping manhole.

"I'll be a son of a—" Gordy squatted by the hole and shouted, "Are you hurt?"

Thomas staggered over to the opening "Olivia! Why did you leave me?"

Damien grabbed his arm and led him from the hole, reassuring him, "We'll get her for you."

Gordy radioed dispatch, requesting an ambulance, and then said, "Looks like you're gonna earn your pay today, Brazil."

She smiled, surprised by the excitement she felt. She jogged to the rig for the life safety rope and medical bag. She donned her helmet and pulled on her turnout pants. Bettina retrieved the junior extension ladder, and she and Damien lowered the ladder into the hole. Brazil draped the medical bag over one shoulder and the rope over the other and climbed down.

Daylight shined like a spotlight on shattered glass scattered on the ground. Broken shards stuck to a torn vodka label. Olivia huddled at the outer edge of the circle of light, and Brazil spotted a bone protruding from the woman's foot. She stepped off the ladder and flipped the switch on her helmet lamp.

"Do you have pain?" Brazil asked.

"No. But I'm lost."

Brazil dropped the rope on the ground and placed the medical bag on top. She crouched in front of Olivia, pressing her back against the rocky wall in the cramped space. The ground was damp but not wet. It was cold and smelled like ancient mud, disturbed after years of stagnation.

"Olivia, right?"

Olivia lifted her chin. She raised her hand to shield her eyes from Brazil's headlamp.

"Olivia. I'm gonna check you out, and then we're gonna get you out of here."

Olivia tried to stand but fell. "My leg doesn't work."

"Don't try to get up. I'm going to help you." Brazil shouted up the shaft, "Looks like a compound fracture. I'll have to splint it." She pulled the SAM Splint from the medical bag and quickly braced the ankle.

"Why are you doing that? It hurts," Olivia said.

Brazil thought, *It's going to hurt a lot more when that vodka wears off,* but said only, "Almost done. Leg's stabilized," she shouted up to the crew.

The arriving ambulance's siren chirped.

"I'm putting her in a life safety knot. We'll have to hoist her out."

Brazil quickly tied the knot to form leg loops and created a seat harness to safely hoist Olivia up.

"Okay, Olivia," she said, "sit back and let us do the work." She climbed up to hand the rope to Gordy and then down again to support Olivia from below. "Pull her up," Brazil shouted.

Olivia slowly rose to the surface. Thomas said, "You came back. Where'd you go, Livie?"

The medics loaded Olivia onto the stretcher and into the ambulance. Thomas knocked on the side door, but the medic gestured to the paper-covered bottle and said, "You can't bring that with you."

Thomas stepped down and watched the ambulance until its lights disappeared in the distance.

On the drive to the station, Gordy commented first. "Fucking Chief Stands with a Brown Paper Bag chose booze over his wife."

Brazil stared at the back of his head, deciding if the fight was worth conflict with her captain. *Saying nothing makes me part of the problem*, she decided. "I don't think it's much of a choice. Alcoholism is an illness."

"He made a choice when he took that first drink, didn't he?"

Brazil's gut fizzed, like the fizzle before a light bulb explodes, and she hissed, "Easy cop-out for the white guy who never has to wonder, 'Is it me they don't like or are they ignoring me because I'm a lazy Indian who can't control my drinking after generations of mass genocide, forced migration, and rape?' You might want a drink once in a while too, with that kind of history."

"Whoa, a little sensitive?" Damien said. "Believe me, if you'd been at the union Christmas party last year, you'd know Gordy can slam down a drink or eight."

Gordy looked over at Damien with one eye half closed, like he was zeroing in a target, and said, "I'm not all white. My great-great grandmother was Aztec."

Damien did a double take and joked, "So that's how you got on the fire department. You checked the nonwhite box on the application. You're Native American?"

"I didn't check the box. I left it blank. And I ain't no buffalo jockey."

"So you are Mexican," Brazil said.

"Guatemalan. I'm one-eighth Guatemalan." Gordy rubbed his thumb over the tattoo decorating his forearm—a circle with an ancient face in the center. "Can we drop the fuckin' chalupa? I'm not a racist. Just statin' facts."

"Nice perk," Brazil said. "Take the benefit of hiding inside of a white guy until a little color works in your favor, and then you pull out the one-eighth card. By the way, the Aztecs didn't come from Guatemala."

"I don't think Brazil is anywhere near Ireland, McFadden. How about you and your pal Bettina give this rig a wax job when we get back to the station."

Brazil sat back. Maybe he was right. When her parents adopted her, they had named her Mary. Mary McFadden had a nice ring, but the name never felt right. On her eighteenth birthday she went to the courthouse and changed her first name to her birth country.

Damien circled the apron to back into the fire station. Brazil guided him in and placed the lanyard in its holster.

Bettina climbed from the till and said, "You might want to reconsider being the poster child for racial justice with that guy. Captain Gordy Guatemala won't forget that slice of dipshit humble pie you served."

Brazil glanced up into the till at the speaker. *Bettina's spy cab,* she mused.

———

Brazil had the vegetables chopped, the rice simmering, and the chicken marinating in the fridge when the alarm sounded. Six blasts meant a fire call. She turned off the stove and hurried to the truck. As she stepped into her boots and pulled her suspenders over her shoulders, she noticed the guys dragging their feet to get on the rig. *Is it smiles or smirks decorating their faces?*

Bettina slid down the pole. Next to her fire gear, old phone-books had been stacked into makeshift stairs leading to the tail-board. Bettina kicked the stairs over but used one phonebook for a boost. She climbed into the till and flipped double birds at the pranksters, then threw wooden blocks from her cockpit. Brazil must have seemed puzzled, because Bettina explained, "Duct taped to the foot horn. Brilliant."

The engine pulled out, and the ladder truck followed. Brazil searched the horizon for signs of smoke. The truck turned the corner and there it was: turbulent black smoke swirled into the sky. She zipped her coat and slipped the straps of her SCBA over her shoulders. Her stomach squeezed. *Definitely a fire.*

The engine pulled past the house, allowing the truck to position at the fire front. Brazil leaned forward, pulling her air tank from its bracket. She tucked an axe into her spanner belt and double stepped to catch up to Gordy. Their first job was to gain entry and begin a primary search.

Gordy tried the door. Finding it locked, he nodded to Brazil. She turned and donkey kicked the lock below the handle. The door cracked, and she kicked again. The door swung open, and black smoke poured through the doorway. She turned to don her facepiece and spied the ladder extending from the truck toward the roof. Damien and Bettina would soon be chopping ventilation holes.

Gordy shouted from inside his mask, "We'll do a right-hand search. Stay close. We're looking for the stairs. Then we go to the second floor."

Brazil followed, keeping her gloved right hand on the wall and following the sound of Gordy's breathing. She knocked a picture from the wall and bumped into what felt like a recliner. She made a mental note: living room. She raised her hand to her face. Like in the maze at rookie school, she was blinded, but this darkness was different. Instead of blinding her with a paper lining, the mask protected her from the deadly smoke. She drew her hand closer to her face. Still seeing nothing, she closed her eyes. With closed eyes, darkness made sense.

Finding the stairway to the second floor, she followed Gordy up the steps, mentally reviewing locations for possible victims. The chops of Damien and Bettina's axes on the roof sounded like the clop of a smooth-paced horse. The dispatcher's voice relayed through Gordy's radio, "All residents are reported out of the building."

"We check the bedrooms one by one anyway," Gordy said. "We need to see for ourselves. As soon as they get the roof open, the smoke will clear."

Brazil opened her eyes. Two durgans from the engine crew wedged past her, dragging the hose. They opened the nozzle, and steam rose, fogging her mask. She brushed the condensation from her facepiece as droplets rained from the watered-down ceiling and smoke rushed through the open hole in the roof.

Gordy tapped Brazil's shoulder. "Open the windows. Look in the closets and under the beds and then meet me back here." He pointed toward a doorway where a firefighter sprayed water into the room.

Looking past him, she noticed the closet door was burned through. The fire, stripped of the cover of smoke, appeared as orange snakes. The firefighter on the nozzle seemed to taunt the orange flames, striking at invisible targets.

He closed the nozzle, and she squeezed around him into the room. She lifted the sash on the window, but it wouldn't budge. She checked outside, below the window, before smashing the glass with her axe and ripping out the screen. Searching for the bed Gordy had told her to look under, she found only the metal springs of a twin mattress between charred wooden slats. Red embers pulsed on the charred wood.

The firefighter on the nozzle saturated the wood. "Let's toss it," he said.

She recognized the muffled voice as Wes from the engine.

"Droppin' like it's hot," Wes shouted before they hurled it through the window.

She met Gordy at the top of the stairs. "All clear," she said.

Gordy keyed his radio. "IC, primary and secondary search of the second floor is complete. All clear."

With the bulk of the fire knocked down, truckies swarmed the second floor, searching for hot spots by demolishing the ceilings and walls. Brazil went back to the charred bedroom, pierced the ceiling with her hook, and jerked down. Plaster fell like hail.

Bettina walked through the doorway with a hook in her hand and suddenly bounced back. "Damn it. I'm caught," she said.

Damien pushed her from behind. "Butt, Tina. It's your fat ass. Turn to the side." He laughed and nudged her.

"Fuck off."

Brazil had noticed Damien spending a lot of time in the weight room trying to bulk up, so she shot back, "She's caught on her spanner belt, Twiggy." She pulled at a piece of wood sticking out of the door. Bettina jerked forward and stumbled into the room.

"Let's open some walls, Twiggle Sticks," Bettina said.

"I'm right behind you, Butt-Tina!"

They all laughed, except for Brazil. While she understood the expectation to poke fun in this macho fire-department culture, Brazil recognized the danger in crossing the line. Seeing Bettina go along with the hurtful comments and pretend, Brazil assumed, to be unaffected wasn't funny.

———

Back at Station 4, Brazil finished cleaning the ladder tools and helped the engine crew wash dirty hose. Damien scrubbed, and Brazil rinsed it down.

"What time's dinner?" Damien asked. "I want to get a workout in before I eat, bulk up these twigs a bit. Can you hold off for about an hour?"

Brazil was growing tired of the requests that came with cooking. She went to the dorm, grabbed a clean uniform, and took a quick shower. Thirty-five minutes later she served dinner.

Damien threw open the dining room door, dressed in shorts with a towel over his shoulder. "What happened to the hour I asked for?"

"The rice is getting sticky. Plus, everyone else is complaining they're starving. I can't make everyone happy."

"She made it; you eat it when it's ready," Gordy said.

———

Three days later, on her next shift, Brazil flipped through the blue-canvas-covered logbook on the coop desk to check her watch duty. She ran her finger along the page and wasn't surprised to see she was assigned to noon watch. After cooking last shift, she had counted on being able to work out before dinner. Hoping to predict the dinner menu based on the chef, she continued down the page—*McFadden*. She flipped the page ahead to make sure she wasn't on the wrong day.

"Damien, it says I'm up to cook again."

He shrugged.

"I don't think it's right. Do you? I mean, I cooked last shift."

"Take it as a compliment. We like your food."

Bettina chimed in, "That's bullshit."

"She is the rookie."

"And she cooked last shift. It's bullshit and you know it."

"I'll do it," Brazil said. "But someone else has to take my noon watch."

"Durgans don't take—"

Bettina interrupted, "I'll take your watch." She whited out Brazil's name from noon watch slot and used a Sharpie to write in *Bullshit*.

At the grocery store, Bettina hopped from the tailboard and said, "It's wrong. You do know."

"I do. But it's not worth the battle. I'm gonna keep it simple. I don't need help getting the groceries," Brazil said.

She strolled the grocery aisles, uninspired and looking for simple but tasty. No mushrooms, not too spicy, under five bucks, and a quick prep. She decided on chicken strips with plum sauce. More accurately grape jelly sauce—a hit with her sons and, she was sure, a firehouse winner.

––––––––––––

The silence at the dinner table lasted until Wes licked the plum sauce from his plate and said, "This is fuckin' awesome."

Brazil cleared her throat, feeling apprehensive, and announced, "This is my last meal. I'm getting out of the clutch."

"You can't just get out of the clutch," Damien said.

Bettina looked up from her plate with wide eyes.

Brazil focused on the *Last Supper*, looking for strength. "What do you mean, I can't just get out? I won't cook and I won't eat. I'm just out." Keeping her eyes fixed on the portrait, she imagined a heaping plate of pot roast to build a mental army against giving in.

Wes followed her gaze to the portrait. "Even Jesus washed the disciples' feet before his last meal."

"That's not happening."

"How about she buys us ice cream sandwiches," Gordy suggested, and winked at Damien.

Brazil's eyes widened—it was a compromise she could live with. "I can do that, Captain Martin. That sounds great. I'll buy ice cream."

––––––––––––

The next shift Brazil kept her word. She bought a box of ice cream sandwiches and a half-gallon of ice cream. She put both in the freezer and went to the TV room, where everyone was huddled around a preseason Vikings game.

"Ice cream's in the freezer, guys, help yourselves."

"We're saving it for after dinner, and then we're all going to eat it out of Gordy's mouth," said Damien.

"Ohhh-kay," she said, and turned to leave.

"You too. You're gonna do it too."

"Yeah, right."

"Good, it's settled then."

At dinnertime an odor of fat exuded from the kitchen, confirming Brazil's decision to skip the camaraderie of shared meals. She was realizing it was a myth—more boys' club than fellowship. It seemed the boys wanted women at the fire station to disappear, and Brazil thought it was best to comply.

Hearing the dishes being tossed into the sink, Brazil peeked into the dining room and caught Bettina's eye.

"Want to work out after dinner?" she asked.

Bettina held up a full bag of trash. "Let me get rid of this and I'll meet you downstairs."

Damien said, "There you are. Come on in here. You ready?"

The whiteboard on the wall behind the dinner table advertised the cost of dinner in big red letters—$4.25. She approached the table surrounded by blue upholstered swivel chairs. In the middle of the table was a pile of one-dollar bills and quarters. Gordy sat at the end of the table with the ice cream. A large serving spoon jutted from the carton. He dug out a spoonful of ice cream and dropped it on his tongue. Damien was up first. He spun Gordy around, dipped his spoon into the melting ice cream in Gordy's mouth, and ate it. Wes followed his lead and then handed the spoon to Brazil.

"Wait," Gordy said. He unwrapped an ice cream sandwich and pulled the cookie from the ice cream. "Use this as a spoon."

She took the cookie, trying to make sense of the absurdity. The ice cream was a puddle in Gordy's mouth. She approached him and sank the cookie into the ice cream on his outstretched tongue. She offered an uneasy smirk. "I won't do it. You guys are crazy."

"So, you're a liar, then," Damien said.

Brazil rushed from the room and bumped into Bettina. Chanting rose behind her, reminiscent of some movie scene right before they rip out the sacrificial heart and eat it. "Liar. Liar. Liar."

———

A masking-tape label covertly stuck on Brazil's helmet granted her first fire-department nickname: McLiar. She confided in Bettina, whose answer for all that was wrong remained a consistent "It's bullshit." However much she advocated for chicks to stick together, Bettina didn't seem to have a strategy when solidarity was needed most. Brazil didn't blame her for avoiding an alliance with the outcast.

Brazil walked into a room and the guys walked out. She had typical rookie firefighting questions, but when she asked a durgan for forcible entry tips, she was mocked for stupidity. Every day showing up to work felt a little heavier. The worst was the evening her son Emmett called the station.

Damien yelled from the coop, "Hey, Liar! Your kid is on the phone."

Brazil pressed the phone to her ear to hear Emmett say, "Mommy, why are you a liar?"

"I'm not, sweetie."

"He said you're a liar?"

"He's joking. Tell me about what you did today. Did you play with Bentley?"

Brazil hung up the phone feeling lonelier after hearing the details of what she was missing at home. She walked to the dorm to spend the rest of her night alone. Bettina was sitting in her cubicle, reading. She looked up from her book and asked, "You okay?"

"I hate my job," Brazil said.

"You should report that shit."

"I'm not even sure what I did. I mean, who would eat ice cream like that?"

"You scare them because you're smart and you don't participate in their bullshit. Then you got outta the clutch. They have PTSD from being rejected at the junior high dance, and you remind them of it."

During Saturday super clean Brazil pulled the chain on the target saw and let it run. The deafening roar of the engine made it seem normal that no one was talking to her. After two weeks of exclusion, she was surprised by a tap on her shoulder. She stopped the saw.

Gordy's hands were on his hips. "Chief's here for you."

She went to the coop, where the chief informed her, "The assistant chief of the department wants to talk with you. Some baloney about recruiting women of color. I'll be driving you to headquarters."

On a Saturday? she thought. *I'm new myself. What do I know about recruitment? Women of color? What color?*

Afraid to question the chief, she said, "I need to hit the restroom and I'm ready."

She stepped into the bathroom and opened the glazed window, hoping fresh air would clear her head. Outside in the station parking lot were three pickups, a Jeep, and two F350s, and closest to the door was her new-but-used Volkswagen Rabbit.

"God, you may as well have led me to Mars," she whispered.

During the drive to city hall, Brazil's anxiety intensified. "The assistant chief is working on Saturday?" she asked.

"I don't question his schedule," the chief said. "He ordered me to come get you, and that's what I did." Pulling up in front of headquarters, he added, "I suggest you follow my lead. Feel free to practice the phrase *yes, sir* on your way up."

Brazil trudged up the marble steps. The lights in the entry cast a gray path. She looked down the hall. The offices were dark except for one bright light at the end.

"Brazil. Come on down," the assistant chief said. He took a seat behind his neat desk and smiled. "Sorry to take you away from your station duties. Have a seat."

He opened his desk drawer and took out a small tape recorder. He smiled again. His glasses had fallen down his nose. He pushed them up and placed the recorder in front of her. "I didn't call you down here to talk about recruitment. There's been a complaint concerning station behavior, and your name came up."

Brazil tugged at her collar and cleared her throat.

He pressed record, sat back in his chair, and said, "Tell me about the ice cream."

CHAPTER 27

Jessie

The tattoo Jessie had planned for her deltoid landed on the inside of her forearm. She pulled up the sleeve of her turnout coat to admire the artwork. She hadn't yet decided whether to fill in the middle of the Maltese cross with the traditional firefighting insignia of hooks and bugles or keep it simple and showcase her favorite, two crisscrossed axes.

Captain Robbins instructed her to practice chopping before dinner, unaware of her obsession with smashing wood. She arranged railroad ties in the garden courtyard outside the station kitchen, donned her helmet, and drove the axe into her target. A melodic *thud* vibrated the station walls.

Ross, the designated cook, yelled out to the courtyard, "Dinner in thirty minutes, rookie."

Jessie propped her axe against a wrought-iron fence and rested on a bench, happy with the damage she'd inflicted on the splintered railroad tie. Dried roses drooped from thorny stems in the garden. Flowering pumpkin vines gave her a feeling more reminiscent of her childhood on the farm than working at a busy downtown fire station. A city rabbit hopped into the garden, oblivious to her presence. She thought of her brother Tag and his pet wild rabbit. And then she heard a *whoosh*.

She felt the air move before she saw the object spiraling past her. The point of an arrow penetrated the railroad tie with a *thunk*, the rabbit's body dangling from its spit.

Captain Robbins hurried through the garden to the pile of wood and jiggled the shaft free. He held up the rabbit and said, "Ever have rabbit stew?"

Jessie's shock quickly spun into anger. She clenched her teeth, trying to control her rage, and searched for an escape. Her vision tunneled, fixed on the fuzzy carcass.

"What an asshole," she heard from the kitchen. Ross stood in the doorway like a beacon, showing her the way out.

Following Ross's voice, she squeezed past him and rushed through the kitchen to the apparatus floor. She dropped her axe next to the fire engine and climbed in. Sitting in the darkness of the back seat, she slid off her helmet and buried her face in the flap.

"Tag," she said to her dead brother. "Why?"

Tag loved that rabbit. He sheltered it in a discarded chicken coop next to the barn where their dad kept his restored Chevy Corvair. Jessie envied the love he showed to such an insignificant creature, and the little rabbit seemed to return the affection.

She was sitting on the step, teasing a garter snake with a stick, when her father came from the barn holding a tattered wire. A squirrel had made a nest in the engine and chewed through the brake line.

"We're not a homeless shelter for rodents," he said.

Jessie recognized that tone and knew someone would have to pay.

"Go find your brother."

"Tag!" she screamed, keeping the snake under her stick.

Tag came bounding out the door.

Jessie looked up. "Do you have a pet squirrel? 'Cause you're in trouble."

Tag stood there, smiling at his rabbit in the chicken coop, as their father scolded, "You can't keep wild animals in a cage, Tag. It attracts other rodents."

Jessie's prisoner wriggled from under the stick, and she adjusted to capture the snake again. Their father led Tag over to the rabbit's cage. Tag sniffed and ran his sleeve across his face. He opened the door to the cage. Hopper sat in the corner. Its whiskers twitched before it bounced into Tag's hands. He drew the bunny close to his chest and let its fur graze his cheek.

"You're too soft," their dad said. "No wonder the boys gang up on you."

Tag placed Hopper on the ground and stomped his foot by the rabbit's tail. "Go on, Hops," he said. "You're free."

Tag turned toward the house, streaming mud-stained tears. Hopper followed close on his heel. Tag turned back, and his eyes brightened to see his loyal pet following. Jessie felt her heart lift.

She imagined how it must feel to have a friend who refused to give up.

The shot from her father's handgun popped like one firecracker the morning after the fourth of July. Hopper rested on the ground, gray head matted in blood. Jessie's snake slithered under the porch.

Jessie hung her helmet on the hook inside the cab. Ross announced dinner, and she joined the chow line. The voices of hungry firefighters faded into utensils scooping mashed potatoes.

Ross's words rose above the babble. "Hey, fucktard. Captain bunny killer. Pass the ketchup."

"Get it yourself—when we're done putting out this fire," Robbins said, standing at the interruption of six short tones.

"The fire lure strikes again," Ross said, nodding at Jessie. "Can you at least turn that magnetic force off at dinnertime?"

Jessie pushed her chair from the table and shrugged. Since she had joined the crew, fires at Station 13 increased one hundred and fifty percent. Firefighters attribute fire karma to the newest crewmember, and Jessie wore the fire-magnet badge with pride.

They sped from the station, and emergency lights dominated the streets, forcing traffic to the side—Jessie's destination mattered more. Arriving at a one-story home with fire shooting out a window confirmed the urgency.

Captain Robbins delivered the size-up. "Dispatch Engine 13 arrived—fire showing on the delta side."

Jessie rushed to the back of the engine, pulled the loop marking one section of hose, and draped it over her shoulder. Five 50-foot sections of connected hose followed her across the grass to the door.

Captain Robbins pointed a finger toward the sky and circled it, shouting to the driver, "Charge the hose line." He pressed his mask to his face.

Jessie stood on the front porch and opened the nozzle, clearing the line. She masked up and stepped over the threshold. Captain Robbins followed. He tapped her shoulder and pointed, saying, "We go left. We need to find access to the basement."

Moving through the room, she turned left into a kitchen or dining room—too dark to know for sure. Another step and the hose jerked her back. She leaned forward for leverage. Stuck.

"I need more slack," she shouted through the darkness.

"I'll be back. It's wedged in the door," Robbins said.

Fire flashed overhead, brightening the room. Jessie opened the nozzle and wet the flames. Smoke dropped from the ceiling, covering her in darkness like a hoodie. She felt the hose release. She stepped. The floor shifted. She stumbled and went down to one knee. Jessie recovered and stood up—and heard a crack.

The floor opened like a sinkhole. Jessie stumbled. The hole expanded, swallowing a chair. She reached out for the edges of the pit, and the open nozzle led the hose in an uncontrolled dance, flopping and jumping, spattering water on the wall, spitting at the ceiling and raining down.

She pushed against wooden beams to keep from falling into the basement. Her shoulders ached. She kicked her legs like she could swim out of the hole. She pushed with her arms once more but slipped further.

"Help!" she yelled.

Robbins shouted, "Grab her arms. Grab her tank. We're gonna lose her."

The hole widened. She reached for the arms grabbing at her but slipped until she held the edge with her fingers. The grasping hands pulled at her coat, and she was being lifted. Firefighter boots came into view on the floorboards. Jessie surrendered to the rescue.

Rising from the hole at last, she stopped with a *thud*, her tank wedged under the floor joists. Frenzied hands tugged again and pulled her coat at the shoulders. And then the hands let go. She reached out and locked gloves with a masked ally.

The gloves slipped off, and Jessie dropped into the crater.

The eight-foot fall into a seemingly bottomless pit progressed in slow motion. Fire blazed around her. Flames engulfed the stairway, her only egress. Jessie closed her eyes. Details from her past flashed in her mind like negatives on a photo reel. Like a character in a TV cartoon, the edges of one figure sharpened and slowly approached.

It was Tag—her brother dropped from the barn rafters. The noose around his neck snapped like a whip. Tag was free from his pain, enslaving Jessie in regret.

The nozzle bumped and bounced above. Jessie stood. Robbins's muffled voice crackled in the chaos: "She fell right into the seat of the fuckin' fire. Grab the nozzle and get the junior extension ladder."

And then Jessie heard nothing.

Surrounded by flames, she felt more than saw blue in the distance. Crystals floated toward her, glistening like stars on a frozen lake. She drew her arms close for protection from the bitter cold. The blue glow hovered before descending and encapsulating her inside a frozen bubble of ice and frost. Tag smiled and said, without making a sound, "I'm okay. I'm happy."

A ladder punched through the hole above her. Flames pierced her protective glacial sphere. Jessie grasped the ladder rung and the fly slipped, trapping her fingers between the rungs. She yelled to firefighters overhead, but her cry was lost in the frenzy of the rescue.

Jessie leaned back, pulling to free her hands. With all her strength she screamed and lifted her forearms. It was impossible.

Glass shattering intensified the urgency of her escape. Broken-out windows would feed fire with air. Jessie turned to the small window, expecting a heat-warped frame, but instead saw Dana crawling through on her belly.

Entering a basement fire through a window with no means of egress is highly discouraged, a risk that demands a high reward. A firefighter in a mayday situation is that justification.

"Can't let our star student go down her first year on the job." Dana pushed up on the ladder, freeing Jessie's hands.

Jessie stepped up on the ladder and looked one last time for Tag. Flames gently moved across wooden beams void of blue crystals and little brothers. She climbed. At the top, panicked firefighters grabbed and pulled at her.

Jessie protested, "I can walk."

In spite of her protests, four firefighters carried her to the front lawn. They pulled off her helmet, her tank, and her coat. A firefighter carrying the pump can pointed the nozzle at the burns bubbling on her neck, but Jessie raised her hand to protest the rusty can. "Maybe get the saline."

Jessie sustained second-degree burns on her neck and forearms. Burns on her arm circled but never touched the Maltese cross tattoo, lending a flare of invincibility. During her monthlong recovery she found serenity tracing the burn marks outlining the ink on her skin.

Jessie made a final visit to the tattoo shop before returning to duty at the firehouse. As she reached into her gear locker to retrieve her fire coat, her sleeve retracted. Tattooed inside the protective bubble of the Maltese cross was Tag's rabbit, Hopper.

Captain Robbins was out sick, leaving the department short of captains. She wondered who would be "put in the seat," riding out of grade. Jessie flexed her forearm, feeling uneasy with a substitute captain. The twitch of Hopper's ears calmed her.

In the back seat of the engine she pressed her mask to her face and took a deep breath, listening for the click of released air. Lights inside her mask indicated a full tank. She lowered her mask as the out-of-grade captain hopped into the front seat.

"I guess they'll let anyone ride in charge," Dana said.

Jessie smiled. "I guess so. I'm glad it's you."

"It's good to have you back, Jess. Listen, we're gonna take it slow today. If we get something, I'll be on the line. You come in behind."

Jessie felt relieved and a little guilty. "I'm okay. It was no big deal."

"Maybe falling through a hole into a lake of fire is no big deal to you, but either way, I'm going in first today."

Jessie finished her morning checks and went to the kitchen. She recognized two of the guys from the ladder truck plus Ross. The other guys she hadn't seen before. "Is today a popular day for vacation or what? Where is everyone?"

Ross sipped his coffee and then hugged Jessie. "You scared me shitless. Robbins reported off sick. Says he has a date with a fishing pole, but I think he's shook by you coming back."

Jessie felt a gush of flattery. She wondered if this is what it took to become one of the guys, a literal trial by fire. "It was no big deal."

The ladder captain chimed in. "When I saw the top of your helmet and no body, all I wanted to know was how the hell you didn't drop." He curled his arm into a bicep, "You got steel pipes, girl."

Jessie sniffed and then snorted. She ran her hand through her hair and felt a prickling sensation at her neckline.

A firefighter Jessie hadn't met said, "I heard a lotta shit. Rumors about what happened. You were there. I wanna hear it from you."

Fuzzy white flakes danced in front of her eyes, obscuring her vision. She took a swig of coffee and cleared her throat.

The next thing she knew she was lying on the floor. She wiped the blood dripping into her hair from her forehead and sat up against the trash can.

"Jessie, are you okay?" the firefighter said.

Dana bolted into the kitchen. "What the fuck?"

"She was talking to me, and then bam, she fell out. She hit her head on the trash can and dropped to the floor. I'll get the med bag."

The captain from the ladder truck leaned in and said, "I think she fainted. Jessie, are you on your period?"

Jessie wiped blood streaming from her nose with her sleeve. "What? No. Fuck you. I ain't no Southern belle. It's none of your damn business." She tried to stand.

Dana crouched in front of her. "Relax. Medics are on the way."

That was the second time Jessie passed out.

CHAPTER 28

Overhaul and Extension: Opening (smashing) walls, floors, and ceilings to find hidden fire. Efficient overhaul prevents every incident commander's fear: a rekindle, requiring a return to the same address to put out the missed fire.

Brazil

Brazil sat facing the chief, scratching at the fabric of her polyester uniform pants. The chief's glasses slid down his nose again, and he peered over the lenses at her.

"The ice cream," he repeated.

Dismissing the battalion chief's *yes, sir* advice, she said, "You want me to tell you about the ice cream. With all due respect, Chief, since I'm here, I have a feeling you know all about the ice cream."

"I'd like to hear it from you."

She clasped her hands on her lap. "I wonder. What was your nickname?" She considered his size. "Hercules, or maybe Sherman. They call me McLiar. If I tell you about the ice cream, I won't be able to set one foot inside that station without getting a new nickname. I prefer Liar to Judas." She whispered under her breath, "I may as well be a shrimp thrown into a pool full of catfish."

The chief nudged the tape recorder closer to Brazil. "This is your one and only chance to tell your side of the story. We've had a complaint. We have to investigate. Were you bullied into eating ice cream from another firefighter's mouth?"

She panned the photographs on the wall. Firemen standing side by side with their hands cupped on one another's shoulders. Did she envy them or pity them? She wasn't sure. She tried to imagine a scenario where her photo would be displayed on the wall and decided that the compromise required to blend in was costly. Brazil had accepted it a long time ago—fitting in is exhausting.

The year Brazil turned eight, there was a family reunion at "the cabin" in Wisconsin. She had hunted at the wood's edge for the perfect marshmallow-roasting stick and used it to write her name in the sandy driveway.

Her mother called, "All members of the clean plate club! Dessert!"

Fifty-foot red pines bent in the wind, cracking as they swayed into one another. Brazil, then little Mary McFadden skipped along the driveway. She heard the trees whisper and looked toward the sky. The wind lifted. The trees bending in the wind seemed to reach for her on the ground. Afraid, she ran. She didn't see her uncle coming toward her and slammed into his legs.

He bent down. "Where's the fire, little nugget?"

"The trees cracked. They're falling!"

"The trees won't fall. They're practicing for winter."

The wind blew; the trees swayed. Mary squeezed her uncle's legs tighter.

"You see that?" he said. "They're leaning on one another. In winter, heavy snow covers the branches. All alone one tree may break, but trees standing together can't fall."

Mary let go of her uncle's legs and took his hand. Together they walked to the dessert table. She reached for her favorite. Her uncle said, "It's chocolate and sweet, like you."

She pulled back her hand. In her suburban town she had been teased as the only Black kid in her school. Kids called her dirty, mocking her, saying she was burnt by God. She envied the white faces of her relatives, gathered around the picnic tables. *I won't be chocolate much longer*, she thought. *When I grow up, my hair will turn yellow and I'll have tan skin just like my family.*

Mary's dad had a mouth full of apple cake and washed it down with beer.

"A true Irishman," his brother said.

Her dad raised his plastic cup. "First born of an original coal cracker. One hundred percent Irish and—"

Her mother interrupted, "It's such a shame that you had to muddy the pond by marrying a Mckraut like me."

Her father put his arm over her shoulder and pulled her close. "Marrying you and your German apple cake has given me a slice of heaven on earth."

Mary licked the frosting off the top of her cake. "Mom, if you're half Irish and Dad is all Irish, does that make me three-quarters?"

Her uncle barreled out a deep belly laugh.

"Honey," her mom said. "You're not Irish at all. Remember? You're adopted."

Brazil stared into the glare of the chief's lenses. She weighed the truth, considering the branches it would break. No matter which way she bent, she doubted she'd have someone to lean on. She leaned in close to the recorder. It was like opening the curtain of the confessional. Brazil was done keeping secrets. Maybe revealing them would finally end the harassment.

On her way out the chief said, "Oh, and McFadden. There's a gag order on this one, so keep it to yourself."

"Yes, sir."

"One more thing," the chief said. "Who's Sherman?"

"Not who. What. The biggest tree on earth."

On the way back to the station, Brazil occupied the silence between her and the battalion chief with busy thoughts. *My side? He wanted my side. How many sides can there be?*

The saw she had been checking waited for her on the apparatus floor. She returned it to its compartment and went to the coop. Damien pushed the mute button on the TV remote.

Gordy rushed into the room and said, "So what did the chief want?"

"Recruitment advice?" She wasn't prepared for an interrogation.

"On a Saturday? No. C'mon, McLiar," Damien said.

"There's a gag order. I can't talk about it."

Gordy argued, "A gag order is exactly why you talk about it."

She squinted, trying to unravel how this made sense.

"Yup," Damien said. "A gag order is how they divide and conquer. Who do you want to stand with? Us or headquarters?"

The guys huddled around her, goading her to join their team. She thought of the red pines bending and whispering, and for the second time that day Brazil entered the confessional—though this time it felt more like an inquisition. Brazil realized that Ice-Cream-Gate wasn't over.

───────────

Over the next few weeks, the guys were summoned to headquarters one by one. Whispers in the station were a loose interpretation of honoring the gag order. When Brazil entered a room, those whispers hushed.

Brazil filled a mop bucket with soap to wash the truck. The rubber of the massive garage door scraped on the concrete. The chief followed a path of sunlight across the floor. Brazil noticed her name on the cover of the folder he carried.

The door to the coop closed behind him. She pushed her bucket close to the door, fully intending to eavesdrop. She peeked through the thin, rectangular window in the door.

"Son of a bitch," the chief said to Gordy. "You couldn't handle this one in house? Anyway, today is your lucky day. She's being reassigned. Have her read and sign the transfer." He threw the folder on the counter, chuckled, and said, "That is, if she can read."

Brazil released an audible gasp that must have been more like a war cry because Gordy and the chief whipped around to face her. She banged the door wide open. The two men flinched as she charged toward them

Maintaining her stride, she snatched a pen from the desk. "I don't need to read it." Brazil signed her name, dropped the pen, and said, "Where to?"

"Gather up your stuff and report to Engine 14," the chief said.

She packed her fire gear into her Volkswagen and filled an empty cardboard box with the contents of her personal locker. Her photo of Bentley and Emmett she peeled off the door and tucked in her shirt pocket—a reminder of the reason she'd joined the fire department. *Get paid while you earn that nursing degree.*

Brazil parked in the lot behind Station 14, unpacked her fire gear, and checked the fire engine equipment. She slapped her yellow magnet next to the other firefighter's nameplate. Reading all the names, Brazil couldn't believe her luck. The red magnet belonged to Bell—*As in Captain Ruby Bell?* She hoped.

Drawn to the smell of bacon, she carried her box from her hatchback to the kitchen. Ruby stood at the stove, tossing eggs with a spatula. The driver, Henry, stood next to her, holding an empty plate.

"Hungry? It's turkey bacon." Ruby said.

Brazil was hungry, but it was the crumb of acceptance that she hungered for most. "I didn't realize you were at fourteen's. It smells amazing in here. I threw my gear on the engine."

Ruby flipped the bacon. "I'm the permanent tramp without a crew. The regular captain is out with a knee injury," she explained.

Brazil held up the cardboard box and said, "Where can I put my stuff?"

Still holding onto his plate, Henry motioned toward the fridge and said, "There's lots of room in the freezer. We don't have ice cream here."

"And I don't have ice cream in this box. I don't see your point."

Ruby spooned a heap of eggs into a bowl and topped them with two strips of bacon. "Put your stuff upstairs. Take an empty locker and join us."

Henry threw his plate onto the counter. It spun like a top, rattling to a stop. "Why are you being nice to her? You do know she's the ice cream girl."

Brazil turned to Ruby, expecting to be defended. Ruby piled eggs on Henry's plate, saying nothing. She understood what Ruby believed, without truly knowing. *Maybe McLiar fits after all,* she thought. *My reputation—born from others' lies—is a myth. So is Bettina's fish tale about women sticking together.*

Brazil started up the stairs in search of her locker. The alarm sounded—six blasts. "House fire. 3791 Lowry Avenue. Caller reporting heavy smoke and flames."

Brazil knew a fire was an opportunity to bond with her crew. The fireground was the place where station nicknames and bullshit reputations came second to the risky work. A firefighter using dirty water to mop the kitchen floor or forgetting to pack the blood pressure cuff for a medical call was forgiven after grinding at a house fire. The durgan leaving the scene with the dirtiest helmet earned the most respect.

Arriving on Lowry Avenue, Ruby reported light smoke showing from an upper-floor window. She turned to the back seat. "Brazil, grab the line. I'm going in to take a quick look."

Brazil carried the nozzle to the door and spread the hose on the lawn. A young woman approached her and said, "I forgot about the candle in my bedroom upstairs."

Brazil nodded and readied her mask.

Ruby returned and said, "Fire's in the bedroom, top of the stairs."

Brazil braced the nozzle under her arm. Ruby lifted the hose behind her, and together they climbed the stairs. Flames swallowed the bedroom curtains. Brazil opened the nozzle and quickly knocked down the fire. She wet the ceiling and the wall, cooling the room. Truckie boots pounded up the stairs.

"No extension. You can put those axes back in your belts," Ruby said.

She keyed the mic clipped at her shoulder. "Fire's out. Shut down the tank line." She turned to Brazil. "Let's pick up and get back to that bacon."

A truckie rubbed Brazil's helmet like a big brother tousling his younger sibling's hair, saying, "Nice job, McFadden."

"Toddlers," Ruby said, and took the nozzle outside.

Brazil draped a section of hose over her shoulder and dragged it downstairs to the doorway. She looked for the woman who had confessed about the candle and found her standing across the street. Brazil made eye contact and waved. The woman looked away.

Brazil scanned the fireground. Flickering fire-truck lights lined the street. Ruby stood with Henry, laughing by the engine. Then Brazil noticed everyone was laughing except the homeowner.

Ruby playfully punched Henry in the arm and joined Brazil on the porch. She lifted the hose from Brazil's shoulder.

"Did I do something funny?" Brazil said.

Ruby spoke without moving her lips. "Check your helmet."

Brazil removed her helmet and discovered a pair of leopard panties stretched across the dome. She recalled the durgan tousling her helmet and realized his friendliness had been merely a vehicle for deception. She removed the underwear and approached the homeowner.

"I'm so sorry. These must be yours?" She stretched out her hand, the helmet ornament balled in her fist.

The woman shook her head no. Brazil considered the scene

scattered with fire *men* and understood the woman's embarrassment. "Oh, right," Brazil said, and tucked the undies in the pocket of her fire coat.

———————

At the station, Brazil draped her coat over the fire engine door. She got busy cleaning hose and hung it in the tower to dry. Then she retrieved the box she had left and climbed the stairs to find a locker. A string looped through the vent of the only vacant locker held the leopard panties. Under the panties was duct tape with *McPanther* written in black marker. She tugged at the knot. The string and the panties drooped, covering her new nickname. She pulled the string back through the vent and tied it tighter. She ran her hand across the tape and said, "Better than McLiar."

CHAPTER 29

Sawzall: *Heavy-duty reciprocating saw with a push-and-pull blade motion. Cuts through almost anything.*

Brazil

Brazil packed Bentley's lunch and then pinned her badge to her uniform. Bentley made siren sounds as he pushed his fire engine across the kitchen floor.

Her mother came from upstairs with Emmett and went to the fridge for apple juice. "It's seven twenty, honey. You don't want to be late."

"Maybe I do. This job is killing me. I'm not sure I can do it."

"What else will you do? This was supposed to be your ticket to nursing school, and you haven't taken one class since you joined that fire department."

"Thanks, Mom. Bentley, grab your backpack. I can't be late for work."

She buckled Bentley into his booster seat. Emmett clutched onto his grandma's leg at the door. "Be good for Grammie," Brazil shouted. "I'll call you before bed."

On the way to Bentley's preschool, Brazil opened the center

console to check on the pack of cigarettes she'd bought weeks earlier, after a fight with her ex-husband. It was her vice, left over from high school and still handy during stressful times. She flipped open the box and peeked inside. A smoke felt like her only friend.

"Mom," Bentley said.

Brazil dropped the open box into her lap, and one cigarette fell to the floor. She adjusted the rearview mirror to see his eyes. "Yeah, honey?"

"Mom, I don't want you to die."

She glanced at the cigarette on the floor and pushed it under the mat with her foot. "I'm not going to die, sweetie. Why would you think that?"

"You said your job's killing you. Is it cuz you breathe fire?"

Brazil repositioned the mirror so he could see her face. She smiled and said, "I'm a firefighter, but I wear a mask and a helmet and a fireproof suit, like Fireman Sam. Fireman Sam doesn't die."

She hated referring to Sam as *fireman*, but it was exhausting to constantly confront the gender roles portrayed in her kids' favorite cartoon, and honestly, Sam the Fireman came in handy with her boys. Embracing Fireman Sam was a worth-it compromise.

Bentley smiled. "Mommy, can we stop at the store and get a Fireman Sam helmet?" Bentley raised his arms in victory and sang the character's theme song.

"Not today, honey. I have to go to work."

———

Brazil entered the station through the back door and was greeted by the pungent smell of death.

"Someone has got to clean out the mousetraps," she muttered.

She walked to the kitchen. Splayed out on the counters, in the sink, and on the table was a half-gutted deer. Globs of innards soaked the newspaper lining the floor.

The white Maltese cross on Henry's blue uniform shirt was speckled with blood. "I got back last night," he said. "I snagged this beauty yesterday. Had to drag him a mile through the swamp to my truck."

Brazil tried to connect "this beauty" with the odor of decay and stiff white legs reaching toward the ceiling. She covered her mouth to stuff her compulsion to gag, then put her face in the crook of her arm and turned to run from the kitchen. She bumped into Ruby.

"Sorry, Cap'n," Brazil choked.

Ruby raised her hands out to the side, palms up. "Is there a problem?"

Brazil stopped. "You're okay with this?"

Henry said, "My wife doesn't like it when I mess the garage."

Brazil retreated to the dorm and remained there for the day, coming out only for emergency runs. She skipped dinner, and at 21:30, a half hour before the customary bedtime at a fire station, she climbed under the covers and closed her eyes.

The intercom in the dorm crackled. "Firefighter McFadden. Report to the kitchen."

She pulled the covers over her head.

Ruby repeated, "McFadden, report to the kitchen immediately."

"What the Hades. I'm coming," Brazil whispered. She threw off the covers and slid down the pole. The smell of rotting deer remained. She opened the kitchen door a crack and wedged her body to the side, peeking in.

The floor was lined with clean paper now, and only parts of the deer remained. Henry stood next to the body, wearing safety glasses and a coverall apron stained with brown blood.

Ruby widened the door and ordered, "Go out to the truck and get the Sawzall."

"What for?"

"We're having a Sawzall school. I want you to get an idea of what that saw can do. This deer is a perfect opportunity."

"I don't want to do that. I'm not doing that," Brazil said.

Henry chimed in, "I think she gave you a direct order, rookie."

Brazil stepped into the room and crossed her arms. "I won't do it."

"Brazil, Henry's right. It's a direct order. Go get the Sawzall. You will cut up that deer, or we can call the chief."

She thought about the last time the chief had been called. *It's protocol when what I'm about to do makes no sense. I'd rather eat ice cream out of a dog's mouth than cut that deer.* She reluctantly walked to the fire truck and slowly opened the engine compartment. She removed the Sawzall from its case. The blade, long like a swordfish's nose, was shiny like it had never been used. The saw felt heavier than Brazil remembered from rookie school.

Donning safety glasses, she shuffled into the kitchen. She tried to make eye contact with Ruby in one last plea to escape the insanity. Ruby looked to the floor and then at Henry. Brazil understood there would be no escape. Ruby had her own demons, not so different from her own. *Is it a weakness to desire acceptance? Is it a sin to fear rejection? Even Peter denied Jesus.*

Brazil approached the deer, set the blade against its hip, above the hind leg, and pulled the trigger. The saw bounced back, throwing Brazil off balance. She stepped back.

Henry offered, "Start the saw blade moving before you make contact."

Brazil raised the saw and pressed the trigger. The deafening *whir* was surprisingly calming. She stepped in and lowered the saw. The blade cut through quicker than Brazil expected. She wasn't prepared for the intensified stench when the leg dropped to the floor.

Ruby buried her nose in a towel.

"Like a butcher!" Henry said in celebration. "Do the other one."

Brazil lifted her glasses and rested them on her head. She turned to Ruby.

"She's done," Ruby said. "Go ahead and put the saw away."

Brazil retrieved her cigarettes from her car. She climbed the ladder in the hose tower to the scuttle hole leading to the roof. She lit a smoke, and her cell phone rang.

"Hey, honey." Her mother's voice felt like warm apple pie. "You forgot to call the boys. Bentley had a bad dream, so I let him call."

"Hi, Mommy. I wanted to make sure you had your fireproof suit on."

"You bet I do, B-man. Go back to sleep. Tomorrow we'll get Fireman Sam's helmet and we'll both be safe."

Her mother came back to the phone. "I'm sorry for pushing you about nursing school. I want you to be happy. If that job isn't right for you, you need to find the one that is."

Brazil couldn't remember what happy felt like.

Little Mary rubbed at her tears, smearing chocolate and dirt across her face. After her mother reminded her that she wasn't Irish, she'd run out to hide. Now her uncle had found her crying behind a tall pine tree.

"Hey, McNugget. Why the tears?"

She stabbed the ground with her marshmallow stick. "I'm not a McNugget. I'm not Irish. Mom said I'm adopted."

"You might not have Irish blood, but you're still our McNugget. Your mom and dad went looking for someone special and found you. That makes you a gold nugget."

"The kids at school don't think I'm special. No one likes me. Is it because I'm adopted?"

"I don't know about that. I do know, if someone doesn't like *you*, they're missing out on a pot of gold. Some people will look hard to see what's wrong with you. Your friends see what's right about you, and your family sees both. Right and wrong, and we love you anyway. Never forget, you will always be our golden nugget."

CHAPTER 30

Jessie

Jessie was now an expert at hiding her blackouts, but this time she'd dropped right in front of the paramedics. Now she struggled to sit up as they wheeled her through the back door of the HCMC Emergency Room. "I can walk."

The medic steering the foot of the stretcher smiled. "You were midsentence when you passed out. Maybe just lie back."

Jessie complied. *Midsentence?* She felt for the badge pinned to her shirt and remembered, *The Home and Garden show. After the engine dropped me off for fire watch at the convention center, I met the medics at the EMS post. We were discussing fire department budget cuts. How it sucked for me to be pulled off the rig for private events so MFD could generate revenue.*

The medic had suggested that the fire department set up a booth for a bake sale. She recalled laughter and someone saying, "Everyone loves firefighter chili."

The ER intake nurse directed the medics to an exam room,

where they transferred Jessie from the stretcher to the bed. The medic's radio chirped, and he peeled the back exam room curtain to leave, saying, "Take care, Jess."

The ER doctor stood on the other side, reviewing notes on a clipboard. Jessie could tell he was a no-nonsense kind of guy. He moved fast and got right to the heart of the matter. He lifted the gauze covering her wound. "Have you ever passed out before?"

Jessie considered answering truthfully: *Let's see, the first time was when I got my MFD rejection letter and slammed my face into the deck. Next was a broken nose at the fire station, and then there was the time that Kim was clearing the table and dropped a stack of dishes. Last thing I remember was the sound of breaking plates; I woke up with my head slumped in my dessert. What a waste of Death by Chocolate. When I dropped in the middle of spin class, the instructor recommended a homeopathic fix, a tablespoon of apple cider vinegar each morning for stomach acid. Finally, Kim insisted I go to a doctor. That led to the PTSD hypothesis.*

Afraid of losing her dream job for emotional instability, Jessie looked into the doctor's eyes. "This is a first for me."

The doctor told the nurse, "Go ahead and get Jessie's vitals and put a few butterflies on that gash. I'll check back later."

The nurse applied the bandages and left Jessie alone in the cubicle. Jessie checked the mirror and traced the bandage over her eye. *How will I explain this one?* After an hour with no sign of a doc or a nurse or another patient, she opened the curtain and found the corridor empty. Jessie tightened the muscle of her forearm so Hopper's ears twitched. "What do ya think, Hop? Time to get outta here?"

She left the hospital and hiked the half mile to the convention center. The fire engine was still parked in front. She ducked through a side door, cut through the building, and met the rig on the other side.

The captain smoothed his eyebrow and pointed two fingers at Jessie like a handgun. "How do you get injured at a House and Home show?"

"It's Home and Garden," Jessie said.

"And?"

"And you missed your calling. You shoulda been a cop. What's with the interrogation?"

"You're on duty, smart-ass. I need to know if I should fill out an IOD report."

Jessie knew the captain would accept the simplest explanation to avoid filling out a report. "It's a scratch. Medics cleaned me up. Overkill. You know how those medics can be. I tripped on the fake grass at the golf exhibit."

The driver pulled away from the curb. "I guess that's why they call it *blades* of grass."

On the second morning of Jessie's three days off, her phone rang. She felt across the bed for Kim; finding an empty space, she rolled over and reached for her phone. The words *FAT DAY* flashed on the screen, meaning the fire department was understaffed and was looking for people to work overtime. Time and a half for twenty-four hours meant a big paycheck. Jessie answered.

The voice said, "Backseat on Engine 14. Want it?"

Jessie left an apologetic message for Kim, canceling their

dinner plans. "I'll take you out to breakfast tomorrow. Promise." She dressed quick and drove to the station, where she dropped her gear next to the rig.

"We got a fat one. Steaks for dinner tonight," said Henry. A firefighter working overtime was expected to kick in an extra twenty bucks toward the dinner clutch.

Jessie climbed into the back seat and checked the magnet board. "McFadden!"

Brazil pushed a mop bucket filled with truck wash over to the rig. Two long-handled brushes extended from the soapy water. "Are you napping in there?" Brazil said. "Help me wash this beast."

Jessie jumped down from the cab and grabbed a brush.

"My mom is bringing the boys in twenty minutes. I've been working my tail end off to finish before they get here. They miss me."

"Go get ready for your kids. I'll rinse the rig."

Jessie wrapped up and washed the last of the soap down the drain. Through the open apparatus door, tiny footsteps slapped against the concrete.

"Mommy! Bentley pinched my baby skin," Jessie heard Emmett say. He rubbed the skin of his arm under his bicep.

Brazil scooped Emmett up and covered his arm with smooching kisses. He wriggled from her arms, ran to the driver's side of the engine, and started to climb. Bentley took the captain's seat. Brazil handed him her yellow helmet.

Bentley clipped the chin strap and announced, "When I grow up. I'm gonna be a firefighter and a dinosaur bone digger."

Emmett sat quietly behind the wheel of the engine, his chubby legs on the seat and his feet dangling over the edge.

Jessie widened the driver's door. "What about you, Em?" she said. "Do you want to be a firefighter like your mommy?"

He smiled and pushed up on the blue frame of his eyeglasses. His smile widened. He rocked the steering wheel back and forth. "I'm gonna be a banana."

"Boys can't be bananas," Bentley corrected, and jumped down from the captain's seat, smacking his sneakers on the concrete. Emmett crouched in the doorway of the FMO seat and launched into the air.

Jessie caught him and eased him to the floor.

"I can do it," Emmett protested.

Brazil's mom laughed and said, "We know you can, Chiquita, but we didn't want you to scrape your baby skin."

Emmett rubbed the tattoo on Jessie's arm. "I like that bunny," he said, laughing. Jessie flexed her muscle, and Emmett's eyes sparkled with the animation of Hopper.

The fire station tones squealed. Brazil took her helmet from Bentley's head, squeezed her boys, and hopped on the rig. She raised her hands in a shrug toward her mom. "Sorry."

"Girl, you go save the world."

Jessie could see the pride in Mrs. McFadden's eyes. Even though she wasn't the target of the comment, she felt the glory. Nothing was more satisfying than heading out in a big red truck to, like Brazil's mom put it, save the world.

Jessie slid into the back seat with Brazil and snorted. "A banana?"

"I made my You Can Be Anything When You Grow Up speech last night—a banana's no wackier than this little girl becoming a firefighter."

Ruby slid into the captain's seat in the front.

Jessie slapped the back of Henry's seat and said, "If it weren't for you, we'd have a certified all-chick crew."

"All-women," Brazil corrected.

"Keep dreamin'. If it weren't for me, you'd have no rig at all. You can't go anywhere without the driver."

The dispatcher's voice sobered the banter. "Caller reporting a jumper on the bridge over the railroad tracks. Golden Valley Road."

Jessie felt a shiver at the back of her neck and imagined Tag, the moment before he stepped off the ledge. His smile from his bubble was gone. He closed his eyes. The hopelessness he must have felt—*I should have known*.

Henry turned onto a dead-end street, and Ruby switched off the siren. In the distance the jumper stood with his back to them on the opposite side of a chain-link fence. He leaned over a precipice, holding onto the metal mesh behind him.

Jessie reached under the seat and uncased the binoculars. The man's fingers clenched white on the fence. His hair fell over his face, and he seemed to be talking.

The dispatcher advised, "Police suggesting you stage and wait for the negotiating psychologist."

Jessie adjusted the focus of the binoculars. He leaned further over the railroad tracks, still grasping the fence. He lifted one leg from the ledge like he was about to jump and then pulled back, regaining his footing. Jessie wondered if Tag had doubted his decision before stepping off the loft in that barn.

"Cap'n. He's gonna jump. I don't think waiting is an option," Jessie said. She handed the binoculars to Ruby.

"Brazil, get the bolt cutters," Ruby ordered. "Jessie, take the med bag and leave it by the curb. Follow behind me in a single file.

Brazil, you're behind Jess." Ruby turned to Henry. "Use the rig to block traffic. Don't let anyone through." She paused, "Except MPD. When the cops get here, let them in."

Ruby quickly explained the plan and led the way. Jessie and Brazil matched her steps, stealthily approaching the fence.

At the sound of their approach the jumper, keeping his eyes on the vertical drop, warned, "I will jump. I miss her so much. Don't get any closer. I swear, I'll jump."

"I'm Ruby."

"Stay away from me."

"Who do you miss? What happened to her?" Ruby took a few steps closer. Jessie and Brazil followed.

"Fuck. Nothing happened to her. I can't be here anymore. Why would she cheat?"

"What's your name?" Ruby inched closer. "It's just you and me."

One hand left the fence to grip a gold pendant around his neck. "She said forever." He tugged at the chain and started to cry. The chain came off in his hand. He dumped it onto the rocks below.

Jessie pushed up the sleeve of her coat to see Hopper. The jumper looked over his shoulder and cried out, "Who else is there? You fuckin' liar."

"Go!" Ruby said.

Together Jessie and Ruby grabbed the jumper through the diamond openings in the fence. Jessie held a fistful of his shirt in one hand and the waistband of his jeans in the other. The chain link cut into Ruby's hands, one clasped around his arm and the other wrapped around his side, pulling his torso into the fence. Jessie leaned back, adjusting her grip from his jeans to his belt.

Brazil made several quick swipes with the bolt cutter, trac-

THE FIRE SHE FIGHTS

ing around them. Seconds later all three fell back onto the curb, leaving a hole in the chain link in the shape of the *Charlie's Angels* silhouette.

The jumper rolled onto his stomach, sobbing. Jessie held him tight. "You're gonna be okay."

The police siren chirped as a squad arrived on scene.

The next morning Jessie packed her equipment with twenty-four hours of overtime complete.

Dana threw her gear bag next to the rig and said, "You can't eat up all the overtime. Spread that fat cash around. I need it after my night at the poker table last weekend."

Jessie laughed. "After my day yesterday, you can have it."

"I heard. I drove past your artwork in the fence on my way in. It's clear—you were the one on the right."

Brazil emerged from the coop and Ruby from the dorm.

"It's the dream team! The only thing missing is Frankie," Dana said.

"And the dream," Jessie said.

"And the team," added Brazil, and shot a smirk at Ruby.

"Hang out. I'll buy breakfast."

"I got a date this morning. Maybe next time," Jessie said.

"I have to pick up my boys."

Ruby followed Dana to the kitchen, and Brazil headed for her Volkswagen.

Jessie pulled out of the lot, excited to spend the day with Kim, and headed home. She slowed to a four-way-stop intersection.

Clear, she rolled forward—and a speeding car cut her off. She slammed on the brakes. "Minnesota nice my ass."

She pressed the gas. Her vision blurred. Images flooded her view like a slideshow. She tried to make out the pictures, but before she could focus on any one image it vanished. Slide after slide after slide flashed and disappeared.

The next thing Jessie heard was a siren. The next face she saw was Dana's.

"We got you. Your car is pinned up against the concrete, but we'll have you out in a few minutes." Dana pulled the cord on the generator and wielded the Jaws of Life.

Becoming the victim in an official fire-department response made it impossible for Jessie to hide her unexplained fainting episodes. She was assigned to a desk job at MFD headquarters.

When Dana visited Jessie's cubicle the next week, she leaned over Jessie's desk and said, "Looks like that twin gash on the other side of your head is healed. When you comin' back?"

"I'm not. They say I have mental problems. It's a desk job for me."

"What did they find on the scan?"

"They didn't do one. They're saying it's PTSD. I guess I'm fucked up."

"I'll tell you what's fucked up: the fire department."

"No. The fire department is right. Think about it. Would you wanna go into a fire with me? I black out every time things get rough. I'm better here."

"Really? The combat challenge champion is better behind a desk? You don't believe that. What are you afraid of?"

I'm afraid an MRI will confirm how messed up I am, Jessie thought. After being dismissed again and again by doctors with no physical explanation and prescriptions to reduce stress, PTSD became an explanation Jessie accepted. What she feared most was whatever it was that had pushed Tag to take his final step. Was the hopelessness that lived in Tag's mind also hiding in hers?

"I'm afraid I'll black out and hurt someone. Physical ability only matters if I can stay awake long enough to put out the fire."

"You're getting that scan. And for the record, I'd go into a fire with you anytime."

CHAPTER 31

Brazil

Making progress on her nursing degree while working as a firefighter was doable—as long as small children weren't involved. Brazil packed lunches while her mom poured milk on the boys' Cheerios.

"Bentley, run upstairs and get your backpack and grab Emmett's monkey stuffy," Brazil said.

Bentley darted from the table. Brazil was at first surprised by Bentley's obedience, but then she realized she had unwittingly created a competition. Emmett chased his big brother up the steps, yelling, "I can get my own stuffy."

A scuffle on the stairway led to the inevitable Emmett scream.

"Quit screaming like a girl," Bentley said.

The boys sprinted back to the kitchen, out of breath. Brazil pointed at their cereal bowls. "Eat your breakfast." She leaned over the counter and said to Bentley, "What do you mean when you tell Emmett he screams like a girl?

"I don't know. Like a girl. It's a saying."

"What does a girl sound like when she screams?"

Bentley shrugged and then pinched Emmett, who screamed.

"Bentley! That is not okay."

"You asked."

"Girls and boys scream the same. You know I'm a girl, right?"

Emmett chimed in, "I scream like you, Mommy."

Brazil wondered if he had heard her scream in the night. In her most recent nightmare, she had jogged to the top of an ice-cream mountain where a deer with three legs smoked a cherry stem. She tried to speak, and the mountain melted. She woke falling into a mouth-shaped chasm. No need for a therapist to interpret that one.

Grandma added, "We all scream for ice cream."

Bentley lifted his spoon from his cereal. "Can I have ice cream?"

"Not for breakfast. Time to go. Mommy can't be late for work."

———

Brazil rolled into the fire station lot a few minutes before the eight-o'clock bell and got busy checking equipment. The bolt cutters, wedged in the compartment, paled in comparison to its roommate. The massive blades of the Jaws of Life claimed most of the space, and rightfully so, with its ability to smash, cut, and tear with one trigger finger. But it was the little bolt cutter, an unsung hero, called in to sneak up on the heartsick lover and save the day. "Sometimes it takes a little guy," she said softly.

The ding of a mask being checked inside the cab startled her. Ruby hopped down from the cab. "Or the little gal," Ruby said. "You could make any bolt cutter feel good about being the little guy. I've been meaning to tell you. I was impressed with your cuts."

Brazil wondered if this was an explanation or maybe even an apology for the deer massacre. *Is this another yes-sir moment? No,* Brazil decided. *The one person I expected to stand by me betrayed me. Not as a captain, but as a woman and friend, I thought.*

"Why?" Brazil said.

"Fast and efficient is why."

"Not the fence. The deer." Ruby's face flushed red. Anger or shame, Brazil wasn't sure. She continued, "I guess I just thought as two women we could count on each other. Now I don't even know if I can do this job anymore. After all you must have gone through in the early days, I assumed you'd be on my side."

Henry emerged from the coop with a mouthful of jelly donut.

Ruby stiffened and said to Brazil, "The chief called before you got here. Put on your white shirt. We're going downtown."

Henry wiped his mouth on the shoulder of his shirt, transferring the sugar to his sleeve. "Just when you thought they forgot about you, the Ghost of Christmas Past hobbles in with his ball and chain. Or, in this case, his ice-cream scoop."

Judgment day was here. It had to be about the ice cream. The guys at Station 4 were fighting their punishment after the ice-cream interrogations—one day off the payroll. She'd trade a year of Tuesdays off the payroll for the chance to start her career all over. Next time she would stay in the clutch and eat the soggy meatballs. Next time, given a gag order, she would remain gagged. She wouldn't be Huckleberry Finned into believing she could lean on her crew. She knew nice guys finish last. Brazil wondered, as a female firefighter, *What comes after last?*

"I don't know anything they don't. What could they want?"

Henry licked jelly dripping from the corner of his mouth. "You do know that when you get called downtown, they already know the answer. You never shoulda reported those guys." He brushed his shoulder, flicking sugar to the floor.

The anger Brazil felt at Henry's after-the-fact advice swirled inside her like a shook-up soda pop on a hot day. She was tired of trying to convince people she wasn't the one who'd complained about the ice cream. No one believes a liar.

"If they already know, why haul my backside downtown?"

"Henry," Ruby said, "wet down the engine. We don't wanna show up at headquarters with a dirty rig."

Dressed in her white shirt, on the way downtown, Brazil felt like Jesus on his way to meet Pontius Pilate. Before tackling the marble steps, she stopped in the women's bathroom and ran into Bettina.

"What are you doing here?" Brazil said.

"Same bullshit as you, I guess. Damien's Cracker-Jack lawyer called us all down here. Damien's trying to sue the department. He's the son of a bitch who makes you eat ice cream out of Gordy's mouth, and he wants to sue."

Brazil blinked. She didn't remember Bettina witnessing the prank.

Bettina continued, "If anyone should be compensated it's you. I warned them when I first notified them about the harassment. This isn't the fifties, and I told them again today."

"You're the one. Bettina, what did you do? You realize my career is ruined. Everyone hates me."

"Me? What did I do? Don't you know? The good ole boys taught the new ole boys well. They already hated you. They hate me too. I'm sorry if you think I ruined your career. You're adopted, right?"

Brazil wasn't sure of the connection, but it had been common knowledge since her white parents attended rookie school graduation.

"That last time you cooked for the clutch. Remember, you made chicken with awesome plum sauce and didn't need my help with the groceries, so I waited in the till. I'm not sure if the dipshits forgot I could hear them through my speaker, or they didn't care. Anyway, Gordy was pissed after you schooled him about the Native guy. He told Damien you're not all Black 'cause your parents are white. An Oreo cookie, I think he said—or an ice cream sandwich. Then you got out of the clutch. That pushed him over the edge. When they made you eat that ice cream, that's when I knew I couldn't make the same mistake twice."

"I'm not sure what mistake you made, but using me to fix what you messed up, to borrow your term, is bullshit."

"Did you ever meet Hector? That asshole assaulted another rookie. I won't say who—it's her story to tell, or not. I was alone in the hose tower with Hector, hanging the mop—just talking. She burst in and almost killed him. I should have known, but I didn't see it. Later, I heard she wasn't the only one. I couldn't let the same thing happen to you. Maybe what they did to you isn't technically an assault, but it's a slippery slope." Bettina opened the door to exit. "It's all about power. It's not right it's coming down on you, but I'm not sorry and I'd do the same thing over again. We chicks have to stick together."

Standing in front of the mirror, Brazil ran her hands over the curves of her hips and smoothed out her uniform. *People are going to look hard to find what's wrong with you,* her uncle had warned. She leaned close to the mirror and said, "Chicks. Really?"

In the hallway she met Henry leaving the men's room next door. He looked apologetic. "Sometimes the best defense is a good offense," he said. This was a side she hadn't seen of him.

"I think I'll go up there and keep my mouth shut."

"How come you let everyone believe you ratted on those guys?" Brazil shot Henry a confused look. "It's the vents. The bathrooms are next to each other. You can hear everything."

"I got one minute to get up there, and I don't need to add AWOL to the list." She turned to go and then hesitated. "I didn't let anyone believe. It's just easier for some to believe than to put the effort in to know."

She barely recognized Damien out of uniform in his neatly pressed suit. The chief who had first interrogated her about the ice cream looked exactly the same in his white shirt and wire-framed glasses. Seeking an ally, she searched the faces sitting around the long white table. Finding none, she landed back on the chief.

Damien's attorney straightened his papers and motioned to an empty chair. Brazil took the seat. He spoke first. "We're here today simply to identify the facts of the events that occurred on . . ."

Brazil didn't need a recap of the events. How could she possibly help Damien's case?

The attorney directed his first question to Brazil. "Ms. McFadden, is it true, after being told by the chief not to talk about the ice-cream incident, you immediately returned to the fire station and in fact told everyone all about your meeting with the chief?"

Brazil quickly glanced at the chief. The fluorescent lights bounced off his lenses, obscuring his eyes. She hoped for an anchor in Damien but found him focused on his shoes. She stared at his bowed head. That day when he had questioned her loyalty, his eyes had remained steady, his chin pointed in the air, asking, Would she stand with the administration or with her firefighting brothers? Brazil looked past the attorney at the blank white wall, avoiding his eyes but not his judgment, and quietly said, "Yup."

The attorney leaned forward. "Ms. McFadden, are you saying you did willingly defy the order of the chief and knowingly break the gag order?"

Feeling the shame in telling the truth and shame for keeping secrets, Brazil said, "Yes, I did."

The attorney continued, "Ms. McFadden. If this were to ever happen to you again"—he paused and looked up from his papers—"where you felt harassed. Would you report it?"

Brazil's head spun, knowing she hadn't reported it in the first place. Her gut vibrated with the fizz from the soda Henry had shaken earlier. She lost her breath and felt like she was drowning from the inside out. Following the soda bubbles to the surface, Brazil straightened in her chair and said, "Hella no."

Brazil was dismissed from the hearing. On the way back down the steps of city hall, she doubted her place in a department where strong brotherhood was more of a wall than a foothold.

On the way back to the station, Henry flung questions at Brazil like she was a clown at the pie-in-the-face booth.

"There's a gag order." Brazil wouldn't make that mistake again.

"I need to make a quick stop at Target," Ruby said.

"It's not exactly on the way," Henry said.

"You got somewhere you gotta be? I mean, we could rush back to the station and wax the rig," Ruby said.

Henry parked on the far side of the lot. Brazil followed Ruby into the store and went to the toy aisle. She scanned the shelves for the Fireman Sam helmet.

———————

Back at the station, Brazil got off the rig to guide Henry in. Damien was standing in the open doorway, still dressed in his suit.

"Can we talk?" he said.

"Not without a witness."

"Listen, I'm sorry."

"I can't even hear you right now."

"Brazil. I need your help."

"Did you just call me Brazil? What happened to Liar?"

"I felt bullied too. We have to stand together."

"You mean like how you stood up for me? Like when I had to explain to my five-year-old son why I'm not a liar? Speaking of liars, why didn't you tell the guys it was me who warned you, not me who reported you?"

"Listen, Brazil. I'm sorry about all that. I am. I've been think-ing about it. The way you were treated wasn't right. But you gotta decide. What's more important here? Revenge, or telling one little lie to support your firefighter brother?"

"Now you're mad at me because I *won't* lie?" She thought about

Bentley worrying that her job was killing her. He couldn't under-stand that it wasn't the fire; it was the fire "men" making her job hell. "I know what's important. It's my kids."

The next morning Brazil packed her fire gear. In the mirrored sur-face of the engine's pump panel she saw Ruby approaching. Ruby handed her a sheet of paper with the heading *Fire Department Transfer Opportunities.*

"I'm going back to five's," Ruby said.

Brazil scanned the transfer announcement to find Engine 5 and a listing:

Captain:	R. Bell
FMO:	vacancy
Firefighter:	vacancy
Firefighter:	vacancy

She returned the transfer slip to Ruby. "Looks like you'll be saving the south side all by yourself."

When Ruby didn't respond, Brazil tucked the slip into her duffel. She glanced at the captain, who was staring at her own reflection in the mirrored panel. She appeared conflicted—angry. Was it sad-ness? It didn't matter. Brazil had no interest in rescuing Ruby from her feelings. She started toward the door.

Ruby called after her, "You asked me why. The truth is—what we did with the deer—what I did. It was wrong. I was wrong."

Brazil turned. "It wasn't just wrong. You were a bully."

"I am sorry. I know there's no excuse. I thought that if somehow, the shit that happened to me as a rookie . . . happened to someone else. I don't know. Misery loves company?"

"Not the company I'm interested in keeping."

"You should be able to count on me. I thought becoming a captain would change things for me—automatic respect. Becoming a captain didn't change the fact that I'm a woman. We risk our lives as much as the men, but we're valued less. What I did to you was done to me. I know it's worse—a woman harassing a woman. Becoming a captain doesn't mean things are changed for me. It means it's my job to change things for you."

Brazil thought, *If Judas had been true, would Jesus have been crucified and all of mankind been denied salvation? God doesn't keep us from making mistakes, free will and all, but maybe choosing to make up for them is the point.*

"So, are you saying cutting up the deer wasn't an official training exercise?"

Ruby's face reddened again. *Repentance*, Brazil thought.

"Maybe as a captain it is your job to change things for me. Or maybe if we stop treating each other how the good ole boys treat us, we can change things together. Changing the world—or, harder, the fire department—none of us can do it alone."

Ruby nodded. "Let me make it up to you. Come to five's."

Brazil checked her watch. "I have to get home. I wanna see Bentley before my mom drops him at school. It's a small window."

She grabbed her duffel and the Target bag with the Fireman Sam helmet and went to her car. She thought about Bettina's words: "They hate you." *Maybe not everyone*, she thought. She threw the bags in the passenger seat on top of her *Health Trends in Nursing* textbook and drove home.

When Brazil parked in the driveway next to her mother's car, her boys came running outside, followed by Grandma. She gave Emmett a squeeze and handed Bentley the Fireman Sam helmet.

"Mom," Bentley said. "Fire*MAN* Sam is for babies." He pulled the Fireman Sam sticker off and put the helmet on. "I'm a fire*fighter*, just like you."

Brazil squatted in front of her son and straightened his helmet. "How did you get so smart?" She glanced over his shoulder to see her mother beaming with pride.

"He gets it from you," her mom said.

"You think? I did enroll in a nursing class for next semester. I decided to take it slow and keep my options open."

Bentley climbed into his booster seat next to Emmett, bumping his helmet back to crooked. Brazil waited for her mother to back down the driveway. The transfer announcement peeked from the pocket of her duffel.

Brazil pulled into the driveway, grabbed the duffel and her textbook, and opened the car door. Wind stirred through the trees on the boulevard, sending leaves to the ground. The breeze twirled into a gust that lifted the Fireman Sam sticker from the driveway and whipped it into the street.

CHAPTER 32

Proton Therapy: *A type of radiation therapy using protons rather than X-rays to treat cancer and benign cysts.*

Jessie

It was typical for Jessie to feel anxious on Proton Zap day, but today was different. Today was her first treatment without Kim. Jessie pushed her head against the picture window, looking down the street for Dana's truck. Instead, she saw leaves kicked up on the sidewalk and Kim coming across the lawn, being pulled by their golden retriever.

Kim opened the door and unleashed Blaze. He raced to the window to stand watch with Jessie.

"Pushing your head through the window won't get Dana here faster," Kim said.

Jessie rubbed her forehead and swiped her fingers over the scars, one above each eye. Today was treatment number five. After Jessie's third session to zap the grape-sized benign cyst pressing on her vasovagal nerve, the doc had reported significant progress.

"They're going to test me after they zap me."

"I hate not being there for you. I will be there on the day you ring that bell."

"I know you will." She pulled Kim close and kissed her.

The golden bell hanging on the wall in the waiting room at the Mayo Clinic inspired Jessie. The hope in a cancer patient's eyes as they read its inscription, *I am a survivor*, for the first time immediately transformed hope into determination. Jessie was convinced that she would beat the tumor killing her dream.

Proton therapy was a new, noninvasive approach to eradicating cancerous and benign growths. The jury was out on how many sessions Jessie would need to shrink the cyst enough to stop the blackouts.

Jessie was already on her way out when Dana arrived in front of the house. She waved to Kim and ripped down the sidewalk.

"No kiss?" Kim said.

"Jess. Kiss your girl and let's go."

Jessie ran back and kissed Kim hard on the lips. "Every day gets me closer to the back seat of the fire engine. I'll call you after."

Jessie climbed into Dana's truck, and she pulled away from the curb.

After a ride spent mostly listening to the radio, Jessie lowered the volume and said, "I've been meaning to thank you."

"No thanks necessary. I'm glad to drive you."

"I mean about making me get the scan. You were right. I was afraid, and PTSD made sense. The blackouts helped me feel closer to my brother. I know it's messed up. I never told anyone this, but you remember the day you came through the basement window after I fell through the floor?"

Dana nodded.

"Before my hands got stuck. I saw Tag. In the basement. He was happy. I didn't want to give up a chance to see him again by fixing the blackouts. I didn't want him to think I was leaving him behind. Like, because he's not here he doesn't matter. Part of me thought that by feeling what he must have felt, I was being a good big sister. But because of the scan, because of you pushing me to find the truth, I realized a good sister keeps going so she can carry the memories of her little brother with her."

Dana pulled into the parking garage at the Mayo Clinic. She said, "Wanting to feel close to Tag isn't messed up. I get it. Not exactly the same, but losing my dad when I was a kid—it hurts less as I get older, but he's always there. Some memories are clear, and I can't shake 'em. A lot of things we can't fix, but a cyst is no match for the combat challenge champion."

In the waiting room, a nurse called Jessie's name. Dana opened a magazine.

"You comin'?" Jessie said.

"Can I? You want me to?"

The nurse said, "It's fine to come back while we get Jessie ready. You can wait out here during the scan."

"Come on," Jessie said. "I want you to see me in my hairnet. I mean, my face net. I'm thinking of dressing up as Captain Proton for Halloween."

Jessie changed into a gown and got on the table, looking up at the fluorescent lights. "Ready for my facial," she said.

The technician placed a white mesh mask over Jessie's face and snapped the edges to a cradle holding her head.

"Captain Proton works," Dana said, "but I think your cape can use some work."

Jessie thought of the heroes fighting cancer. She clenched her teeth, trying not to move her mouth while protesting, "I can't think of a cooler superhero cape than one that ties in back."

The technician lifted one of the snaps. "Okay, Jess, hold still." He adjusted the mask and re-snapped Jessie's head down. "I'm gonna ask your friend to wait outside."

Inside the tube, laser beams surrounded Jessie. She imagined riding in the back seat of the fire engine. She closed her eyes and saw Tag. He wasn't inside a frozen bubble, and he wasn't hanging from a barn rafter. Tag was running through a field, giggling and looking behind him to make sure his big sister was still chasing him.

"All done," the tech said.

The blue glow of laser lights dimmed. The fiberglass cradle slowly carried her from the tube and back to the harsh light.

"The doc will meet you in the conference room," he said, and then he smiled. "Throw your cape in the bin."

On the way into the conference room, she imagined the cyst shrunken to a tiny dot, and her hope swelled in proportion. The doctor and the nurse stood with their backs to the door, discussing pictures tacked on white-lit screens. The white of their coats made them seem almost invisible before the X-ray of Jessie's head. The nurse hadn't been in the room for her previous reading. Jessie worried: it always takes more people to deliver bad news than good.

Jessie cleared her throat. The nurse turned, and Jessie tried to read his smile. Was it a forced smile saying "I'm sorry, we'll keep trying"? Jessie didn't think so—the smile looked real.

The doctor turned next and said, "Looks like today is your day to ring the bell." She handed Jessie the mesh mask. "A souvenir if you want it."

Jessie took the mask. The doc handed her an envelope, and when she peeked inside, she saw the words *Return to work, no restrictions.*

Jessie banged through the door to the waiting room like a child escaping her bedroom on Christmas morning. Patients sat quietly on their waiting chairs. Dana was directly across the room.

"Take a video," Jessie said. "I want Kim to see this."

She jogged across the room, pulled down on the rope hanging from the golden bell, and clanged it three times. The room erupted in applause.

On the drive home, Jessie dug in her pocket and said, "Hey, look, I brought your lucky penny."

"That penny is worth a million bucks. First the combat challenge, and now you're cleared to get back on the rig."

"I didn't use it for luck. I use it as a token. It reminds me you're rooting for me."

"And you're a beast who doesn't give up. And you got crocodile skin."

"You were right. Some of the guys are ruthless. I'm sure it was worse for you and Ruby. But the fire department is no match for the thick skin I got growing up in my family." Jessie traced Hopper's ears in the center of her tattoo. She needed courage to say what was coming next. "I've seen you as a mentor. I wanna be a friend. I think about you and the gambling. I worry."

"I'm good at it."

Silence isn't uncomfortable between friends discussing what's real. It's a gift. It's the pause required for genuine reflection.

Dana sighed. "The last thing I did with my dad was play cards. The night before he died. Sometimes I tell myself I gamble because it reminds me of my dad. Truth is, I don't think about my dad when I'm playing poker. I don't think about anything. I don't feel anything except hope to win the next hand. But I get more from losing. The dread I feel out of nowhere, I can't explain that. Losing everything, the dread makes sense."

"You seem happy most of the time."

"I am happy. And I think if I lose the dread, the happy goes too. Can't have one without the other."

"Like the crocodiles. They have thick *and* sensitive skin. They feel the ripples moving the water. It's how they survive."

"You sure ran with my crocodile advice."

"It's what I do: nothing half-assed. I'm pretty sure it's a lot like gambling. I'm all in. Tidal waves are unmanageable—but maybe we both give the ripples a chance."

CHAPTER 33

Wye: A gated ball valve (shaped like a Y) where one 2-inch hose feeds into two 1-inch hose connections operated with shutoff handles. Enables firefighters to add hose to reach a fire too far for the initial tank line.

Ruby

Ruby didn't have much confidence she would stick on Engine 5. She woke early, allowing time to drive to five's and then to a different station without a captain. She brought Tyler some coffee and peeked into Dana's room next. "You gettin' up?"

Dana pushed off the covers. "I'm up. Let me know where they tramp you."

Engine 5 sat alone in the dim shadows of the single firehouse. Dirty hose was spread out next to the floor drain, and the odor of scorched metal let Ruby know they'd recently returned from a car fire. She was anxious to learn where she would be sent after the guys refused to show.

In the coop, the offgoing captain sat at the computer, finishing reports. His face appeared haggard and drooping under the fluorescent lights.

"Busy night?" she said.

"Four calls, timed perfectly to get us up every ninety minutes. We reloaded the rig with clean hose. I didn't have the heart to make the guys hang the dirty stuff. They're beat."

"I wonder where they'll send me," she said.

"Chief dropped off the lineup late last night. I shoulda called so you could come in later, but I figured you might be in bed. Looks like you got your crew."

He pulled a scratch paper from the wall and held it out for her. "Here you go. Your first very own lineup."

I have a crew! She could barely believe it. A female captain of a permanent crew would be squeezed between glass slides under a microscope. But, for Ruby, it was worth it.

She snatched the lineup from his hand. Instead of the list of names, four different tuna can labels had been taped to the paper.

CPT: Chicken of the Sea
FMO: StarKist
3Man: Geisha
4Man: Bumble Bee

The offgoing crew stood in the doorway, snickering. Ruby's cheeks flashed with anger. As unsettling as the meaning of the tuna-fish crew was, she understood she was the target of another adolescent prank. Ruby flew out to the apparatus floor. She wouldn't stand there for them to see her demoralized.

The offgoing captain followed her. "Wait," he said.

He pushed the lever to open the apparatus door. It rattled. The protective rubber scraped along the floor, and sunlight outlined three figures standing on the apron. Dana stood with her gear bag flung over her shoulder. Brazil and Jessie flanked her, their bundles of fire gear resting on the concrete.

Dana pulled Winnie from her gear bag. The Saint Flora medallion winked at Ruby from the collar. "I didn't have the heart to leave her home, knowing the fun we would have today."

Ruby glanced at the lineup. She could almost forgive the reference to foul-smelling tuna vaginas. She had her crew—made of the three best firefighters on the department. *Hell, on the planet.*

She read the lineup. "You're StarKist," she said to Dana. "And Jessie, you're Geisha. That leaves Bumble Bee. That's you, Brazil."

"We got ourselves a chick rig," Brazil said.

After a shocked pause, Ruby, Dana, and Jessie burst out laughing. Jessie dropped her gear next to the engine. "Did you call us chicks?"

On his way out, the offgoing captain said, "Good luck, Captain Bell." He smiled. *I'll take it,* she thought, at last feeling respected.

S to the power of three— No, S to the power of four. Sweet, Strong, Smart, and Sisterhood.

The first-ever all-women crew readied their gear on Engine 5, and together they washed the dirty hose. Ruby dragged two sections toward the hose tower, where Dana held the hoisting hook. The light from the fixture at the top of the thirty-foot tower reached the ground bright, like sunlight starting a new day.

"We did it," Ruby said, and secured the hose onto the hook.

Dana pulled the rope. "Told you I'd drive for you someday."

"We did it for them." Ruby lifted her chin toward the apparatus floor, where Jessie and Brazil splashed water on hose and each other. "That's what fitting in looks like."

"We did it for us and not to fit in. That's what belonging here looks like."

The station lights flickered, and the engine rolled out of the station. The day's calls left them with barely enough time to shop for the clutch and no time to perform the mandatory daily training session.

That evening Ruby worked at the computer, logging the details of the emergency calls, while Dana prepped her signature stir fry.

Jessie joined Dana in the kitchen. "Need help?"

"I got it."

Jessie gestured to her wristwatch. "No, I mean it's seven o'clock. I'm starving. Do you need help?"

Dana threw a dishtowel at Jessie. "Smart-ass. It's ready. Get Ruby and Brazil."

The crew lined up to heap stir fry onto their plates and then tucked in around the table. The customary three minutes of silence at the fire station dinner table was broken by Jessie.

"This is the best chicken I have ever had at the firehouse. So tender and tasty."

Ruby and Dana smiled like they were enjoying an inside joke.

Brazil said, "It's tofu."

"It's chicken. Tofu tastes like wet socks," Jessie argued.

"Only when Tyler makes it," Dana said.

Ruby defended, "It's taken him almost ten years, but with practice he's gotten better at tofu. And speaking of practice, I need to put a training in the computer, so after dinner let's meet by the rig. We'll do knots."

"I was gonna work out after dinner," Jessie said. "I get a dead weight in my stomach if I don't work it off."

"I need to call my boys before bed," Brazil said.

"Twenty minutes, and then training."

Dana, Brazil, and Ruby stood in a semicircle, holding short lengths of rope. Winnie sat on the tailboard of the engine like one of the crew. "Let's start with the running bowline. Where the hell is Jessie? Brazil, go get her, would you?"

Brazil trotted to the 1970s microphone on its pedestal. She hesitated and then covered the once-white button, now stained with black grease, with the tail of her shirt before announcing, "Firefighter Jeroncyk, report to the apparatus floor. That's an order."

The sound of fast-paced sneakers hitting the stairs assured Ruby that Jessie was on her way. A moment later she completed the circle, wearing just her workout shorts and sports bra.

Dana bowed her head, feigning concentration on her piece of rope, and then peeked from under her dark eyebrows, fighting the tug of a smile.

"Really?" Ruby said. "I know we're comfy—like Brazil says—as a chick rig, but uniform, please."

Jessie snapped the strap of her navy sports bra. "It's blue."

Ruby smiled. "Get your uniform on and grab a rope. I'm interested in seeing a running bowline, not rock-star abs."

First came the click. The lights flickered; the fire tones vibrated in six loud blasts. Winnie jumped from the tailboard and dashed into the station.

Jessie pulled out the T-shirt tucked into the waist of her shorts, wiped the sweat from her lip, and stepped into her fire boots. All four rig doors slammed in unison.

The possibility of a fire—their first fire as a crew—beckoned the engine at full speed. Dana blasted the air horn. Like the sea parting before Moses, traffic yielded, clearing the path to the promised land and the supreme calling of a firefighter—the fireground.

Dana turned onto the block. Black smoke obscured streetlamps, and the air was thick with the toxic odor of burned possessions. She pulled past the burning house, making room for the soon-to-arrive ladder. The chief had already arrived and was out of his Suburban, pointing at the house.

"Hey girls," he shouted, "it's right here!"

"You mean that one?" Dana said. "The one with the flames blowing out the windows?"

The house was set back from the street and required a longer hose lay than the 250 feet of the tank line. Jessie flaked the line on the front lawn while Brazil attached the wye and added two sections of hose. She opened the wye handle, ensuring that water would flow to the nozzle.

Sirens wailed, announcing the arrival of a ladder truck and a second engine. Ruby cinched the straps on her air tank and met Jessie at the door. Brazil raised a thumbs-up and joined Ruby and Jessie. With the hose ready and her firefighters at her side, Ruby keyed her radio. "Charge the tank line."

Dana's voice came back. "You got water."

Jessie stood on the step and pulled the trigger to clear the line. A stream of water shot into the air and then fell. Water trickled from the nozzle in drops. The hose went flat. Ruby radioed, "Dana, we need more pressure."

"I'm at one seventy-five."

Peering across the lawn, Ruby tracked the flat hose back to the wye. A truckie stepped over the hose. The hose leading from the engine to the wye was stiff with water. Beyond the wye the hose went flat. *Did he kick the shutoff?*

"You two wait here. I think the truckie hit the shutoff with his boot."

Ruby followed the flattened hose to the shutoff and turned the handle, releasing water back into the hose. Her radio crackled. Dispatch added new information: "The homeowner reporting her toddler is inside. Repeat, possible child inside."

Adrenaline spiked, energy surged, hearts raced. Truckies shoved axes in their belts and bolted with Ruby across the lawn to the home.

Jessie cleared the charged line and shouted to Ruby through her mask, "Brazil heard a cry. I told her you'd want us to wait, but she went in."

"Dispatch reported a trapped child. Let's get in there with the water." Ruby covered her face with her mask.

Before they could enter, Brazil appeared in the smoke-filled doorway, carrying a soot-faced toddler. Smoke swirled around the little girl's blonde curls. With the child in her arms, Brazil manifested the drama glorified on a movie poster, a heroic apparition. This, Ruby knew, was the reason why.

Ruby took up the hose and nodded Jessie inside. *The courage to fight the fire pales in comparison to the courage required to feel valuable when treated as less-than,* she thought.

Together they chased the flames to steaming retreat. Seeing Brazil there, fearless and with nothing to prove, Ruby understood,

The Fire She Fights could finally be extinguished by knowing she was—that they were—good enough.

Next shift, while Ruby and the crew were having coffee, the chief stopped at the fire station, armed with his clipboard. "Captain Bell, meet me in the coop."

He handed Ruby a coaching and development form. "Your firefighter entered a burning building alone and without the protection of water. I realize it was for good reason, but it's against our SOPs and she needs to sign this C&D form acknowledging poor judgment."

Ruby reviewed the form. "Chief, you do realize that her good reason was a child calling for help. This should be a medal, not a disciplinary letter."

"It's just a formality. We all know what she did."

Ruby crumpled the paper. "You can drag me outside right now, stand me in the middle of Bloomington Avenue, and run me over with the fire engine before I'll ask Brazil to sign this bullshit."

It was like justice intervening in the universe when the station doorbell rang. The homeowner from the fire waited at the door, her three-year-old girl on her hip and her six-year-old son at her side.

Looking uncertain, she said, "I was told the crew that rescued Macy would be here today."

The chief made a quick exit. Macy wriggled from her mother's arms and ran to Ruby.

"Thank you for finding me in the fire."

Ruby tousled her curls. "Actually, it wasn't me. It was Firefighter Brazil."

Ruby called the crew into the coop. One by one, Dana, then Jessie, and finally Brazil turned up. "This is Brazil. She found you in the fire."

Macy ran to Brazil and hugged her leg. The mom nudged her son to shake Brazil's hand. He looked at each woman's face in turn, Ruby and then Dana, Jessie, and Brazil.

"Go ahead, shake her hand. She saved your little sister."

The boy looked at the ground while shaking Brazil's hand.

"I'm not sure what's wrong with him. Usually, I can't keep him quiet."

Brazil winked at the mom. She knelt in front of the boy and said, "No worries, boys can be firefighters too."

He smiled and ran out to the apparatus floor to admire the fire truck.

All five women filled the station with laughter. Macy just stared— too young to appreciate the road Ruby, Dana, Brazil, and Jessie had paved for her.

AUTHOR'S NOTE

From 1986 through 2009, the percentage of women firefighters in Minneapolis increased or held steady. Starting in 2010 and continuing through 2020, the percentage of women declined.

This graph illustrates a proper question:

What the Fuck?

Percentage of Women Firefighters MFD
1986-2020

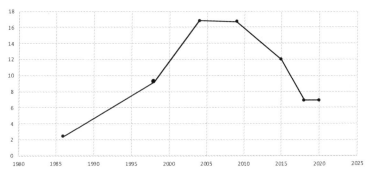

*Percentages based on numbers from the official Minneapolis Fire Department sworn personnel lineup. (Includes sworn personnel working desk jobs)

Ruth Bader Ginsburg said, "When I'm sometimes asked, 'When will there be enough [women on the Supreme Court]?' and I say, 'When there are nine,' people are shocked. But there'd been nine men, and nobody's ever raised a question about that." In 1991 Minneapolis staffed its first all-women fire engine crew. Thank you, RBG, for cracking open the door. May we continue to widen the path and close the gap.

Despite our numbers steadily declining over the last ten years, I have hope. Minneapolis recently promoted a Black man as chief. He appointed a Black woman as his second in command. The most recent recruitment poster advertising open Minneapolis firefighter positions features a Black woman, and she looks fierce. Like the woman on the poster, we must be vigilant to keep from sliding back from the advances we fought so hard to make.

ACKNOWLEDGMENTS

Thank you to my wife Renee for being my true partner, and for mapping the path that makes sense. Thank you for being by my side and whispering advice in my ear, reminding me to go outside. Because of our walks and because you entertained me with tap dancing, this novel never lost its stride.

Renee's sister, Denise Pardello—thank you for reading chapters and then offering a perfect mixture of compliment and critique. Thank you for weighing in on my choice of words, my cover, and the design, and for being my first backer. Your enthusiasm consistently catapulted this novel's energy toward success.

Captain Casidy Anderson—your passion for justice excited me to keep writing and then to revise and revise again. You have inspired me with your stories and our friendship. Thank you for believing with me—in the importance of women's voices at the table, and among the fire.

Tom Swain—your fellowship at the University of Minnesota enabled me to attend graduate school. Our friendship that grew in its wake has been motivational—there is always time to do what matters.

My professors at the Humphrey School—the idea to write this novel began with encouraging words from Gary DeCramer. Jodi Sandfort modeled the importance to "do what you say you will do."

Jodi, your conviction for our actions to parrot our words has made a difference.

Thanks to Mary Carroll Moore from the Loft Literary Center for nudging me just enough to keep writing little islands, then to connect them with characters people care about. It's amazing how one comment can make or break another's trajectory toward their mission. You said, "I believe you will finish this book," and I did.

I'm thankful for the UCLA Writer's Program, where I worked with thoughtful students and learned to write with a purpose. I'm especially thankful for you, Robert Eversz, for offering amazing critiques to improve my writing and continuing to support me through introductions and genuine interest in my success.

My therapist, Rosemary Kliever—it has been a journey. Thank you for guiding me through the trauma that comes with the many years of being a firefighter; and equally important, helping me to find the courage to relive it as I wrote this novel. Your encouragement to cling to the reason I was writing—to honor women firefighters—reminded me of my purpose and gave me peace.

Thank you, Scott Carnahan from Fire Wire. Your generosity in allowing me to share your photos empowered me to convey the message—women firefighters are in the fray, and we are badass.

Thank you to my Women of Words writing group, where I found resources for editing; thank you, Connie Anderson. To the women who showed up every month to support and share our similar challenges and successes, I look forward to our next meeting and our next book.

Wise Ink—the village that surrounded me to bring this novel into the world. Thanks to Victoria Petelin, for your advice from the start. Emily Mahon, for revising the cover until she was perfect. Thank you, Dara Moore Beevas, although unrelated by blood, for guiding me like we are family. Most of all—thank you, Kellie Hultgren, for your incredible editing and giving even me a clearer picture of what this novel is about.

Thank you to the women of Minneapolis Fire for putting yourselves out there by showing up for video recording and allowing me to use your photos to say: *We are here.*

Thank you to the women of Minneapolis Fire who trusted me to tell our stories. After listening to your experiences, I am more convinced than ever—we all have a story to tell and more books to write.

Thank you, Mom, for being my first true hero. For making sure I am more than sweet, more than strong or smart. Thank you for letting me be me.